LOVE AND WAR

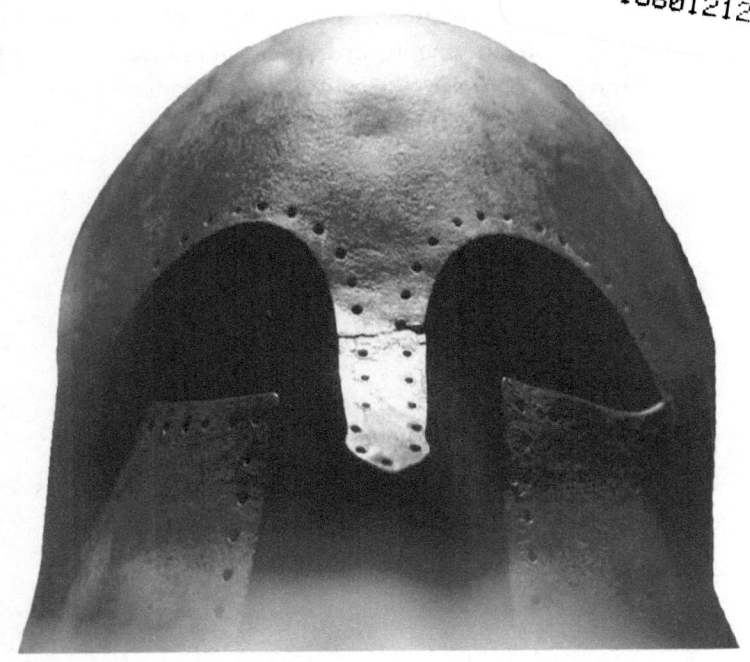

M. L. Hollinger

The Javik series Book Two

TotalRecall Publications, Inc.
1103 Middlecreek
Friendswood, Texas 77546
281-992-3131   281-482-5390 Fax
www.totalrecallpress.com

ISBN: 978-1-59095-286-3
UPC: 6-43977-62863-3

Library of Congress Control Number: 2014955308

Printed in the United States of America with simultaneous printings in Australia, Canada, and United Kingdom.

FIRST EDITION
1 2 3 4 5 6 7 8 9 10

To all of my old Boy Scout troop pals.

World renowned Author M. L. Hollinger

received an Aeronautical Engineering degree from Purdue University in 1957 and went into the Air Force right after college. He worked on several space program projects including; Titan III Space Booster, Space Shuttle, Star Wars and several other special studies for the Air Force. He attended the Air Command and Staff College and the Air War College. He served in Viet Nam from 1971-1972. His decorations include The Bronze Star Medal, Meritorious Service Medal, Air Force Commendation Medal, The Vietnamese Honor Medal First Class, The Vietnamese Gallantry Cross and five unit excellence awards. He retired from the Air Force in 1980 with the rank of Lieutenant Colonel and came back to Indiana where he joined the Indiana Corporation for Science and Technology. He is now fully retired.

Acknowledgement

I gratefully acknowledge the support of my wife and family in this project. They provided many helpful suggestions and a good deal of editing support.

Preface

This is the second book in the Javik series and continues the parallel stories of Javik and Allana. While Javik is at war, Grazhda and Tao Shan confirm that Allana is heir to the throne of Gorgos, an island kingdom far to the South. Allana is finally convinced to undertake the quest for her throne even though she is not too sure about what she must do to complete that quest. Javik returns from war to find her gone but encounters many problems before he can go after her.

The story continues in the next book, *The Queen of Gorgos.*

Introduction

Javik goes off the war. While he's away the old witch, Grazhda, tells Allana she will be Queen of Gorgos and tells her Tao Shan has the key to her true identity. She consults Tao Shan who confirms she is of the royal house of Gorgos.

Allana encounters Grazhda again, and the witch shows her visions which almost convince her to seek the throne of Gorgos. She tells Tao Shan of this encounter, and he offers to help her learn about Gorgos.

A raid on his village produces a bonus for Javik in the form of a large war dog, Mordah. Mordah's master is killed in the raid, and Javik claims the huge animal. With the help of a villager who knows about training dogs and a potion from Grazhda, Javik turns the dog to his service.

A List of Characters

Javik: A boy learning to be a warrior in a cruel, medieval world.

Dana: Javik's mother.

Browdat: A wealthy war leader in Javik's village who adopts Javik.

Goldar: A 'war leader' in Javik's village who marries Dana and becomes Javik's foster father.

Tao Shan: The best mentor in the kingdom. Javik has agreed to further training with him after Mauhad.

Sigurd: A fellow student at Tao Shan's school and now a close friend of Javik.

Noka: Javik's old roommate at Tao Shan's school.

Grazhda: A witch living near Javik's village and feared by all.

Allana: An escaped slave girl Javik encounters in the forest and falls in love with.

Bogard the Red: Another of Javik's former schoolmates.

Margan the Minstrel: A traveling troubadour who provides Javik with information about Allana.

Polla: A village girl who traps Javik into marriage.

Gilda: Javik's mother-in-law.

Garen: Javik's son.

Mordah: Javik's war dog.

Barinosh: Once an admiral in the now defunct Gogon fleet

Varuda: Once madam of a high class bordello who helps Allana gain wealth and power.

Vargon: King of the Turrek bandits.

Chapter 1

Mauhad was over. The older boys in the village who completed the ordeal were now considered to be men and could take wives and establish their own hearths. They were also free to pursue any career they chose, and many became farmers, tradesmen, merchants or politicians. Only a few remained on the warrior path, but every boy was now, at least, moderately proficient in the weapons of the day — pike, sword, ax, mace, longbow and crossbow. Should war arise, they were ready to leave the fields and the shops and take up arms to defend their village and their country.

Completion of the manhood test was an occasion for feasting and revelry. The strong beer the Berglauni called qush flowed freely as boys and their male relatives celebrated well into the morning hours. As the sun rose, the village streets were quiet well past the time when they were normally bustling with activity. In the longhouses the revelers were suffering the punishment related to such debauchery. The Lord Browdat was no exception.

The war leader's head felt like it would not go through the door of his room as he walked from his bed to the latrine area of the longhouse. He had consumed more qush last night than in the whole preceding year, and he was not used to that kind of anymore. He smiled as he thought of Javik. Here was a son to be proud of. He evaded the searchers completely for seven days; no mean feat considering who was searching for him. On top of that, he defeated a Sentii war leader in combat. This boy would bring honor to his house.

Tao Shan stayed at Browdat's house rather than return to his in the middle of the night. He was looking forward to a good breakfast prepared by the skilled women of that hearth. The wise old fox had moderated his consumption of qush and was as alert as ever.

"Good morning, Lady Frieda," Tao Shan bowed as he entered the dining area of the longhouse.

"You are such a gentleman, Master Tao Shan. Why don't you take my husband as a pupil for the next year?" Frieda jested.

"I fear he would be a difficult student, madam. Do I smell bacon?" Tao Shan sniffed the air.

"You do. It is the first of our hogs to be butchered this fall. Sit down, and I'll serve you."

Tao Shan's mouth watered at the thought of fresh bacon to go with his wheat cakes. A hung over Browdat padded in behind him.

"Good morning, Lord Browdat. How fare you this fine day?" Tao Shan boomed his greeting deliberately knowing the condition of the war leader's head.

"Not well, mentor. Please keep your voice to a whisper until I have downed three pots of good bark tea. I'm afraid I overdid the qush last night."

"It's not every day a man's son passes Mauhad," Tao Shan complimented. "You were justified in celebrating."

"He's a fine boy, Tao Shan, but don't let him know I said that. He has much to learn yet of the outside world."

"I agree with you, sir. We must keep him safe in the coming war. The Berglauni will always need leaders of his potential."

The conversation stopped as Javik, who was every bit as unsteady as his adoptive father, staggered to the doorway.

"Well, the new warrior arises," Browdat mocked. "How many tankards of qush did you slaughter last night?"

"Too many, I fear, sir," Javik answered. "My head is full of demons trying to hammer their way out."

Javik showed the effects of too much qush. His six-foot, muscular frame was slightly stooped, and his shoulder length golden hair was a mess of tangles. Only his neatly trimmed beard remained to prove he was once well groomed. His deep green eyes, usually alive with sunlight were now dull and bordered with red. He stepped into the room.

Tao Shan smiled but held back a laugh. "It is good to celebrate, but you have also learned a valuable lesson from it, I see."

"Yes, sir. Too much qush is not good for you."

"Yes, yes," Browdat observed. "Too much qush can rob a man of his judgment and make him do and say things he would not do while sober. Mark the lesson well, Son."

Tao Shan turned to Browdat, "I hope you recall one promise you made last night."

The women arrived with trays of food, delaying Browdat's answer. Javik and Browdat only picked at their breakfast, but Tao Shan dove in eagerly.

"She would fix bacon this morning," Browdat fought back the nausea brought on by the greasy smell of the meat.

"It's delicious. Aren't you going to eat yours?" Tao Shan asked Browdat.

The big warrior pushed his bowl toward the mentor, and Javik did the same.

"What's this about a rash promise I made last night?" Browdat asked Tao Shan.

"You told me you would pay for Javik to spend another year in my longhouse," Tao Shan spoke between mouthfuls of bacon.

"I don't remember such a promise," Browdat grumbled his reply. "He can pay for it himself now. He has a slave to sell and a rich Sentii sword."

Javik answered before Tao Shan could respond. "I have no slave, sir. She purchased her freedom last night."

Browdat rubbed his hands together in anticipation of profit. "How much did she give you?"

"One copper coin, and I threw that away," Javik said.

"What?" Browdat blustered. "That girl was worth over 100 crowns. How could you do that, son?"

Tao Shan broke in. "I can't believe you haven't noticed they're in love with each other. I guess you were also too drunk to take in the announcement of their engagement last night."

"What? Engaged? He can't marry a slave girl. I won't have it," the war leader protested.

"She's not a slave any more, Father," Javik said.

"But, she was just yesterday," Browdat fumed. "You will not marry that girl. I forbid it. You must marry well and bring gold and land to this house, now that you are my son."

Once more Tao Shan interrupted. "Lord Browdat, the lovers have also agreed to wait until the question of war is settled. You and I know there will be war, and Javik must go. Give this matter some time to cool off. You can address it again after peace is restored."

"Aha! If he's to spend another year with you after the war, how can he be a student and also support a wife? If he marries, he must set up his own hearth, and that takes gold. Another year with you takes even more gold. The whole thing's impossible." Browdat leaned back in his chair with a satisfied look on his face.

Javik rose and faced his adoptive father with a defiant expression. "I will marry her, Father. I respect you as a war leader and my father, and I love all in this house dearly, but I will not be denied the woman I love, no matter what the cost in gold or family." He strode from the room in search of Allana.

Browdat's expression changed from smug to wonderment. "By Zhou! That boy is just as rash as his father. Go after him, Tao Shan, and talk some sense into his thick head."

"My lord, you cannot conquer love with logic, but I'll speak to him." The mentor rose and followed Javik.

Outside the longhouse he found Javik leaning against a tree exhausted emotionally.

"Javik, may I speak with you?" Tao Shan called.

Javik looked at his old master and smiled a bit. "I will always listen to your council, wise teacher."

"Come, walk a bit with me." The mentor took Javik's arm and led him down a forest path.

"Your father is right, you know."

"I know, that's why it makes me so angry. He's always right."

"Only partly right this time. If you truly love Allana, you must marry her and fortunes be damned, but you must be in a position to set up your own hearth before you can do that. I'm certain there will be war, and now that you are a warrior, you will win plunder and a share of the spoils. While you're gone, Allana will earn money teaching sling for me. I'm sure you will be in a better position when peace comes. If you win enough gold in the war, you may even be able to train with me and keep your hearth also."

"If I have a hearth to provide for and a wife and family, how could I train full-time with you?" Javik said.

"Full-time is not necessary. Full time, I could accomplish

what I desire in only seven months, but the same goals may be achieved in a year at, say, three days a week. How does that sound to you?"

"It's a very good plan. We'll wait until after the war, but my father will be no more amenable to our marriage then than he is now, I fear."

"Time and circumstances change many things. You must not think Browdat cannot be moved. Perform well in the war, and you may see a change in his attitude."

At that moment Allana appeared ahead on the path with a basket on her arm full of ripe berries. She waved at Javik and Tao Shan. "Javik, how good to see you among the living this morning, and good morning to you, Master."

Javik reveled in the silver laughter of her voice. Her hands and her apron were stained with the juice of the berries, but she was still beautiful.

She ran to Javik and threw her arms around his neck. They kissed as Tao Shan watched.

"Ah, true love," Tao Shan said, and the lovers broke off their kiss and turned to him. Allana released Javik and started to embrace Tao Shan.

"Whoa! I'm wearing my good tunic, and your hands are a mess," he said.

"Sorry, Master, but I feel I must thank you as much as anyone for my new freedom. If you hadn't brought me to your house, I probably would have perished at the next harsh winter."

"No need to thank me. You brought me one of the best slingers in the country to teach my students."

The mentor saw he was one too many persons in the scene. "I must be on my way now. Javik will tell you all about the events of this morning. I hope you agree with my plan as much as he does. Goodbye." He walked on along the trail, leaving the pair alone.

"What's he talking about, Javik?" Allana asked.

"I had a row with my father this morning. He doesn't want us to marry, and I'm afraid I defied him foolishly."

"Javik, you must go back and apologize to your father immediately. He's a good man who only has your best interests at heart," Allana said.

"Humph! He's only thinking about how much gold and land my marriage would bring him if I married some rich, ugly thing."

"I'm sure he's disappointed in me as a bride for you. After all, I was a slave. Let me go with you to see him. Surely, after you apologize and he sees how much we love each other, he will relent."

Javik took her face in his hands and smiled at her. "Who could resist those eyes? Let's go."

They returned to Browdat's longhouse and found him being scolded by Frieda. When they saw the two enter they stopped abruptly, and Frieda left the room.

"I wish to apologize for my defiance, father." Javik dropped to one knee before the war leader.

"Get up, Javik. I certainly forgive you. I've had nothing but grief from Frieda and your mother ever since you left. Come, sit down, the two of you." He indicated chairs around the large table.

Javik began to speak after they were seated. "Father, Tao Shan spoke with me and showed me the error of my ways. I realize that I must set up my own hearth once I marry, and that will require some gold. Allana and I have agreed to wait until after the war to marry."

"You're still determined to marry in spite of my objections?" Browdat asked.

Allana took over for Javik. "My Lord, I know I am not the wife you would have for Javik. I cannot bring a dowry or rich lands to your house, but I can give you grandchildren to brighten your life now and soften the blows of old age. I love your son with all my heart and soul, and I vow to make him happy in all ways. He will do well in the coming war. We are delaying our marriage, and we ask you to delay your judgment of us until then also."

Javik could see the old war horse's eyes soften a bit as he studied the beauty of the woman pleading with him. He was not surprised when Browdat spoke.

"Very well, Javik has yet to prove himself in battle, and no noble house would grant him their daughter until he's done so. I agree to hold my judgment until the war is over, and we return safely home. Now go and tell the women to leave me alone about this matter."

Browdat picked up his mug and drained it. He slammed it on the table and called to Sasha for more qush.

Allana moved to Browdat and kissed him on the cheek. "Thank you for understanding, my Lord." While the war leader blustered, she went to join the women, only pausing to do the same to Javik. Javik excused himself and left to find a less tense environment.

* * * * *

Several days later the rider came from the capital with news of war with Wallandia. Browdat entered his house just as the family was preparing for the noon meal. He kissed Frieda and turned to Javik.

"Javik! We are called to the square. Goldar wants all men to assemble there now." He emphasized the word "men."

"Will I need my weapons, Father?" Javik asked.

"No, this is an organizational meeting. Goldar will make the weapons assignments today and set the marching date."

"Then, I'm ready." He stood to leave, but stopped to kiss his mother before following Browdat out the door.

Dana waited until he was gone before she buried her face in her hands and wept.

* * * * *

Goldar stood on a small platform with the other war leaders of the village gathered around him.

"The Wallans are on the march," Goldar announced. "We have been ordered by the King to meet the men from two other villages at the fallen oak by tomorrow noon. We will then march to join the rest of the army near Wallandia Moor. If we are lucky, we'll be there before the Wallans and set an ambush for them. Our levee is for twenty horsemen, fifty infantry, thirty archers and fifty pacemen. I expect to bring many more than that in each category. Most of you know your weapons and your captains. We will assemble here at dawn ready to march. Fugnor will have two wagons here for the baggage, but I expect each man to bring only what he needs. Those of you who have not been assigned will stay here. The rest of you are excused until morning."

The group broke up with considerable grumbling intermingled with a few shouts about slaughtering the Wallans. Javik's village was well acquainted with war, and only the young men looked forward to it.

The remaining group consisted of the boys who recently passed Mauhad and a few men who had moved into the village in the last year. Goldar turned to the men first.

He pointed to one. "What was your weapon in your last village?"

"Pike, sir," he answered.

"Good, we will probably be short on pacemen. Report to

Mikka at the shrine of Verna in the morning."

"Aye, sir," the man acknowledged as he turned to go.

"And you?" Goldar indicated the next man.

"I can handle a pike as well, Captain," he replied.

"Then you know what to do," Goldar said.

The man nodded his understanding and moved off to join the first pike man.

The remaining two men were leaning on long bows.

"I see you are archers," Goldar said.

"Yes, sir, we fought with the King at Biddlestown three years ago," the taller one replied.

"Good, you will report to Jundar at the meeting elm."

The only ones left were the boys, and Goldar did not bother asking any of them for their weapons preferences.

"All of you will be pike men. We have few enough of those, and it is the safest place to put you for your first combat. Your mothers would skin me alive if you didn't return safely to them. Which of you knows how to handle one?"

"I do, Sir," Javik raised his hand. Tao Shan spent a great deal of training time on the pike, anticipating it would be his students' first assignment in battle.

"Tao Shan teaches pike well, I know," Goldar smiled. "Do you think you could show these other boys, er, I mean men, a bit about it?"

"Yes, sir!" Javik shouted.

"Good, draw pikes from the armory and form them up on the meadow. I will check with you later to see how it's going. Dismissed!"

The boys trooped past the long building the village used to house its supply of weapons and each boy, now a man, was given a long ash pole topped with a shiny steel point. Javik's first job was showing them how to carry the awkward weapon without skewering one of their fellows or tearing the roof off the armory.

Once on the meadow, Javik's real task began. The new men seemed to have no resentment concerning Javik's command. They knew he had trained with Tao Shan, and that gave him a certain degree of authority by itself.

Most of them were Javik's friends, but even those who were mere acquaintances knew who he was. Tolda, Javik's father, was a famous warrior, and the heroics of his death were well known. He had no trouble drilling them in the use of the pike. He even included a march through the forest to get them used to moving among the trees with a weapon three times as long as they were tall.

Goldar was pleased as he rode up to see the group assembled in perfect battle order.

"Well done, Javik!" he called. "They almost look like veterans."

"Thank you, sir. They've trained hard and listened well."

Goldar dismounted and led his horse closer to the pike men.

"This will be your first combat. Don't be ashamed if you feel fear. Only the foolish have no fear of combat. Your mentors have done what they can to prepare you, but only your first battle will make you warriors. I'm confident you will all bring pride to our village. Just remember that the first duty of a pike man is to stand firm against whatever comes against him. Go home now and prepare yourselves. We march at dawn."

Javik walked back to Browdat's longhouse and placed the pike in the ground near the entrance. He would have to get his baggage together now.

Dana met him at the kitchen.

"Won't you have something to eat, Son? You've been drilling all day."

"Yes, Mother. I am hungry."

Dana busied herself preparing a platter for her son, but talked as she worked.

"How many times have I seen your father drill before battle. He was so handsome on his horse."

"I'm afraid I will only be carrying a pike, Mother," Javik smiled.

"You will have your horse in due time. All warriors must start with the pike." She set the plate before him and seated herself across the table.

Javik dove into the meal. He had almost forgotten to be hungry while he drilled, but now that the food was before him, he was ravenous.

Dana reached across the table and took his left hand in both of hers.

"You are all I have left, Javik. Come home to me, Son."

Javik looked up to see tears running from his mother's eyes. He stopped eating and placed his free hand on top of hers.

"I will return, Mother. I must return for your sake."

"And Allana's?" Dana prompted.

"Oh yes, I couldn't forget her. We agreed to wait to see if war would come before we married, and I think that's best."

"I'm sure it is. It will give Browdat time to think about the marriage. Now that he sees how much in love you are, he will relent."

"I hope you're right. I do love her so."

Dana patted his hand with hers. "It will all come out right, I know it."

* * * * *

That evening, Allana entered his room as he was packing.

"I've made you a sling, Javik." She presented him with a leather bag containing the thong and several smooth stones.

"I'm afraid I'm not your equal with this," Javik smiled.

"You can practice when you get bored," Allana said.

"How can a man be bored in war?" Javik laughed.

"My old master used to say that war is days and days of boredom mixed with moments of stark terror," Allana replied. "He was a Sentii war chief and should know what he was talking about."

"I suppose he's right. Tao Shan said much the same thing."

The room fell silent as Javik continued to pack. He didn't know what to say to Allana. He'd never done this before. Allana solved his problem by throwing her arms around him.

"Oh Javik, please come home safely to me."

Javik embraced her and lifted her face to his. He almost cried himself at the sight of tears streaming down her cheeks. He kissed her and wiped away her tears with his fingers.

"I promise to come home to you so we can be married at last."

"Oh, Javik, I'll live for that day."

* * * * *

That evening, after the dinner table was cleared, Browdat rose to speak.

"My family, hear me!" he lifted his goblet of wine. "Your men are off to battle on the morrow. Here's a toast to the success of our army."

The family rose and joined their lord in the toast. "To our army!" they shouted in unison.

Browdat refilled his goblet and indicated to the servant he should fill Javik's also.

"To my son, I give you this ancient charge of our people. 'Dead or alive, return only with glory,.'" He drained his cup and Javik followed suit. As the warm, red liquid burned his throat, he realized this was no training exercise. After today, a mistake could be fatal. The gravity of the situation hit him like a stampeding horse.

It would not be Master Ling pulling his punches or Tao Shan stopping his sword thrust at a mere skin prick. The men he faced in battle would be intent on taking his life, and they would be quick to take advantage of any mistake on his part. The enemy army would be made up of seasoned warriors – not green boys like himself. His first encounter could even be a war leader. The realization made his spine weak and dryness spread up his throat and into his mouth. He had only known fear like this once before when Browdat's knife was poised to begin his painful execution. There would be no Margan to save him this time.

That night, Javik lay in bed unable to sleep for several reasons. His mother cried as she bid him goodnight, which only intensified his apprehension, but Allana kept popping into his thoughts. He could only pray he would survive the war and return to her arms.

* * * * *

Shortly before dawn, Browdat's loud call drove the sleep from Javik's head.

"Get up, son. We must be on the march."

Javik rolled from his bed and began to dress for battle. He put on the leather undergarment for his chain mail, then the mail itself. Over the mail, he put the covering with the mark of Browdat's family on the chest. He felt as if he carried half the weight of the world on his shoulders, and he wondered how long he could march in this garb. No wonder Tao Shan filled their packs with so many stones.

Next came the sword belt. The sword the King gave him hung from the wide leather on his left side, with Zuban's dagger at his waist on the right. He tied Allana's sling pouch on the left just in front of the sword. Finally, he added a pouch containing his fire tools, salla and a few coins from his meager stash.

The weight of the weapons was nothing compared to the burden of their significance. The sword once belonged to the King's brother and represented both the valor of that warrior and the King's esteem of Tolda. Zuban's dagger symbolized the heavy responsibility of being Browdat's son, while Allana's sling pouch was a constant reminder of the great bond of love between them.

Carefully, Javik unwrapped the helmet - another of the King's gifts. It gleamed brightly as he raised it to his head. There was no mirror in his room. He could not tell if it was on quite straight, but it felt good. He moved to the dining area.

Dana gave a start as he entered the room. Browdat heard her suck in her breath and looked up from his bowl. He smiled broadly.

"By Zhou, all the Wallans will need is one sight of that to flee in terror," he roared.

Allana was as awed as Dana, but she approached Javik and gave a slight adjustment to his helmet.

"You are a fierce warrior, indeed, Javik." She smiled at him proudly.

"My son, a warrior." Tears streamed from Dana's eyes as she embraced Javik. "I knew this day would come, and I was both dreading it and looking forward to it. Sit down, my boy and eat well. I'm afraid you will not taste food like this for a long time to come."

Javik set his helmet on the table in imitation of Browdat and awkwardly adjusted his sword as he sat down.

"You'll get used to that, Son." Browdat smiled at him.

Javik ate like a hungry bear. The excitement of going off to war made him even more ravenous than usual.

Drums began to beat in the village square, and Browdat rose from his bench and donned his helmet.

"We must go, Javik. The muster is called."

"Yes, sir," Javik responded. He went to his room to get his shield and baggage and found Allana there.

"I will miss you, Javik. Come back safe to me." She threw her arms around him and kissed him passionately.

"I'll be home soon," was all Javik could find to say without crying like a baby himself. He lifted the shield, freshly emblazoned with a red wolf's head, slung it across his back and lifted his baggage bundle to his shoulder. Once more he kissed Allana before leaving her, possibly forever.

Dana met him outside the longhouse. She knelt before him.

"Be well, my son. Fight bravely and bring honor to the village and the house of Browdat."

Javik was surprised by her calm demeanor. She had done this many times with his father, and learned to hide her emotions well. He lifted her to her feet and embraced her.

"Good bye, Mother. I will come back to you soon." Javik embraced his mother about to shed the tears he managed to hold back from Allana. He could not cry now. Warriors were not supposed to cry.

Browdat held Frieda close to him and kissed her. It seemed strange to Javik to see the display of emotion from the huge, gruff war leader. He turned from his wife and called to Javik without looking at him. "Come, Javik. We don't want to be late for the war. You that way, and I this," he pointed the way they each should go.

Javik shouldered his pike and marched off without looking back. If he had, he would have just caught the one tear Browdat could not contain, falling down his face and vanishing into his black beard.

CHAPTER 2

Allana ran into the forest. She didn't have a destination. She didn't seem to notice the brambles tearing at her dress or the slap of low-lying twigs against her face. Tears streamed down her cheeks blinding her to any danger ahead. Nothing mattered now that Javik was gone away to war. She didn't see the exposed root of the great beech tree that sent her sprawling to the rotted leaves on the forest floor. She lay there sobbing for what seemed to be a long time before a sixth sense told her she was not alone. She turned to see a stooped-over woman standing just at the edge of the clearing.

She'd seen her before, but only as a dark shadow, moving furtively through the forest—an ominous shadow, provoking nightmares after each sighting. Now that she saw the hag clearly, all fear left her. What did she have to fear from a decrepit old crone like this?

"Hail Queen of Gorgos," the old woman said.

Allana looked at her with a quizzical expression. "Why do you call me that? Who are you?" Allana asked.

The old hag laughed merrily. "I address you as your subjects will in time."

"I've seen you in the forest before, haven't I?"

"You may have. Your Javik knows me well, but I don't suppose he's told you about Grazhda."

"No, he hasn't mentioned you. Are you related to him?"

Again, the old woman laughed. "Our fates are tied together but our blood is not the same. His father once saved my life, and I'm bound by honor to repay that debt to his son."

"What does that have to do with me?"

"You are Javik's beloved. As he values you, I must see that you come to no harm, but you will soon embark on a quest of great peril before you seat yourself on a throne."

Allana started and backed away from the crone. "Throne? I'm a recently freed slave, not a royal."

"You don't really know who you are, child, but you will soon find out your true identity. Tao Shan has the key to that."

Allana smiled at her. "Tao Shan needs no 'key' to tell me who I am. He knows full well where I came from. You speak in riddles."

"No, I speak the truth. You will see." She cackled merrily as she melted into the dark forest like an early morning fog.

Allana stared after her. "Queen of Gorgos, bah. That old woman is crazy."

* * * * *

The next day after her sling lessons, she approached Tao Shan. "Master, may I have a word with you?"

"Of course, what is it?" he replied.

"What do you know of an old woman who lives deep in the forest?"

"Are you speaking of Grazhda?"

"Yes, she said her name was Grazhda."

Tao Shan snorted his disgust. "Why do you ask about that old witch?"

"I encountered her in the forest, and she said some strange things to me."

He took her arm and led her out of earshot of the boys and the servants. "I know she is a powerful witch who can curse or bless. Javik told me of his meeting with her. What did she tell you?"

"She called me 'Queen of Gorgos' and said I would soon embark on a quest of great peril. Is she mad?"

"Many think so, but many have seen her predictions come true. I know you said you were originally from Gorgos, how did you know that?"

"I was cared for by an old woman who was with me until I was sold to Grucheaux. She told me I was from Gorgos. Why would the old woman call me 'Queen'?"

"I have no idea, but there are many tales about her telling people strange things that seem to come true. This is the strangest I've heard, though. A slave girl and yet a queen?"

"She said you held the key to my true identity, Master."

"Again, I have no idea what she's talking about. I wouldn't let it bother me, if I were you. Your future is here with Javik when he returns." He placed an arm around her shoulders and hugged her briefly.

"I know, thank you for hearing my story, Master."

"Feel free to speak to me any time, Allana." With that, he went into his apartments, leaving her trying to forget about the encounter with the witch.

* * * * *

Tao Shan sat down in his library and poured himself a goblet of wine. He sat back in his chair and contemplated the racks of scrolls.

Someone should deal with that witch. She's frightened too many people in this village with her curses and strange utterances. I remember John the butcher. When he refused to give her some sheep entrails, she cursed his wife's womb. The poor woman died giving birth to their next child, and he grieved for her the rest of his life. He was afraid to marry again for fear the curse would apply to any woman he wed.

The cook everyone called 'Worm' entered the library and broke his train of thought. "Master, shall we serve venison tonight or the roast pig?"

"You'd better serve the pig. The venison will keep for a bit longer in this cooler weather."

"Thank you, Master." Worm turned to leave, but Tao Shan called him back.

"Worm, didn't you once serve in the Gorgon navy?"

"Yes, Master. I was an oarsman for five years before the pirates captured me and sold me into slavery."

"Sit down and tell me all you know about Gorgos, please."

"The supper, Master. I must see to it or there will be none." Worm pointed toward the kitchen area of the longhouse.

"Go tell Thorne to take charge of the meal then come right back here."

"Yes, Master." Worm left and Tao Shan remembered Allana's words. He held the key to her true identity. What could the witch mean by that? He poured another goblet of wine.

Worm returned, and Tao Shan pushed the second goblet toward him. "Please sit and have some wine. Telling a story is thirsty work."

Worm took a chair opposite his master. "Thank you, Master. It is."

"Now tell me of Gorgos."

"Not much to tell. Theres a good brothel on Verba street in Thatos, and my favorite inn was the Golden Conch in Harrish. The Gorgons were good to their oarsmen. We doubled as warriors also. The taxes were low. I'd saved some money before the pirates captured my ship, but it did me no good. What would you like to know?"

"I'm curious about the royal family."

Worm took a drink of his wine before answering. "I was only a poor oarsman. I knew nothing of the royal family. I know they didn't have kings, only queens. The crown passed from mother to eldest daughter. While I was captive of the pirates, I heard the island was sacked by the Voldunee. That's all I know, Master." Worm finished his wine in one gulp.

"Thank you Worm. By the way, what is your real name?"

"I think it's Nicola, Master, but I've been called Worm for so long, I'm not sure."

"Very well, we'll continue to call you Worm. You may go now."

"Thank you for the wine, Master." Worm rose and went back to his duties in the kitchen.

A kingdom ruled only by queens, very curious. I wonder what Grazhda knows?

* * * * *

That evening after the evening meal and lights out for the students, Tao Shan lay in his bed wide awake. Grazhda's words kept swirling through his brain. *I have the key to Allana's true identity, eh. The old hag knows something. I don't believe in her magic. It's all mumbo-jumbo and trickery, so she knows of something I possess that might be helpful to Allana. It's not something I know, or I would have thought of it by now.*

He went through a mental inventory of his possessions without finding an answer. He'd collected many curious things in his travels, but none were related to Gorgos. Unable to sleep, he rose and donned a heavy robe before lighting a candle and moving to his library.

The fire was burning low, and he added a log then moved the kettle over the fire to heat water for tea. While he waited for it to boil, he sat at his long table and studied his collection of scrolls. *The answer has to be in here, but where?*

He stood and moved to the diamond-shaped scroll racks covering one whole wall. He stared at the first row for a moment. *Why didn't I label these a long time ago?* He picked a scroll from the top rack and unrolled it a bit. *Weapons, I must have a dozen scrolls on weapons. Where's my history collection?*

He followed the same routine at several of the racks cursing a bit after each try. Near the end of the row he finally found his history section. *Ah, here's what I'm looking for, "The Royal Houses of Gaia.* He moved back to the table and unrolled the scroll. The royal house of Gorgos was near the middle of the document.

Yes, this confirms what Worm said—only queens. What's this? Each member of the royal line was tattooed at birth with the royal crest. Unrolling it further he found the drawing of that crest. It consisted of two serpents arranged in a circle with each snake consuming the other. Inside the circle a golden conch shell sat on a field of sable. *Interesting crest. It says each royal child was tattooed on its rump at birth. Well, it looks like there's one way to prove Grazhda wrong and settle Allana's mind. Tomorrow we will see if she really is a royal.*

He rolled up the scroll but left it on the table. He went back to bed with a smug smile on his face.

CHAPTER 3

The next morning Tao Shan called Allana to his office immediately after she reported in. He led her to the library and had her sit down.

"What is it, Master?" she asked.

"After you told me about Grazhda I couldn't get the witch's words out of my head. She said I had the key to your identity, and I lay awake thinking of what I might possess that held that key. I knew of only one way to prove her right or wrong. I searched my library for a scroll containing the history of all known royal houses, and I found a section pertaining to Gorgos. What it told me may be that key she spoke of."

"What is that, Master? Her words also kept me awake last night. If you have a way to unravel her riddle, please tell me."

"Do you have a tattoo besides your slave tattoo?" Tao Shan leaned toward her in eager anticipation of her answer.

"I do, but I can't show it to you. Grucheaux often remarked about it when he abused me." Allana's face turned beet red.

"What does it look like?" Tao Shan was almost salivating at this point.

"I've never seen it. It's not in a place I can see without a mirror."

The old mentor rubbed his hands together in glee then moved to a chest. He found a small mirror and handed it to Allana. "Here, go someplace private and look at your tattoo, then come back and describe it to me."

"Yes, Master." Allana took the mirror and headed for the latrine area. All the way there she wondered what difference a tattoo on her rump would make, but the mentor seemed very excited about it, and she owed him a great deal for taking her in so she could be close to Javik. She inspected her tattoo and returned to the library.

"Well?" he asked as she came into the room.

"It's very faded, but I could make out a red circle around a black spot with a golden center," she said.

Tao Shan beamed with delight. "Come look at this." He opened his scroll to the Gorgon royal crest and motioned for Allana to come closer. "Does it look anything like this?" He pointed to the drawing.

Allana gasped in surprise. "Yes, it does. This is more detailed, but I think it's the same thing."

"You'd best sit down to hear the rest of this," he said.

Allana took a chair and waited for his explanation with wide eyes.

"Grazhda was right. You could be the Queen of Gorgos. This scroll says that all the children of the royal family were tattoed with that mark when they were born."

"But how could a slave be a royal?" Allana asked.

"The woman who cared for you, did she ever mention anything about your tattoo?"

"No, she never told me anything except that she and I were from an island far away. She used to tell me stories about how beautiful it was, but never anything about my parents. She only said they died proudly." A tear formed in her eye as she remembered those days, and she brushed it away with her sleeve.

"How old are you, Allana?" Tao Shan asked.

"I don't know. I can remember four winters since I was sold to Grucheaux, but before that, I have no idea."

"When did you start your monthly cycles?" Tao Shan asked.

Allana bristled a bit at the question, but decided female menstrual cycles were nothing new to Tao Shan. "Just before I was sold."

Tao Shan thought for a moment. "You would have been 12 or 13 winters when they started, but no more than 14. This scroll says that the kingdom of Gorgos was destroyed 17 years ago. That would make you the right age."

"For what?" she asked.

"The story goes that a female child, only a baby, was saved from the Voldunee by a nursemaid and her husband, but it tells nothing about their fate. That baby could have been you."

Allana's face revealed more disbelief. "I don't remember any man with the woman who took care of me."

"He would have been sent to the mines, but I can't believe she never mentioned him."

"She never spoke of a husband."

"Well, in any case, you are definitely a member of the royal line. Does this make any difference to you?"

"Yes, in a way it does. Lord Browdat objects to Javik marrying a slave, but he could have no objection to his son taking a royal wife. Otherwise it makes no difference at all. I'm no queen. I wouldn't know how to go about being a queen. My place is here with Javik. He will return someday, and we will be married and have many children. I will be queen of his hearth, that's all I want."

"If you want me to speak to Browdat, I will."

"After Javik returns, we will ask for Lord Browdat's permission to marry. You may tell him about it then, but please tell no one about it until then. Thank you for this. I wouldn't want Javik to defy his father even to take me as his bride. This solves the problem nicely." Allana rose and moved to Tao Shan. She bent down and kissed him gently on the cheek before leaving the room with a smile on her face.

CHAPTER 4

Two days later, Allana was gathering sling stones from a creek bed near Tao Shan's longhouse when a dark shadow over the water caused her to look up.

"Grazhda, you frightened me," Allana said.

"Hail Queen of Gorgos. Did Tao Shan confirm what I told you?"

"He did, and I'm happy for that."

"Oh? So you plan to claim your throne?" The old witch raised one eyebrow at Allana's words.

"No, but it does overcome any objections Lord Browdat might have to my marrying Javik, and I'm happy for that." Allana sat back on a large rock near the stream.

"How can you ignore your heritage? You must go to Gorgos and be crowned queen." The old woman bristled and seemed to grow two hands higher in her anger.

Allana only laughed at her. "You're a foolish old woman. Why would I leave this village and every happiness I ever hoped for to pursue a kingdom that lies in ruins?"

Grazhda pointed to the stream. "Look."

Allana started as the previously rippling water turned to a smooth pond. She stared into the pool as the image of a woman materialized on its surface. "Who is this?" she asked Grazhda.

"She will tell you," Grazhda said.

The woman wore a white robe and a golden diadem. A rich

golden necklace hung from her neck, and rings with precious jewels adorned each of her fingers. Her hair was raven black like Allana's and her skin was like fine marble. Deep black eyes radiated authority, but they softened considerably as she looked at Allana. "Allana I am Queen Oriana, your mother. I'm so glad to see you well and happy."

"How do I know you're my mother? I don't remember her at all."

"I gave you to Jodash and Norma when the Voldunee came. They promised to take you to safety. Are they still alive?"

"I don't know. I remember Norma, but she had no husband then. After they sold me away from her, I had no way to know if she lived or died."

Grazhda smiled as she watched a tear run down Allana's cheek.

"You're a slave?" the woman asked as anguish spread over her face.

"Not any more, my beloved killed my old master in combat, and he's granted me my freedom. We will be married when he comes home from war."

Relief softened Oriana's expression. "Is your husband-to-be a warrior? Does he have a mighty army at his back?"

"Javik is a warrior, but he commands no army."

"Then he will be no help to you in regaining the throne of Gorgos," Oriana said as her face fell a bit.

Allana bristled. "Javik is a fine warrior. Why do you speak of a throne? You are only an illusion anyway." She ran her hand through the calm water, and the image disappeared for a moment, but it returned quickly.

"Listen to me, child. I have but little time here. You must believe me." She held up the pendant hanging from her necklace. "You bear this crest tattoed on your rump, the same as I do. Is that not true?"

Allana saw it was the same design, only much clearer than her tattoo. Suddenly she was interested in what this apparition had to say. "It's true. What do you want to tell me?"

"You must regain the throne of Gorgos. Our people suffer greatly under the yoke of slavery. They're scattered across the lands bordering the Great Ocean, but they remember Gorgos. They ache for their homeland. If they knew you were alive, they would have some hope of being rescued from their plight. You are the only one alive who can save them. Don't leave them to suffer chains and whips any longer. Go to Gorgos. Return it to its former glory, and remember I love you always, and I'll be beside you in everything you do, though you will never know it. Goodbye my precious child."

The stream returned to its previous state, and Allana stood staring at it for a moment before turning to Grazhda.

"Why did you do that?"

"To show you your fate, Your Majesty."

"My fate, bah. How can a slave girl be a queen?"

"But, you are already a queen. A kingdom is there for you if you have the courage to claim it. As your mother said, thousands of your subjects languish in slavery. They have no hope now, but you could free them."

"I know what it means to be a slave, and I would rescue all of them if I could, but I'm only a poor woman with few skills and little cunning. Even if I wanted to be a queen, I have no idea of how to go about it, much less the gold or the army. It's impossible."

"Speak to Tao Shan. He will give you good advice. Goodbye for now. We will talk again soon. Just know that if you decide to accept this challenge, you will have my full support."

The witch walked into the forest and soon vanished while Allana sat on the rock thinking about what she'd seen. *Tao Shan says all wizards and magicians are charlatans, but I've never seen any of them do what I saw just now. I know there was some trick in it, but it was so real.* Allana smiled as she thought of the lovely lady in the water. *If that really was my mother, she was certainly beautiful. Javik says I'm beautiful. I quess I get that from my mother.*

* * * * *

She waited a few days before approaching Tao Shan again with the latest from Grazhda. She didn't want to appear to be a nuisance, but he seemed to sense something was troubling her. He approached her one day after her sling class.

"You've looked worried lately. Is something bothering you?" he said.

Allana packed her slings and stones, avoiding eye contact. "I saw Grazhda again, Master."

"You did? You must tell me all she said. Come into my rooms." He led her inside to the library table.

"Now, tell me all about it."

Allana sighed and related her experience. "How did she do that, Master?"

"I don't know, but it's the greatest trick I've ever heard of. The part about the medallion is interesting. I didn't think she knew anything about the royal crest of Gorgos, but she could have a scroll like mine. How do you feel about the encounter?" He leaned back and studied her as she answered.

"I don't know. I can certainly sympathize with people living in slavery, and I would rescue them if I could, but I'm so ignorant of these matters. If I tried to free them, I'd be killed before even one was free."

Tao Shan saw the thoughts behind her eyes and the sad expression. Here was a woman who was truly torn between her own happiness and the possibility of doing something truly great.

"What the image in the water asks of you is a daunting task, but a noble one. I know you are capable of accomplishing what the vision asked, and I know your misgivings about taking it on. You alone must decide, but if your decision is to try it, I will certainly help you."

"How is that, Master?" Allana's face took on a curious expression as she leaned forward in her chair.

"Javik is to train with me for another year when he returns. The tutor I have in mind for him would also be very helpful in preparing you for your adventure. You could train together, and Javik would be a great help to you in this quest."

"I know he would, but I must think more about this. It's quite overwhelming."

"Yes, I'm sure it is, but you are a formidable woman, Allana. Nothing is beyond your capability."

"Thank you, Master. I will give it some thought." She rose and left for Browdat's longhouse and solitude.

CHAPTER 5

Javik's feet felt like they were two sizes too big for his boots, and his back cried out for relief from the weight of his shield. The strap cut into his shoulder in spite of the lamb's wool tied around it. He could use the pike as a staff at times, but it often caught in a low tree branch and jerked him to a halt. When would they stop marching? The sweat poured from under his helmet in spite of the nearly freezing temperatures. He knew that if the column did stop, the sweat would rob the heat from his body and deliver it up to the all-devouring cold.

Autumn's color had given way to the bleak landscape of winter in the highlands. Only the black trunks of trees showed against the carpet of brown leaves on the forest floor. All the foliage was gone from the thick brush, and only scrawny wisps of branches remained. The dull gray sky hung low and seemed to intensify Javik's fatigue.

The other men around him seemed to be faring no better. The spring was gone from their step, and the boisterous marching songs had died out entirely. Javik now understood Tao Shan's comment that war was hardship followed by pain followed by death for the fortunate. He was beginning to think death might be preferable to another two days on the march, but a vision of Allana drove him on.

The armor, so bright only two days ago, was now as dull and gray as the sky. The pikes once held high in pride now rested on the shoulders of the weary pike men. Even the horses were showing signs of fatigue.

Tao Shan tried to prepare him for this. He forced the boys to march carrying rocks in their packs. They marched rain or shine, snow or sleet, through mud knee-high and through the swirling dust of summer drought. Never, though, had he felt like this before. The pace here was much faster and it seemed he carried twice as much as Tao Shan ever required. Those had been good times, when fellowship with the other trainees was sweetened by the fervor of youthful yearning for things they did not understand.

Javik thought much of his life had been consumed in longing for things he wanted desperately and working hard to achieve them, only to find their attainment brought more pain and a new longing for something else. He wanted to be a warrior like his father and trained with one of the best mentors in the kingdom only to find himself worn out from marching back and forth through the forests of Berglaundia without ever striking one blow in glory. Now he longed for the fire in his mother's section of the longhouse and a bear hide to wrap around him as he slept the sleep of the dead.

"Rest stop!" The command echoed down the long column from the commander at its head.

"Finally!" Gronan exhaled. "I didn't think we were ever going to stop." He fell in a heap of baggage and weapons, laying flat on his back against the frozen ground. Gronan was another one of Tao Shan's pupils. He was from a neighboring village, and carried a pike just like Javik.

Javik found a pile of fallen leaves and used them to help insulate his body from the ground.

"Get up, Gronan. You'll let the earth sap all the heat from you if you stay there," Javik advised him.

"Let me die, Javik. I'm in no shape to face the Wallans after all this marching, anyway."

"Leave him be." It was old Ian who spoke. He gathered up some twigs nearby and was starting to set them up for a fire. "He'll get up when he's cold enough."

According to Browdat and Goldar, Ian was too old to go to war but the old man insisted on being part of the army. Goldar finally gave in because of Ian's outstanding record of courage in battle and the fact that he was expert with a pike. Javik was surprised by the old man's ability to keep up on the march. The only drawback of his advanced age was the number of times he left the column to relieve himself, but he always resumed his place in short order.

"No fires!" The instruction was relayed down the line of march. They had not been allowed fires since morning. Their last hot meal was at the noon stop the day before, and cold rations served for food the previous night after setting up camp.

"Damn!" Ian spat as he kicked the stack of twigs into disarray. "No need for the Wallans to kill us. Our own chiefs will take care of that."

Javik almost agreed with Ian, but he knew the commander of this army. Goldar would not push them beyond their limits, and he would not prohibit fires unless there was a good reason.

"We must be close to the Wallans," Javik said.

"Aye, I can almost smell 'em," Ian sniffed the breeze like a dog and cackled at his own joke.

"What is battle really like, Ian?" Gronan asked. Like Javik, Gronan was fresh from Tao Shan's school and had never before been in battle.

"Didn't Tao Shan teach you whelps anything?" Ian mocked.

"He tried to tell us," Javik said. "He painted horrible stories for us and even showed us his wounds, but I don't think he felt there was any way to make it real for us."

"You're right, lad. You have to live it. I can tell you all the stories you want, but it won't prepare you for it. Just trust in your own strength and your pike and sword and try to remember everything you've been taught. If you're good, and a little lucky, you'll come through it in one piece." Ian spoke in a flat voice with a hard edge. He stared past the boys with the sorrow in his eyes telling of many lost companions and the hardships suffered in his long service to the King.

A horseman approached, and Javik recognized him as Wain, one of Goldar's lieutenants. He stopped near Javik and called for the soldiers to gather round him.

"We will await the Wallans on the moor yonder. Goldar commands that we form up for battle now since they may attack at any time. You pike men follow me. I'll show you where to set up your lines." Wain turned his horse and the weary men rose to follow.

"Looks like all night in battle formation," Ian groaned. No fires and no tents for us. It'll be a cold meal and a colder night. He cackled again at his own dark humor while the pike men struggled on in the low afternoon sun.

Wain positioned the pike men along the line Javik anticipated after seeing the moor. The broad meadow spread down to a gully he assumed hid a small stream. The woods they just left were matched by another on the opposite side of the gully but closer to it. Wain said the Wallans were approaching the moor through those woods. The pike men stood as a bristling barrier to the advance of this invading army. There was no way around them. To the left was the swampy source of the stream flowing through the gully. To the right, the stream vanished into a narrow gap in the high cliffs.

Javik had never been in this part of the kingdom. It was

beautiful, but soon it would be the site of his first battle. He shivered not so much from the cold as from the thought of actually killing a man in hand-to-hand combat. He had no doubt about his ability to kill after killing Grucheau, but vengeance drove that thrust. This time, he would be looking into the eyes of a man he did not hate. The poor fellow probably had a wife and children to mourn him and didn't want to die any more than Javik. He shook the thought from his mind. He remembered Tao Shan's admonitions about feeling sorry for the enemy or thinking of anything other than his death and one's own survival. If you did too much thinking in battle, you could be the one killed first. All the same, it was a shame anyone had to die, but better some Wallan than he. War was a tragic thing, but he would much rather return to Allana than lie rotting on a field far from the village.

Javik snorted in disgust at himself for forgetting his mother. She too, wanted him to return safely for more important reasons than Allana. Allana was a beautiful, young woman and could easily find another love, but his mother lost her love to war, and the loss of her son to the same cause would surely kill her also. He must survive more for her than for Allana. He vowed to keep reminding himself that this was his primary mission.

Wain appeared again. "You men may eat and sleep now, but no fires. We don't want the Wallans to know our strength until they come out of those trees." He pointed with his sword. Our scouts now expect they will be here by morning. They have stopped for the night."

Javik chewed on some cold dried fish while he waited for the stale bread the cooks would bring around. He had some goat cheese in his pack and his canteen was full. Tao Shan always told him to keep a full canteen and, particularly, to make sure it was full before any battle. He remembered the mentor saying war was thirsty work, and a thirsty man was thinking more of his next drink than his next opponent in battle. Javik made plans to fill his from the stream in the gully before he went to sleep.

He shivered through the night – grateful it did not rain. The leather battle dress under his chain mail was little enough protecttion from the cold without being soaked through as well. The dawn came as beautiful as any in his memory. If this were the last one he would see, it would be enough. He watched the golden lining of the clouds melt into the bright blue sky above as the sun began to warm his face. He realized only then they would be fighting with the sun in their eyes. Tao Shan warned him to avoid such a situation if possible, but he had no choice here.

The cooks passed out something he recognized as the remnants of the hot meal from two days ago. The cold kept the meat from rotting, but it did nothing for its flavor or tenderness. It seemed to grow in size as he chewed it. He cursed the day he first wanted to be a warrior.

The sound of drums on the other side of the gully interrupted his self-pity. The Wallans soon emerged from the woods in battle order. At the sight of Javik's countrymen, they broke into fierce war chants and battle cries. Javik felt his mouth go dry and was glad of his full canteen. They marched to the ditch and threw ladders across the narrow points while others climbed down the slopes into the creek bed. At that moment, Goldar rode out of the swamp area followed by his horsemen.

The thunder of the hoof beats was nearly deafening, and the shouts of the horsemen sent shivers down Javik's back. He felt sweat between his hands and his pike and quickly wiped it away with the cloth he kept tucked into his belt for just that purpose.

He could see Goldar and Browdat at the head of the charge. Tundig, Goldar's huge warhorse, churned the earth into great clods spraying out to either side, while Browdat's smaller mount glided over the turf without seeming to disturb it. Goldar swung a huge battle-axe and shouted encouragement to his men. Javik could hear Browdat bellowing curses at the Wallans as his long sword flashed in the sunlight. They were the fiercest sight he had ever seen.

The Wallans were taken completely by surprise. Evidently, they had scouted the swamp and decided a mounted attack was impossible from that location. Goldar's men knew the places where the footing was sufficient for horses and used that knowledge to good advantage. The horsemen were badly scattered as they emerged from the trees, but they quickly assembled into fighting groups and cut through the Wallan ranks like scythes through grain. They did not stop to give battle but swept across the field felling the Wallan warriors with sword and lance as they rode. Once across the field, they turned behind the line of pike men. A few fell, but nearly all made it to safety while the Wallan dead and dying littered the ground.

It was then Javik heard the cries of the wounded for the first time. He did not understand their language, but agony is the same in any tongue. The enemy was stung but not crushed. They resumed their march only to be met with a shower of arrows from the trees behind Javik. More fell under the deadly rain, and this broke the advance. The Wallans fell back to the tree line leaving the fallen where they lay. Here and there, two would lift a third between them, but most were abandoned. Some of the wounded began to crawl into the shelter of the ditch or back toward the trees. Only a few made it to their destinations. Most gave up and lay groaning on the cold ground.

An answering shower of arrows emerged from the Wallan lines, but it fell short of Javik and the pike men. The battlefield grew quiet as the wounded fell into faints or died from loss of blood. The drums began again as the Wallans advanced once more. This time there was no thunder of hoofs only the tramp of thousands of feet and the steady rhythm of the drums. As they marched, the Wallans clashed their swords and axes against their shields in time with the drums while a guttural death chant rose slowly in the chill air.

As they reached the ditch again, Berglauni infantry raced from the swamps placing themselves between the ranks of pike men and the advancing Wallans just at the lip of the gully. With the advantage of higher ground, the warriors were able to stop the Wallan infantry advance, but the Wallan archers moved up behind the advancing lines and began showering the pike men with arrows. Javik held his shield above his head and winced as each metal point pinged against it. An arrow hit the ground just in front of his left toe, and he moved his shield slightly forward. He heard a gasp and turned to see the man behind him fall with a feathered shaft protruding from his thigh. Javik felt responsible for the man's wound, but remembered Tao Shan's words. "Battle is chance – each man must face the roll of the war god's dice and accept the outcome. Be glad if it is not you who dies even if five hundred others perish on the same roll."

The screams and groans were closer now. Javik saw the Berglauni infantry giving ground slowly. Like a rising tide, the hideous melee advanced toward the pike men. Javik knew he must hold his line so the enemy could not create a gap for the cavalry. A horse was a virtual engine of death by itself. Its great bulk knocked a man to the ground then the hooves rained down pain while another rider's lance skewered the beaten body like a rabbit on a spit. No, his pike must hold fast to keep the horses away.

Javik could smell the blood now. The dull, metallic scent seemed to blend with the sweat-soaked armor and the odor of fear from each man around him, creating a vile perfume of battle. Javik's people always fought while retreating so the enemy would have to step over the dead and wounded, slipping in the blood-soaked mud while the Berglauni fought on dry ground. Javik planted the end of his pike's shaft firmly in the ground behind him and lowered the point so it would meet an oncoming man at chest level.

The first Berglauni warriors passed his position, moving rapidly to the rear and giving Javik room to work. Some of the archers moved up behind the pikes and began to pour arrows into the Wallan lines at point blank range. A huge man with a black, wooly beard loomed in front of Javik's pike and struck the point with his sword. Javik felt the blow all the way to his heels, and the shock drove his pike to the man's knee level before he could recover. By that time, Black Beard had moved around the point and headed straight toward him.

As if by Javik's command, a second pike point appeared to block the warrior's way. The man behind Javik had kept his point high until it was needed. Two arrows bounced off Black Beard's breastplate, but a third struck his neck and stayed there a moment before the warrior pulled it out and threw it away. The hot blood from the wound turned his curly black beard auburn, but he came on striking upward at the new point blocking his path. Javik knew he must now concentrate on the next man in the enemy line and leave this one to the other pike men and archers, but it was hard for him to take his eyes off the bulk looming over him now. Black Beard forced the second pike up and out of his way, but another appeared immediately.

Javik knew there were four rows of pikes and hoped one would soon find its mark.

Javik raised his own point just in time to impale the next Wallan. He was smaller than the first one, almost skinny, and his nose protruded beyond his helmet like an eagle's beak. Eagle Beak had no breastplate and let his shield stray just enough to allow Javik's pike point in. It was not an intentional move – more like a reflex action. Javik made a mental note of the move for use in the future. He now had Eagle Beak on the end of his pike and Black Beard standing so close on his left he could hear him breathing heavily.

Javik was about to draw his sword to kill Black Beard when the last pike found its mark just below the warrior's breastplate. With one mighty scream, the huge warrior fell on top of Javik, his great weight, forcing the boy to the ground and spattering Javik with his sweat and blood.

Black Beard tried to raise himself while groping for his knife. Javik could see the broken shafts of two arrows sticking out of joints in his armor and a large cut down one side of his head, gushing blood. The fatal pike had penetrated deeply into the Wallan's stomach, but Javik knew he could live for hours with those wounds. He must finish the job himself or be killed.

The great bear of a body was blocking both Javik's sword and his dagger. He would need another weapon quickly. Black Beard managed to pull a wicked looking knife from its sheath and was about to plunge it into Javik. Javik's left hand groped for a rock and found the giant's sword instead. The Wallan had dropped it with the point aimed back at his own face. Javik grasped the blade and drove it with all his might at the blood-soaked head. He felt the edge of the blade cut into his palm as the point entered his enemy's left eye. Black Beard's hideous scream nearly burst Javik's eardrums, but he dropped the knife and fell on Javik, limp and helpless, though he still breathed laboriously.

Javik struggled to free himself of the body and found his pike was still imbedded in Eagle Beak. The man was bleeding heavily, but still moved his hands along the shaft attempting to remove the point. Javik pulled it out with more strength than he thought he had and raised it again to confront a new threat. The next man stayed just out of reach of the point with his shield high, he was not eager to enter the fray. His eyes showed the terror of the carnage, and Javik could sense his unwillingness to die.

The ground shook under his feet, which could only mean cavalry. Theirs or ours – he could not yet tell. The battle continued on either side of him. The coward in front of him did not advance of his own accord, but was thrust forward by the crush of men behind him. Javik lowered his point and forced it into the unguarded thigh of the coward. He went down with a scream, and the man behind him tumbled forward out of control, ending up with his back to Javik. The pike behind him plunged into that man's back while Javik withdrew his point and presented it to the next fighter. *Would they never stop coming? How many could he kill before someone killed him?* He was getting tired. His arms were like lead, but he forced them to move the pike as he was taught.

"Fall back! Fall back!" The command was in Wallandian, but Javik knew what it meant. The warriors in front of him began to give way as Javik noticed the cavalry he'd heard was their own. It charged in from the right and cut its way through the Wallan infantry. The pike men cheered loudly as the horsemen swept in front of them. Javik could now take some time to survey his surroundings.

The large warrior lay still with his one eye wide open and

the other a gaping hole. The coward lay moaning and begging for mercy. The second man to feel Javik's pike was also lifeless and sprawled on his back, one hand on his chest. He had torn open his own tunic to see the extent of his wound before he died. The Berglauni infantry came back through the pike men and gave chase. One stopped just long enough to dispatch the coward.

"Fall back to a new line." It was the voice of the captain. He began to move back, but the man beside him said, "Get that sword! It's yours, you know. You killed him." He pointed at the sword Javik used to kill the giant. It was covered with blood, but he could see it was a fine weapon. He picked it up and pulled the sheath and baldric from the dead Wallan.

They formed new lines, but the battle was over for the day. The Wallans retreated into the forest as the Berglauni drums sounded recall. His people were not quick to pursue their enemy into what might well be a trap, so a rest was called to clear the field. For the first time Javik felt the pain in his hand. He looked at it and saw the wound was not deep, but it would need attention.

The hand could wait, however. Javik's first priority was collecting booty from the dead Wallans. He returned to where Black Beard and Eagle Beak lay and searched them for valuables. Eagle Beak's purse contained only a few coppers and a stone image of one of the Wallan gods. The totem had done him little good. Black Beard's purse was heavy with silver coins and two gold pieces of Wallan stamp. Javik also removed the big man's breastplate and helmet as well as Eagle Beak's helmet. He cleaned the sword using eagle beak's tunic before placing it back in its sheath. He tossed the coward's leather helmet aside. It was worthless, but Black Beard's knife was a prize indeed.

Javik picked up the fearsome knife and studied it carefully.

The grip was shaped to fit the big man's hand as if it had been poured using Black Beard's flesh as a mold. The guard was solid bronze and carved into intricate patterns of a strange nature. The blade gave the weapon its terrible aura. It was double edged with one side sharp and the other side serrated like the edge of an elm leaf. A dark groove ran down the middle of each side, and Javik suspected it contained some form of poison. He cut the sheath from black beard's belt and re-sheathed the weapon.

Javik now had a pile of considerable bulk at his feet. He slung Black Beard's sword over his shoulder and stuck the knife in his own belt. The coins went into his purse, which was nearly empty in any case, but the breastplate and helmet would have to be carried along with his own pike and shield. A Berglauni warrior was busy stripping another Wallan nearby, and Javik watched as he threaded a rope through holes in the various pieces of booty and then drug the whole package to the next body. Javik had been too busy to notice, but he now saw the field was filled with Berglauni warriors looting the dead just as he was doing.

Javik took a belt from one of the bodies to serve in place of a rope. He arranged his booty using Black Beard's breastplate as a sled and dragged his prizes back to the area where that night's camp was being set up.

Berda met Javik at the edge of the camp.

"Javik, you've been hurt!" Berda noticed the blood dripping from Javik's hand.

"It's not bad, Berda. I will find a healer soon. First, I must get these things to our tent. Have you set it up yet?"

"Yes, Javik. I set it up while I waited for you. I'm afraid the battle never got to my side of the field. I had no chance for booty like that." Berda pointed to the armor and helmet on the ground behind Javik.

"This is not the real treasure. I'll show you the valuable things at our tent. Show me the way so I can get this hand taken care of."

Berda led his friend to a small tent. Several men were clustered around a nearby fire, warming themselves after a hard day's work on the killing ground. Javik shoved the armor inside the tent and took the knife from his belt.

"I have never seen a knife like this one," Javik said as he pulled out the blade.

Berda sucked in his breath. "Ohh, it is a wonderfully terrible knife, Javik." He rubbed his finger along the dark groove in the blade. "This is poison, I'm sure. My father told me about such things, but I never expected to see one."

"It would have been my last sight had it not been for this." Javik pulled the baldric from his shoulder and unsheathed Black Beard's sword. In spite of the dried blood, the blade flashed brightly in the firelight.

"Wow!" Berda exclaimed. "That sword is worth some money, Javik. You're a lucky man to have taken that in battle."

"That's a fine sword you have there, young man. Care to sell it?" The boys failed to notice one of the men from the fire move up beside them. He was one of the healers named Ethen.

"I might be willing to speak of a price after I've cleaned it and inspected it thoroughly, and after you look at my hand." Javik held out his palm to show the healer his wound.

"Come over to the fire, and I will see to it," Ethan nodded toward a chest he had been using as a seat.

Javik re-sheathed the sword and slung the baldric over his shoulder. He was not about to leave such a valuable item lying around, and he was not sure Berda was mature enough to warrant his trust in such matters.

The healer rummaged in his trunk and produced several jars and a linen bandage. He poured some water into a brass bowl and added carefully measured portions from two of the jars. Tearing off a part of the bandage, he used it as a swab to clean Javik's wound.

"Agh!" Javik reacted instinctively to the sharp sting of the potion in his open cut.

"Yes, it does burn some, but this will cleanse the wound and keep the evil spirits from entering it," Ethen assured him. The healer spread a salve from another of his jars over Javik's hand and wrapped it tightly with the rest of the bandage.

"That will be one silver coin," the healer held out his hand, palm up. Javik found the appropriate coin among the new horde of money in his purse and passed it to the healer.

The healer moved to dump the contents of his bowl, but Javik stopped him. "May I use that to clean my sword?" Javik unsheathed the new weapon to the collective gasp of the other men around the fire.

"Here, let me help you with that. I don't want you to soil the new bandage." The healer took the weapon from Javik and began to wash off the dried blood. With the grisly film removed, the sword reflected the firelight with a dazzling brilliance. There were no nicks in the blade in spite of the heavy combat it had seen that day. The hilt was wrapped in soft leather tied in place with gold wire, and the pommel was a large, blue stone veined with red and silver. The sheath was as fine as the sword.

"It's beautiful," Javik gasped. "I've never seen anything like it." He took the sword from the healer and hefted it. It felt like an extension of his arm, but it was heavy. He would need to train with it for some time before he could use it well.

"You have a fine sword at your side there." The healer

pointed to the King's sword. "Let me buy this one from you and save you carrying it around. I'll give you top price for it."

Javik studied the blade and noticed an inscription. "What does this say, healer? I can't make it out."

The healer tilted the blade to get a good angle with the campfire. "Kuan jumo na thrupor," he muttered. "It's in an old language of one of our tribes. I'm not really sure, but I think it means something like 'My Life Before My Honor.'"

"This could well be the blade of one of our warriors killed by that Wallan dog," Javik said. He ran his hand along the blade trying to read the steel's memory of battles past. "What tales this blade could tell, eh?"

"I can see you have become entranced by this thing," the healer laughed. "You have made it too valuable for me to afford. Take it with you young man, and when you tire of its weight and wish a fine wench instead, let me know.

They had a hot meal that night and a chance for a good night's sleep, but Javik sat up by the fire and studied the new sword. At least two men had died with it in their hands. How many souls it had liberated from their bodies he could only guess. Were it not for the discipline of the pike men, he would be one of them. Now it belonged to him. "My Life Before My Honor", it was a good motto.

"Where did you get that sword?"

Javik turned to see Goldar standing behind him. "I killed a Wallan today and took it from him, sir."

"What did this man look like?"

"He was a huge man with a black, curly beard and deep blue eyes. He was wearing a full breastplate, and his helmet had a dragon crest. He fought bravely." Javik would never forget the sight of the light going out in those eyes.

"By the gods, you've killed Horick and re-claimed the sword

of Aelin the Red. That must be the reason they left the field so hurriedly today. Browdat must know of this. Aelin was a kinsman of his." Goldar held out his hand toward Javik. "May I see it?"

"Certainly, sir." Javik handed the sword to the war leader, and Goldar's face took on a new radiance as he hefted the superb weapon.

"By Zhou! It's everything the legends say of it. How did you survive the onslaught of such a fearsome blade?"

"The discipline of the pike men saved me, sir. I would be dead by now had someone behind me failed his duty."

"No pike could down Horick by itself. His armor was too strong for that. There must have been something else, perhaps an arrow you failed to notice?"

"It's true, sir, that no pike or arrow killed the man. In truth, it was his own sword that did the deed."

"What?" Goldar reacted incredulously.

"He dropped the sword as he fell on top of me. It was the only weapon at hand for my defense. He had drawn his knife and was about to strike when I used his own sword to slay him. That's how I wounded my hand. I had to grasp it by the blade to use it."

Goldar examined Javik's bandaged hand. "Then the weapon is truly yours, Javik."

The war leader handed the sword back to Javik who re-sheathed it. "I'm glad to see you alive, Javik. I promised your mother I would look after you, but I couldn't find you until just now. Browdat is looking for you, also."

"How is my father?"

"He is well and has no wounds. I must tell him where you are and that you carry Aelin's sword. Stay here, and I will get him." Goldar strode off toward the camp of the war leaders.

Javik knew well the story of Aelin the Red. In the days when Berglaundia was only a tiny fraction of its present size, the people were constantly at war with the Wallans over good hunting and fishing grounds. The battles raged for three generations as the Berglauni grew stronger and the Wallans weaker. Just when the Berglauni were about to taste victory, a plague decimated the Berglauni without affecting the Wallans. The Wallans saw it as their chance to eliminate the Berglauni, and launched an all-out offensive against Javik's ancestors.

The key battle was fought for control of the same moor Horick died on this very day. All was going well for the Berglauni until Wallan infantry attacked from the swamp Goldar's cavalry used for cover. The Berglauni left was weak, but Aelin the Red commanded that sector.

Aelin was said to be a huge man, well over sixteen hands high. His name came from his fire-red hair and beard and his ruddy complexion. It was said he had slain a hundred men in his lifetime, and his bravery in battle was legendary.

As the Wallans charged, Aelin wheeled his cavalry to meet it. The war-horses burst through the Wallan lines disrupting their order and panicking many of the weaker warriors into flight. To Aelin's dismay, many of his riders pursued the fleeing Wallans instead of turning to help the weak Berglauni infantry in their battle against the superior Wallan force.

Mustering what remained of his horsemen, Aelin charged back into the fray, but was quickly unhorsed by a Wallan pike man. The battle was going badly, but Aelin bravely stood his ground, slaughtering Wallans right and left. A fierce Wallan champion felled the hero just as help arrived to turn the tide of battle. The Wallan only had time to claim Aelin's sword before retreating back into the swamps.

It must have been one of Horick's relatives who killed Aelin.

Javik felt a new weight added to his shoulders now that he knew the history of the weapon. How much must he be expected to carry? The burden of Tolda and Browdat was enough without the added responsibility of a legendary sword. Javik felt his boyhood slipping away rapidly.

He heard Browdat long before he emerged from the darkness and into the firelight. "Thank Zhou you've found my son, Goldar, but what is this nonsense about the sword of my kinsman, Aelin?"

"You will see for yourself soon, Lord Browdat," Goldar laughed as the two men appeared before Javik.

Javik rose to meet his father and dropped to one knee in deference. The big man scooped him up like a rag doll and embraced him passionately.

"Thank Zhou you're well. Your mother would have my balls on a platter if I didn't bring you safely home to her."

"I am well, Father. My wound is trivial."

"Let me see," Browdat demanded.

Javik showed him the wounded hand and retold the story of Horick, handing Browdat the sword at its conclusion.

Browdat turned the sword over in his hands and admired the beauty of the weapon. "This is truly Aelin's sword. It has returned to his family after all these years, and my own son has done the deed." Browdat turned to Goldar. "Aelin never named his sword, Goldar. Don't you think its new owner should name it?"

"I think that would be proper," Goldar assured him as he smiled at Javik.

"Tao Shan says a sword must earn its name," Javik replied with as much humility as he could muster. "I have only used it to slay its owner in a very ignominious fashion. It should belong to a war leader."

Browdat handed the sword back to Javik. "You have earned the right to carry it, Son, and no one may take it from you except by killing you in battle. You are a marked man now. I hope you can live with the burden." He slapped Javik on the back. "You look big enough to take care of yourself, though."

"Father, I would feel much better if the sword were in your hands. I have the one the King gave me, and I have no need for two swords. Please take it and keep it safe."

Browdat rubbed his beard thoughtfully and finally broke the silence. "I will buy it from you, Javik. This weapon is easily worth the price of your year with Tao Shan and fifty gold pieces besides. What say you to that?"

Javik almost fainted with delight. He knew the weapon was valuable, but had no idea it could demand such a princely sum. With Tao Shan paid for and the extra gold in his purse, he could set up his own hearth and give his mother the independence she deserved. His dreams had come true.

"Oh, Father, tonight you've made me the happiest warrior in Berglaundia." He threw himself at the great man and almost broke into tears in his happiness.

"Easy there! You're a warrior now, Javik, and you must behave like one. There is a proper ceremony for the exchange of a sword in our customs. Instruct him, Goldar," Browdat boomed as he turned his back on the two, pretending he was paying no attention to them.

"I know the ceremony, sir," Javik said. "My father taught me that much."

Browdat turned back to face Javik who unsheathed Aelin's sword and held it in his hands, arms outstretched to Browdat. The big war leader knelt in front of him, and Javik felt very awkward seeing the great man in this position.

"Lord Browdat, I present you with this unnamed sword in

exchange for your payment and for the honors you have bestowed upon me, your adopted son. I shed my blood to show that it is willingly given." Javik ran his good hand along the edge of the blade creating a small cut. He spread the blood on the sword.

Browdat ran his hand along the other side of the blade. "I, Browdat, accept this weapon I have not earned in battle as a token of my son's respect and gratitude and in return for the payment agreed upon between us and witnessed by Goldar." The big man spread his blood on the sword and let it mingle with Javik's. "May this be the only time the sword shall taste the blood of either one of us."

Javik handed the sword and its scabbard to his father.

"Father, I thank you for all you have done for my mother and me."

Browdat rose, and Javik thought he saw a tear in one of the great man's eyes.

"Thank you, Javik, for being a son a man can be proud of." Browdat turned to Goldar. "Is there any qush around here? This calls for a drink!"

Several other men appeared, attracted by the presence of Browdat and Goldar, and witnessed the sword ceremony. They gave a spontaneous cheer at Browdat's suggestion of a drink.

Before Goldar could go in search of one, a keg of qush rolled into the firelight and tankards were pressed into the hands of Browdat, Goldar and Javik. The keg was opened with a great rush of foam before a spigot could be inserted to stem the flow. The tankards were filled, and Browdat raised his on high.

"To our victory and the glory of battle, and to my son the new warrior!"

The men cheered boisterously as each joined the war leader in his toast. The keg was emptied before the set of the moon.

* * * * *

The next day the Wallans were gone. During the night they had stolen back to their own borders leaving only graves behind. Javik walked among the mounds. Most were only marked by a pile of stones surmounted by a helmet or a tunic, but one was next to a tree carved with the name "Horick" and the inscription, "Death to he who carries the sword of Aelin."

Javik shuddered. Somehow the word would get back to Wallandia that he carried the sword. Their fiercest warriors would now seek out Javik on the battlefield. He had killed only four men, and he was already a marked man. Then he remembered the words of Tao Shan, "The gods never give any man a burden too large to carry, but many lack the courage to pick it up."

CHAPTER 6

After her encounter with Grazhda, Allana's sleep was haunted by images of starving children and gaunt-faced adults. *I am their only hope. There is no one else with a legitimate claim to the throne. I know it's folly. I should stay here and marry Javik when he returns. I know that's the prudent thing to do, but is it the right thing? Grazhda seems so certain I will reign on Gorgos, and Tao Shan thinks I can do it. He's offered his help if I decide to try. What should I do? I think I should seek the counsel of the Lady Dana. I'll speak with her in the morning.*

* * * * *

The next day she caught Dana as she helped prepare breakfast. "Lady, what do you know of the witch Grazhda?"

Dana looked about furtively before leading Allana outside. "How do you know about Grazhda?" Dana asked.

"I've seen her twice in the forest. The first time she called me 'Queen of Gorgos'. I didn't believe her, but Tao Shan proved what she said was true."

"You are a princess?" Dana stared at Allana in disbelief.

"Yes, Lady. Grazhda said Tao Shan could prove it, and he gave me a mirror so I could look at my tattoo. Then he showed me a scroll containing the royal crest of Gorgos. The tattoo is the same as the crest. The scroll said all royal children were tattoed with the crest at birth."

Dana's face brightened. "This is marvelous news. Lord

Browdat can have no objection to your marriage to Javik now."

"That's not all, Lady. I saw her again a few days ago."

"What did she say then?" Dana seemed to be very interested in the encounter.

"She showed me a vision of my mother."

"Your mother?"

"That's who the image said she was. I've given it a lot of thought, and I think the vision was true. Mother begged me to return to Gorgos and restore the kingdom."

"Grazhda is a powerful witch. She protects our village because my husband, Tolda, once saved her life. She told Javik he would be a great warrior. Her blessings and curses are well known to all. Her advice should not be ignored. Does she want you to go to Gorgos also?"

"Yes, I believe she does, though she hasn't said it in so many words."

"Then you should go. When Javik comes back he will want to join you in your quest. The two of you, together with Grazhda's blessing, will be well equipped to take on such a task."

"I don't know. Tao Shan has offered his help, but I'm so torn. I see my people suffering in my dreams, and I want to help them, but I also see Javik and I happy here in Holliga. What should I do, Dana?"

Dana placed one arm around Allana and embraced her. "Poor child. I don't see that you have any choice, but be sure you know what the old hag wants in return. She never blesses without demanding payment."

"I will go into the forest after my lessons today. Perhaps she'll find me again?"

"Let me know what she says. She always speaks in riddles, but I may be able to help you decipher her words."

"Thank you, Lady. I will, but please tell no one about this. It must be a secret between us."

"You have my word on that." Dana embraced Allana. "Please let me know what you decide to do."

"You will be one of the first to know, Lady."

Allana returned to Tao Shan's and prepared for her sling lessons.

* * * * *

Allana was almost afraid to go into the forest. She knew Grazhda would find her and press her for a decision on Gorgos. She didn't know about all of the witch's powers, however. One night she dreamed of a palace. She walked through its corridors to a large bedroom and approached a mirror. The image was her, but she wore the same white robe her mother wore in Grazhda's vision, and a golden diadem like hers adorned her head. She raised her fingers and saw many rings. When she looked back at the mirror, Grazhda's image appeared behind her.

"Hail Queen of Gorgos?" Grazhda said.

Allana turned to face her. "I don't want to dream of you."

"Yet you dream of wearing a crown."

"All I can have are dreams."

"The throne of Gorgos is yours. All you have to do is reach out for it." Grazhda moved her right hand as if snatching a crown out of the air.

"If it were that easy, all women would be queens. Besides, it will take much gold to buy a crown, and I have none."

"Gold is an easy matter." She held her left hand up in front of her face and rubbed her thumb against the first two fingers. "Javik has Grucheau's sword. Bring it to me, and I will see that you have all the gold you need to buy a throne."

"I couldn't do that, he'd kill me when he found out."

"Kill you? The love of his life? I don't think so. Besides, you won't be here when he comes back, and many things will keep you apart until the time comes for you to rule Gorgos with him by your side. But, gold is only a part of the task. You must bring all of your guile and cunning to bear on the mission of regaining your throne."

"But, I have no skills other than the sling, and I'm not skilled in deception and subterfuge."

"You will need another mentor for that, and I will see that you find one."

"And Grucheaux's sword is all you demand in return?"

"Not quite, but that payment will come after your quest is successful. I will only tell you that what you must give me will cause you no pain in acquiring it, nor any pain in parting with it. Think it all over, and when you decide to act, I will come to you again. Farewell, future Queen of Gorgos."

Allana awoke in a cold sweat. *Was that only a dream? It was so real. All she demands is Grucheaux's sword, but that belongs to Javik. It would be thievery to take it without his consent, even though he would gladly give it to me if he knew it would help me gain a throne. The other demand was very mysterious, but the way the witch spoke, it would be a trivial matter to me, and the demand will not come until after I'm Queen. I will speak to Tao Shan once more.* She went to sleep again and dreamed of Javik.

* * * * *

The next afternoon, Allana approached the old warrior with the problem.

"Master, I've decided I should take up this quest. Grazhda said I would have her full support, but I worry about what she may want in return." Allana told him Grazhda's demand.

Tao Shan sat back and tented his fingers while he mulled over the situation. "The old witch wants something you may not want to give up. That's why she's being so vague about it."

"What could that be? I have nothing of value," Allana said.

"Not now, but if you should reign on Gorgos you would have both wealth and power. But, she already has power, and wealth is not a problem for her." He sat back and sank into deep thought again. Suddenly he snapped his fingers and leaned across the table.

"I've got it. She wants something you and Javik will have. She wants a child."

Allana gasped in horror. "A child, my child?"

"Yes, don't you see? She is not immortal, much as she'd have you believe she is. Someday she will die, and there will be no one to carry on in her place. She must train someone to take over her domain, and she'll need to start the child early."

"I've lost a child already. I don't want to lose another one even for the throne of Gorgos. I know Javik would never agree to such a thing."

"She knows that too, but I'm pretty sure that's what she wants."

"How could that be when she said the thing would cause me no pain in gaining it?"

Once more Tao Shan sank into deep thought. "I don't know. It was just the first thing that came into my mind. It may not be that at all." His face took on a more serious expression, and took one of Allana's hands in his. "Do you really want to be Queen of Gorgos?"

It was Allana's turn to think. She looked off to one side and frowned, but after a while a smile began to change her expression. "I do. Is that silly?"

"Not at all. You are the last of the royal house of Gorgos. Only you have a legitimate claim to the throne, and only you can bring your people back to prosperity. I know of no higher calling than the quest before you now. Know that you have my blessing to pursue that dream as well as 500 gold crowns."

Allana gasped at such a sum. "Master! You are very generous."

"It's only a loan to be repaid after you are Queen. I will place that sum with the Argani, and you will have a letter of credit good in any realm between here and Gorgos. The Berglauni do not do business with the Argani, but those kingdoms standing between you and your throne know to honor their word."

"I've never heard of the Argani."

"You will probably come to know them very well in the future, but that's secondary." He took Allana's hands in his and looked her in the eye. "Take this quest. I know you will succeed."

"What about Javik?"

"You should take him with you, of course. Until he returns, you will train with my tutor. Then, you two will train together until you're ready to embark on your quest. I'll send a message to Bandor tomorrow. You can begin your training in two days."

CHAPTER 7

Allana walked into Tao Shan's library a bit hesitant to meet her teacher. Tao Shan told her he was a bit on the old side, but he'd mentored many princes in his long lifetime, and this was the man he'd called upon to continue Javik's education. The old man rose and bowed as she walked in.

"Your Highness, my name is Bandor. It will be my pleasure to pass on to you what knowledge I have concerning royal conduct."

Allana smiled as she sat down at the table. "You may call me Allana, Bandor. I am not yet a true princess."

Bandor sat opposite Allana. "Tell me about your life to this point," he said.

Allana related her life story, including the meetings with Grazhda. Bandor nodded from time to time to indicate his interest. When she finished he sat up more erect than she thought possible at his age. "I've never taught a princess, but I've tutored many princes in my travels. I've often wondered if a country might be better off with a female ruler. Now I have the chance to train one from the ground up, so to speak. I feel this is an opportunity where I must exceed my own expectations of quality."

"You'll find me an eager student, sir. Shall we proceed?"

Bandor passed her a scroll. "I want you to read this after your sling class today and be ready to discuss it at our session tomorrow. We will meet each morning at this hour and be finished by noon. You will go about your normal duties for the rest of the day, but I will always have a scroll for you to read each evening. Do you understand?"

"Yes, sir."

"Good. First, I must tell you that princes and Kings rule by might, but a princess or a queen must rule by guile. You would be no match for most warriors in any kind of combat, but you hold an advantage over them beyond any strength even the mightiest warrior possesses. That strength is your beauty. Take care of your face and form at all times. Perhaps there are some women in the village who can help you?"

"There is one, sir. The Lady Dana has been very kind to me. She is a lovely woman herself and knows all the secrets needed to bring out the best in any woman. I can confide in her."

"Good, let her teach you all she knows about such things. Now let's begin with some simple scenarios."

Bandor posed a dozen situations to her and asked how she would respond. Then he critiqued her responses adding suggestions about changes in her voice inflections as well as the course of action she proposed for each one. He released her at noon as he promised.

* * * * *

The first carts carrying wounded men rumbled into the village two days later. Allana watched as the bloody and broken warriors were carried to the common house where the healers established a hospital. As one cart passed, she heard a man call her name.

"Allana, come see me when you can," he shouted.

She recognized him as one of Tao Shan's students from the last Mauhad and ran to catch up to his cart. "Gregor, are you badly wounded?" she asked as she drew even with the vehicle.

"I'll tell you all when you come see me. Come soon, I have

some important news about Javik."

"Is he well?" she shouted as she ran beside the cart.

"Yes, he's well. The news is good news. Come see me later."

"I'll be there tonight," Allana shouted over the noise of the wheels and the clatter of the horse's hooves. She watched as two more carts passed her before continuing home.

That evening she sought out Gregor in the common house. She was not prepared for the scene before her there. Two dozen men lay on cots, filling nearly the whole space of the large central area. Many were asleep, but some moaned piteously. A few were missing an arm or a leg. A scream from a room off to her left caused her to start. She peered into it and saw one healer cutting the lower part of one man's leg away as four other healers held him down on a table. She shuddered and moved on. The sounds and the sights of the broken warriors were overwhelming, but the smell was worse. She was used to the body odor of Tao Shan's students, but here the smell of sweat was mixed with that of blood, vomit and festered wounds. She spotted Gregor and moved quickly to him.

"Allana, thank you for coming," he said as he raised himself on one elbow.

"Are you badly wounded?" she asked.

"A Wallan arrow found my leg. The healers with the army thought it might be poisoned, so they sent me home. They think they can save my leg, but I've been very sick until Willum the healer gave me a potion a while ago. I feel much better now, thank you."

"You said you had word of Javik."

"It's good news. He's recovered the sword of Aelin the Red."

Allana looked at him with a blank expression, and Gregor realized she had no knowledge of the sacred weapon. "Aelin was a legendary warrior from this village. It was said his sword was made with metal given to him by Zhou, and that made him invincible When he was killed, it was said it was because he violated Zhou's will. Now it passes to Javik since he killed its present owner. Your man will be honored above all other warriors in this village."

Allana smiled and nodded her head to one side. "This is wonderful news, but it may pose a problem for Javik and I."

"Oh, how's that?"

"Browdat objects to our marriage now. He may be even more opposed to it now that Javik has earned this great honor. I'm sure many of the rich houses will want him as a son-in-law once he returns with such honor. Their daughters can bring rich dowries, but I can bring nothing. At least not yet."

"What do you mean, not yet?"

"I can't tell you now, but if all goes well, Lord Browdat will beg me to marry Javik."

"Very mysterious, but I won't probe any deeper." Gregor lay back in his bed breathing heavily.

"Are you allright?" she asked.

"Yes, I'm afraid Willum's potion is making me sleepy now."

"I'll leave you to rest. Is there anything I can bring you?"

"Thank you, but my sister sees to my needs. I just wanted you to know the news about Javik."

"Thank you, Gregor. I'll visit you again soon." With that, Allana kissed him gently on the forehead and rose to leave.

"That's the best medicine I've had since I was wounded," he said.

Allana smiled at him and returned to Browdat's house and her bed, but she lay awake in spite of all her efforts to sleep. *What more can come between Javik and me? First, it was my position as a slave, now it's his position as an honored warrior. There is only one answer. I must gain the crown of Gorgos to be worthy of him. I must give Grazhda what she demands and learn well from Bandor. I can only hope Tao Shan and the old witch are right. Only a crown will bring me Javik and happiness.*

Allana rose from her bed and dressed. She went to Javik's room and found Grucheaux's sword under Javik's bed wrapped in oily rags to prevent rust. The rest of the longhouse was sleeping soundly as she crept from the building and stood in the light of a full moon. The night air was crisp, and she wished she'd taken a heavier wrap.

You're a foolish girl. You have no idea where to find Grazhda, and the hour's so late. Go back to bed. She started to return to bed when a white stag emerged from the forest. It stood there staring at her for a moment before turning down a familiar path. It had gone only a few meters when it stopped and looked back at Allana.

I think he wants me to follow him. She moved to the path, and the stag walked on. After a short while she stood in front of a small cabin close against the mountain. A candle burned inside the only window. The stag snorted and vanished into the dark forest.

I wonder who lives here. I don't remember ever seeing this cabin before, yet I know the path the stag led me on. As she wondered, the cabin door opened to reveal Grazhda.

"Welcome to my humble home, Your Majesty," the old woman cackled. "Come inside."

Allana stepped warily into the small house, but was amazed to find out the inside was much larger than the outside.

"Sit down, if you please, Majesty."

She took one of the wooden chairs next to a heavy table stained with dark splotches of things she didn't care to ask about.

Grazhda seated herself opposite Allana. "I see you've made up your mind," the witch said.

"I have. I've decided to attempt this quest."

The witch cackled her pleasure. "Have you brought the sword?" She pointed to the bundle in Allana's arms.

"Yes, this is it." She held the package out to the witch who took it in her gnarled hands.

Grazhda laid the bundle on the table and carefully unwraped the weapon. The flickering light from the fireplace made the blade glow with an almost luminescent quality.

"Isn't it marvelous?" Grazhda asked.

"It's only a sword. I've seen it many times when I was his slave."

"Ah, but you don't know its significance. Do you know the story of Tolda, Javik's father?"

"Lady Dana told me he once saved your life."

Grazhda took the sword and held it to her lips. "This sword extracted the final breath of life from Tolda. I can feel his spirit inside the steel. Tolda was not a common warrior. His bloodline goes back many centuries to a very powerful wizard. He carried the seed of another wonderful wizard in his loins, and this has been passed on to Javik. I wanted Javik, but Tolda would not have it. Javik has now trod the warrior's path and will not turn back. I must try to find the great wizard in his son." She lay the sword back on the table, and it seemed to ring as it came to rest.

"I fear the meaning of your other demand should I be successful." Allana said.

"I told you, it will cause you no pain in obtaining what I demand, nor any in giving it away. What do you have to fear?"

"I will believe you for now. I have no other choice."

"Good, now we will get down to business."

Grazhda busied herself rummaging through some drawers in a nearby chest. She soon produced a paper.

"Here is a letter of credit for 500 gold crowns. Any Argani will honor it. You will find the one you desire in Ulum. His name is Gallam. Anyone in Ullum will know where to find him."

"And the mentor you mentioned?"

"Her name is Varuda. You will find her begging in the marketplace. You will know her by her ravaged face."

"A beggar?" Allana's eyebrows rose at the idea.

"She was not always a beggar. Once she was the queen of prostitutes in Ulum. She spurned a bandit king of Magda, and he had acid thrown in her face after he destroyed her brothel and took all her whores as his slaves. She is a master of all the arts you will need to establish the finest brothel in the land of Zargaia."

"You want me to run a brothel?"

"Why do find that offensive? It is an honest profession."

"I will not sell my body. I had to unwillingly submit to Grucheaux, and I vowed I'd do that for no man if I were ever free. You ask too much." Allana stood and reached for the sword, but Grazhda grabbed her hand.

"Sit down, child. Hear me out."

Allana resumed her seat, but her expression was total defiance.

Grazhda moved to a mirror covered by a black cloth. She lifted the cloth and Allana saw it was the mirror in her dream.

"Come look in this mirror."

Allana walked to the mirror and gasped when the image changed, showing her stark naked. "Do you see that? What man would not sacrifice all he had to sample the ambrosia of that body? You have all of the assets necessary to gain the support of the greatest kings."

Allana sighed. "I know what you're implying. I was a slave

and forced to suffer the attentions of my master. I have no intention of subjecting myself to that degradation again."

"Have I said you must? Men are simple things. They will shower you with gold and jewels, trying to bribe their way into your bed. You must become expert at playing them up to the point where you get what you desire, and they do not."

"And Tao Shan will teach me how to do that?" Allana laughed. The thought of Tao Shan being able to teach her feminine wiles and sexual prowess was hilarious. The idea of being a queen was certainly attractive, but she doubted her ability to manipulate men the way Grazhda described.

"You are but the bait in the trap. You need not submit to any man unless you see great profit in the act. Use your gold to buy slaves to service your clients. You will gain many powerful allies if you listen well to Varuda, and you'll need allies to regain your throne. You will also grow rich in the process, and you'll need that gold once you reach Gorgos."

"What would Javik think? He'd never consent to marry me after he found out I owned a brothel."

"He loves you, and he will forgive you anything. Don't worry about him. Besides, he must spend a year with Tao Shan after the war, and you've already decided to proceed without him. Now that he has Aelin's sword, many wealthy families will offer their daughter's hands to such an honored warrior from a noble house. You must gain your throne to win him. You've already decided that."

"Then I will go to Ulum and seek out this Varuda."

Allana rose and moved toward Grazhda to embrace her, but the witch pulled away. "None of that. Go now, and remember your promise."

Allana left the curious house and returned to Browdat's longhouse.

CHAPTER 8

Javik was weary of war. The pleas of the wounded haunted his sleep and the smell of death lingered on everything he owned. It seemed no amount of water would wash away the stench of wasted lives. He'd killed many by now, but he found no glory in it. He killed to save his own life or some other warrior's life. He had seen friends fall, with him helpless to aid them. Karl and Berda managed to survive with only minor wounds, but too many hearths would mourn for sons buried where they fell.

Besides the plunder from Horic, Javik managed little more in the way of personal gain. The army captured one of the Wallan baggage trains, and that loot would be divided among all of the soldiers. Javik knew his share would be small, indeed, but he had his greatest prize from his first battle. Browdat's purchase of the sword of Aelin the Red would put him in a position to marry Allana and establish his own hearth. The extra year he'd promised Tao Shan would be an easy matter now.

Allana, he often dreamed of her.

Javik sat by the campfire absent-mindedly staring into the flames. Many times he thought he could smell the aroma of her raven hair and feel her arms around him. His body ached to possess her. He'd seen the other men frequent the camp followers, but he couldn't bring himself to follow their lead. He often dreamed of the raven-haired girl, and he was hard-pressed to purge her from his mind before battle. The last thing he needed was a mental image of Allan distracting him at a crucial moment.

"Javik, we march to battle again tomorrow!" Berda slumped down by the fire followed closely by Karl.

His friends' attitudes brought a much-needed smile to Javik's face.

"Do either of you remember how we couldn't wait for our first battle?" Javik said.

"Humph," Karl said, "Now I can only hope for the last one before we can go home."

"I thought we'd gain our fortunes in war, but I've only got five gold pieces from that skinny one I skewered yesterday," Berda announced. "How did you do, Karl?"

"Only a few coppers. You and Javik have all the luck."

"It doesn't matter now, the important thing is we're alive," Javik said.

"Well, we can certainly understand why you want to get home," Karl said as he punched Berda with his elbow and winked at Javik.

"She's all I think about, but I don't know if Lord Browdat will consent to our marriage,"

"He has to see how much in love you two are," Karl said.

"All I can do is hope, but I intend to marry her no matter what," Javik said.

"I'd hate to marry without my family's blessing," Berda said.

"When you fall in love you'll understand that being with her is the most important thing in your life. Without the woman you love, life becomes a journey through a wasteland," Javik said.

"Whooo, very philosophical, but I'm hungry," Karl said. "Do either of you have anything to eat?"

"I have some dried fish," Berda said. "You're welcome to some, if you want it."

Karl made a face, convincing Berda he was not interested.

"I ran out of food two days ago," Javik said.

"We should get a hot meal before we start marching tomorrow. I don't think we'll get another very soon," Berda said. "The Wallans are burning their fields behind them and taking all of the livestock."

"Our foragers come back with less and less, and our hunters bring in only meager game," Karl added.

"I think I'll try to get some sleep," Javik said as he rose to spread out his sleeping skins.

"Me too," Karl said as he punched Berda.

"Oh yes, me too," Berda said.

Javik lay looking at the stars and wondering if Allana would ever be his wife. He fell asleep and dreamed of her.

CHAPTER 9

Allana continued her studies with Bandor. The winter pressed on, and the mountain passes became clogged with snow. Any thought of proceeding on her quest would now have to await the spring thaw.

News from the war was good and bad. Good in the sense that the enemy was suffering defeat after defeat, but bad because the men would not be home soon. The army would camp for the winter in Wallandia and press on to sure victory in the spring. The men in the hospital either died or recovered and returned to the war. Those too badly maimed to fight returned to their hearths to live as best they could within the charity of the village.

She was becoming more and more skilled at finding solutions to Bandor's problems, but she knew she had much more to learn. Grazhda no longer haunted her dreams, and she'd not seen the old hag since delivering the sword. No one had yet noticed it was gone, but no one was interested in Grucheaux's sword now that Javik was responsible for returning Aelin's sword to Browdat's house.

* * * * *

The dreary months of winter passed slowly for Allana, but spring was early, and word soon came that the passes to the South were now open. When the first flowers appeared through the melting snow, she approached Tao Shan with her decision.

"I knew you would want to go as soon as we heard about the passes," he said. He opened a drawer and produced a small purse. He handed it to her. "Take this gold for your trip expenses. I will also furnish a horse and pack mule, as well as the supplies you'll need to reach Ullum."

"That's, that's very generous of you, Master." Allana found the words unequal to the gratitude she felt in her heart.

"You can repay me when I visit Gorgos and bow before its queen. I'll also send Ling to accompany you to the city. He is a fine warrior, though a slave now. You'll need some protection from thieves and brigands besides your sling. Stay on the main roads, but don't stop at the inns. They're full of thieves and cutthroats. Camp in the forest. Ling is a good bodyguard. I know you'll make it to Ullum, but do you have any contacts there?"

"Yes, Master. Grazhda told me to contact a woman there named Varuda. She also placed 500 crowns with the Argani in my name. I can't believe you both have been so generous."

"She will expect repayment just as I do. Do not forget your obligations here once you are successful. We're investing in your quest because we have great confidence in you. What should I tell Javik when he returns?"

Allana bit her lip, and a tear ran down one cheek. "Tell him I love him, but I want him to honor his commitment to you. He will be more help to me after that training, and I'll need time to raise money and collect allies. Besides, he won't think much of what I must do to accomplish those goals."

It was Tao Shan's turn to raise an eyebrow. "What do you mean?"

"Grazhda told me this Varuda was once queen of the prostitutes in Ullum. She wants me to establish a brothel there with Varuda's help."

"A brothel, eh?" Tao Shan's tone was more curiosity than disgust. "I see. The old witch is very clever, but how do you feel about that?"

"I don't like it, but she says I will only be the bait in the trap. I should buy slaves to service my customers and hold myself aloof from the proceedings."

"I couldn't have given you better advice. Play that game well, and you will soon be in a position to demand great favors of powerful men and acquire gold by the chest-full. When do you want to leave?"

"As soon as possible, Master. I want to be well away in case Javik should return early."

Tao Shan thought for a moment before answering. "I can have everything ready in two days."

Allana rose and embraced the mentor. "Thank you, Master. I won't forget your kindness."

She left Tao Shan's longhouse and returned to Browdat's. She needed to let Dana know her plans also. She found Dana busy mending garments in the common room.

"May I speak with you a moment, Lady Dana?" she asked.

"Certainly, sit down." Dana stopped her sewing and placed the tunic she was mending aside.

"I'll be leaving our village in two days, Lady, and I've come to ask your blessing on my quest."

"Where are you going, what will you do?" Dana asked.

"I'm going to the city of Ullum in Zargaia. I will live there for a while until I can move on to Gorgos. Grazhda told me of a woman there who could help me in my quest."

"You're being very vague about all of this. For what reason?"

"I don't want to give you any more information now. Just know that all I do will be to help me gain the throne of Gorgos."

"Don't you want to wait for Javik? He could at least be your bodyguard."

"No, Lady, I want Javik to stay here and finish his training with Tao Shan. I will send for him when I need him. As for a bodyguard, Tao Shan is sending one of his servants to see me safely to Ullum."

"Know that I do give my blessing, though it is with a sad heart. I fear you will not live to see Gorgos. You are a woman alone with no powerful friends beyond our borders. You are very brave to take on such a quest."

"I'm not brave. I'm not sure of the wisdom of this myself, but I will follow my dream to Ullum and see what transpires there. I managed to survive in the wild for two years with no help, and Tao Shan and Grazhda both gave me enough gold to be comfortable in Ullum for a long time. I can't fare any worse in a city than I did in my cave. I'm lucky in one respect. I know that if I fail I can always return here to you and Javik."

Dana embraced Allana. "As long as I live, you will have a place at my hearth, and I know Javik would have you for his wife in an instant. Just be careful."

"Thank you, Lady. You will always have a special place in my heart."

The women parted tearfully

Two days later Allana was on her way to Ullum with Ling riding beside her.

CHAPTER 10

The sparkling song of the women reached Javik's ears long before he could see the village stockade. He remembered the many times it welcomed his father home, and he thought he could detect his mother's voice in the merry chorus. He listened for Allana, but there was no trace of her delightful accent. He thought of the women whose songs would change to wails of grief once they learned their men were not in the long column of warriors marching along the snowy road to home. They would look in the wagons carrying the wounded only to be disappointed for the last time. He was glad to escape with only a minor wound to show for his first adventure at war.

The horrors of battle dimmed in his mind as the army crested the last hill. He was glad to see the family banners flying from the stockade walls with the victory flag atop the village common house, and his heart leaped inside him. He scanned the women lined up along the stockade wall searching for his mother and Allana, but they were too far away yet to make out faces.

The men broke into song in response to their women, and the lusty voices reflected the joy of being alive after their ordeal. Javik joined in heartily. The war lasted less than a year, but it seemed like an eternity. The older men told him he was lucky it was all over in just a few fights. Many of them were veterans of long wars where less than half of those who left ever returned to their hearths.

The first horsemen were now close to the stockade wall, and their women rushed out to them. Javik saw Frieda, Browdat's wife, but his mother was not with her. The women's faces became a blur now as they surged toward the column seeking their own loved ones. They ran down the line searching every face with worried eyes and grimly set mouths until they spotted their men. The man marching in front of Javik was nearly bowled over when a heavy-set woman locked him in a bear hug and wailed her greeting as tears ran down her cheeks in torrents.

Javik searched in vain for Allana, but he spotted his mother just as she broke into a run to reach him. He stepped out of the column and spread his arms to embrace her, but she fell to one knee in front of him and bowed her head.

Javik blushed beet red as he lifted her to her feet. "Mother! What are you doing?"

"You are a man now, Javik, and I must show the respect due a warrior from a mere woman."

Javik pulled her into his arms and felt a warmth flow to him from somewhere deep inside the woman who gave him life. "You are no 'mere woman'. You are my mother, and there will never be any need for you to bow to me."

"Javik! What would the other women think if I did not honor my own son? It's good to see you home safely."

"Where is Allana, Mother? I haven't seen her yet." Javik asked.

Dana's face fell as she dropped Javik's hand and turned slightly away. "She's gone, son. She left two months ago."

Javik's face contorted into a mask of anguish. "Why? Where did she go?"

"Grazhda told her she was a princess, and Tao Shan found a scroll confirming that title. She became convinced she had to find her people and try to help them regain their homeland. She said a princess's place was with her people. She spent the winter with Tao Shan, but she left when the southern passes cleared."

Javik stopped to let all of this sink in. "A princess? Grazhda's involved? This is serious, indeed. I have to go after her, I have to help her."

"No, Javik, she doesn't want you to come after her. She told me you were to finish your training with Tao Shan. She said she'd send for you after that."

"Mother, you don't understand. I love her, and now I've lost her. I have to find her."

"I understand your feelings all too well, my son." Dana looked at him with a stern expression tempered with deep sadness.

Javik suddenly understood that her loss was much greater than his. Allana was still alive, and they might be together again some day, but his father would never return from the underworld.

"I'm sorry, Mother. I only wanted you to understand how deeply I love Allana."

"I know that, son. It was a hard decision for her. She didn't want to leave you, but she felt it was her duty to see if she could help her people."

He knew it was useless to argue with Dana, but he could not give up Allana so easily. He would think about it for a while. Allana had nearly three month's head start, and he only had a vague idea of where Gorgos might be. He would need Tao Shan's help, and, of course, Browdat's permission to leave in search of her.

"You're right, Mother. I need to speak with Browdat and Tao Shan before I do anything."

"In the morning. Come home now and rest. Everyone is waiting to hear about the battles." Dana's smile glowed with new pride in her son, the warrior.

"I'm really hungry. Is there any food at home?" Javik could feel the emptiness in his stomach now that things were back to some semblance of normal.

"Javik, do you ever think of anything besides your stomach?" Dana spoke in a voice half disgust and half jest. "Come, there's plenty of food waiting for hungry warriors at the longhouse."

Browdat was not at the longhouse when Javik and Dana arrived. He would be busy seeing to his horses and making sure the families of the dead were consoled. Javik dropped his weapons and pack and stripped off his chain mail. His shoulders ached from the burden, and as he returned to the common room, he felt as if he was floating a few inches above the floor. The heavy wooden tables were laden with all of Browdat's favorite dishes, and Javik dove into the feast with gusto to the amusement of Dana and the servants.

"Tell me of the battles," Old Sasha asked.

"The first was a glorious day for Berglaundia," Javik began between mouthfuls. "You should have seen our cavalry in action. When the Wallans emerged from the forest, they were swept away by a furious charge. I thought they would surely turn and run away after that, but they regrouped and came at us again." Javik grabbed another bite before resuming.

"And you should have seen my son in action." The booming voice of Browdat announced his arrival. Frieda ran to his arms while the servants cheered their master.

"Welcome home, husband," Frieda managed through her

tears of joy.

Dana rose and knelt before her lord. "Welcome home, Lord Browdat."

"Rise Dana! Your boy has proved himself a man many times over in the last few months. Look what he has won for my house." Browdat unwrapped the sword of Aelin, unsheathed the blade and laid it on the table. A chorus of admiring "ooohs" met the sight of the gleaming blade.

"It is the sword of Aelin the Red," old Sasha gasped as he picked it up in both hands to inspect the trophy.

"My father rode beside him, and I saw this blade many times as a boy," the old man continued. "It is home, at last." He kissed the pommel stone and ran an admiring hand down the inscription on the blade."

Dana beamed with pride and held her son close to her. "Perhaps you will bring back Tolda's sword one day?" she whispered in Javik's ear.

Javik turned her face up to see the tears begin to fall from his widowed mother's eyes. His father, Tolda, was killed during a raid on the Sentii, and though Javik had managed to slay his father's killer, Tolda's weapons and armor still hung on the wall of a Sentii longhouse.

"Someday, Mother, I swear," Javik whispered.

Frieda came into the room with more qush. She filled Browdat's mug then sat next to him with a mug of her own. "Well, husband, you have no reason to deny Allana to Javik anymore."

"How's that, woman?" Browdat asked.

"The girl is a true princess and heir to a throne," she began to laugh, but Browdat cut her off.

"A princess? How is that?" he said.

Dana spoke, "It's true, Lord. The old witch, Grazhda, told

her she was a princess, and Tao Shan found it to be so."

"Bring her in. I want to bless the union of my son to a royal family," Browdat said.

"She's gone, father. She's gone to Gorgos," Javik said.

"Then go after her. By Zhou, this is the best news I've had in years."

"She doesn't want me to follow her," Javik said.

"What? I thought she loved you and you loved her," Browdat said.

"That's true, but I will honor her wish and my commitment to Tao Shan. My mother says she will send for me when she's ready to marry."

"Then we'll wait to see what transpires in the time to come. For now, more qush."

The celebration went on into the night with much qush flowing. Javik was bone weary from marching and his heart ached over the loss of Allana. He was glad for the qush induced stupor and staggered into bed, but dreams of the beautiful wild girl who turned out to be a princess haunted his sleep.

CHAPTER 11

The next morning, Javik awakened to the bustle of normal longhouse activity long before he was ready to face the world. His head throbbed with the effects of too much qush, and dreams of Allana that robbed him of proper sleep. He rose and dressed before joining the family in the common room. Browdat was absent, but Frieda and Dana were busy directing servants about in an effort to clean up from last night's party. Dana noticed her son come in.

"Good morning, Javik. How are you feeling this morning?" she cooed in mock sympathy.

"My skull is too-wide to fit through the doorway, and the devils inside are pounding to get out. I would swear to touch no more qush as long as I live, but I know it would be a false oath. Where is Lord Browdat?"

"He's in the village meeting house with the other war leaders dividing up the spoils. Don't you want some breakfast?" Dana asked displaying a wide grin in reaction to her son's misery.

"Food is the last thing on my mind right now, Mother."

"Here, have this," Frieda thrust a mug of qush toward him.

Javik turned his face away from the aroma of the strong Berglauni beer and fought back his nausea. "Do you want to kill me, Lady Frieda?" he asked.

"Didn't Tao Shan teach you that you should always take

some of the feathers from the arrow that wounds you? Drink this! It will help," Frieda insisted once more pushing the mug into Javik's face.

Reluctantly, Javik drank as much of the dark liquid as he thought he could stand and placed the mug on the table while he leaned against it for support. He was surprised to find it was much easier to fight off the urge to vomit after the qush.

Frieda inspected the mug and shoved it back toward Javik.

"Drink it all," she commanded.

Javik looked at her with a sheepish expression and drained the mug.

"Good! You'll feel much better in a little while, and then you'll want some food. Mellia will keep some warm for you until the noon meal," Frieda smiled as she dumped the mug into a barrel of soapy water.

"I need some fresh air," Javik said. He walked out of the longhouse and into the street. The villagers were busy with their daily chores. It was as if there had never been a war, and he was glad of that. War was terrible.

He turned down the street to the village square and met a different picture. Here, two families were draping black cloths over their doorways, and the sounds of mourning could be heard from inside the longhouses. He strode more quickly toward the square thanking his god, Zhou, for being among the living. Berda greeted him.

"Good morning, Javik. Is your head as large as mine?"

"Oh, good morning, Berda. A lot of qush was downed in Browdat's house last night, and I'm afraid I had more than my share."

Berda laughed. "My father made me drink a raw egg in a mug of milk this morning. I almost didn't get it down, but I feel much better now. Besides, if you were drinking with Lord

Browdat, it would be very difficult to drink more than your share."

Javik laughed, and thought he felt his skull crack. "Lady Frieda made me drink more qush, but her antidote has not taken effect yet. Are you going to the meeting house?"

"Yes, I'm anxious to see what my share of the loot amounts to. You're lucky, I hear the Lord Browdat paid a handsome price for Aelin's sword. I wish I had a share of that prize."

"Browdat gave me a lot of gold for it, enough to pay for Tao Shan's lessons this year with some left over. If you need some money, I will be glad to give you some of the surplus."

"No, my share of the spoils will be enough. My father will get triple my share, and that will be plenty for our house, but thank you, Javik."

The pair joined a crowd in front of the meetinghouse just as Goldar emerged followed by Browdat and the other village war leaders. The crowd fell silent as the big man raised his arms.

"Warriors of Holliga! I'm afraid the spoils of this war are not what we would have expected. We only captured one baggage train, and the Wallan warriors were a poor lot, but the ransom for the two war leaders we captured will help make the loss of our comrades less painful. To each family who lost a warrior goes ten gold pieces."

The assembled men cheered this announcement. The gold would go a long way toward helping the families of the dead adjust to the loss of their breadwinner. Once more Goldar signaled for silence.

"To each wounded man goes five gold pieces." Again, the announcement was greeted with applause and shouts of agreement.

"Captains get five gold pieces, and Sergeants receive four. Each warrior receives three gold pieces and the arms and armor he captured. Each war leader's share is twenty gold pieces. The rest goes to the king. Are there any questions?"

"Yes!" an archer Javik knew only by sight called. "What of the sword of Aelin the Red?"

His question was echoed by shouts of agreement.

"Aelin's sword was won by Javik in combat. It was his to do with as he wished, but he allowed Lord Browdat to purchase it from him."

The crowd fell silent for a moment as Browdat stepped forward holding the sword in question over his head. He turned for all the men to see it then set it down on a low bench.

"It is here for all of you to inspect," Browdat shouted. "Each of you has earned the right to touch the blade if you wish." Browdat unsheathed the sword and laid it next to the scabbard. He stepped back as the first man knelt before the relic and kissed the pommel stone.

The next man hefted the blade and admired its inscription before kissing the blade. The one after him used the blade to make a cut in his arm and caught the blood in a small vial. The vial would be a powerful talisman for protecting that man in battle. The sword had already tasted Javik's blood, and the wound in his hand would serve as his talisman. Another man touched his sword to Aelin's and kissed the inscription on the blade. Each man assembled at the meetinghouse performed his own ritual before Browdat re-sheathed the weapon and held it on high once again.

"Aelin's sword will repose in my house forever. Never again will an enemy of the Berglauni boast of its ownership."

The men cheered a long time in response while Browdat turned from side to side. Goldar finally called for silence again.

"All men may claim their shares tomorrow here at the meeting house. Well done, men. The king is proud of all of you."

Another round of cheers greeted Goldar's words, and the crowd dispersed. Javik and Berda noticed Karl and called to him.

"Karl! Over here!"

Karl enfolded Javik and Berda in a bear hug. "Can you believe we are men now?" he asked.

"It's hard to take it all in," Berda said. "My mother actually bowed to me this morning."

"Mine too," Karl said. "I didn't know what to do."

"How could life be any better?" Berda said.

Javik's face fell, and his friends knew the cause.

"I understand Allana left the village," Karl said. "I'm sorry, Javik."

"Allana gone?" Berda said. "I thought you two would be married soon."

"I thought of nothing else all the time I was gone," Javik said. "My mother says she's gone to find her people. Once she found out she was a princess, she began to think more of her people than me."

Javik saw his friends' look of surprise at the same time he felt the hand upon his shoulder. He turned to see Tao Shan.

"How are you, Javik?" the old man asked.

"I am fine, Master," Javik said as he bowed to the greatest mentor in the kingdom and his teacher.

"You need not call me master any more, Javik. You're a man now. I heard you were wounded."

Javik showed Tao Shan his hand. The scar was now completely healed. "It was nothing, sir."

Tao Shan inspected the wound and grunted his approval. "A good healer treated this, I see. It will give you no problems in the future. Introduce me to your friends, Javik."

Javik made the introductions as Karl and Berda stuttered

their honor at meeting such an icon of Berglauni warrior culture even though Tao Shan was not a Berglauni.

"Javik, may I speak to you in private?" Tao Shan asked.

Javik looked at Berda and Karl who took the hint.

"I have to be home now to help my father polish our chain mail. See you later, Javik," Karl said.

"I promised my uncle I'd go hunting with him. Bye Javik," Berda said as he turned toward his longhouse.

"Your friends are very tactful, Javik," Tao Shan said. "Walk with me to my house."

The pair walked in silence for a while until they were out of earshot of any villagers. As they passed through the gate in the stockade, Tao Shan opened the conversation.

"Allana has gone to find the people of Gorgos, Javik."

"I know, sir. My mother told me."

"I don't know what she told your mother, but she asked me to speak with you about her reasons for leaving."

"My mother only told me Allana asked me not to follow her."

"Allana and I spoke quite a lot about her situation once she knew her true heritage. She was convinced that some remnant of her people remained, and equally convinced it was her duty to find them and make them into a nation once more. I said her people would be scattered to the four winds, like she was, and most of them would be dead by now from the harsh life of slavery. Those still alive would probably not remember their native land any more. She acknowledged all of that, but insisted that she must make an attempt to find some remnant of Gorgos. I think the old witch Grazhda had a lot to do with convincing her to go."

"It is so pointless, sir. She will be killed or enslaved again without protection. What chance does a woman have without a man by her side?" Javik was almost in tears as he spoke.

"Don't underestimate her ability to survive, Javik, and if Grazhda's involved, she may have more protection than we realize. You saw for yourself how she evaded the Sentii, and you know from experience her prowess with a sling. Combine that with Grazhda's blessing, and you have no need to worry about her."

Javik felt the back of his head where he still bore the scar of Allana's sling attack. "But, she was hiding in the forest then, not wandering through strange lands seeking to free slaves."

"True, but she felt the call so deeply I could not dissuade her from her quest. She told me she could not enjoy happiness with you here in Berglaundia while even one of her subjects was enslaved. She could not share your bed or enjoy her children if she thought that somewhere one of her subjects was being raped and her children taken from her. She would be no good to you as a wife while she felt that way, Javik. Your life with her would be one miserable day after another until you let her do what she must do."

"If she would have waited for me, I would have helped her. I've seen war now, and I know how to kill. I could protect her," Javik said.

"Could you? You are a strong lad, and skilled with many weapons, but you still have much to learn about the world, Javik."

"And, Allana does not?" Javik's voice held a note of contempt.

"No, Javik. Allana has seen the cruelty of the world. She knows how evil men can be. She's had to use her wits to survive, and she knows how to be invisible when she has to. She told me of her plan, and I agreed it was sound. She trained with Bandor several months before she left, and he's the one who will conduct your training in the coming year."

"How could a girl's plan be sound? Women know nothing of war."

"They know about men, Javik, and they know how to conquer in ways a man knows nothing of. Women do not win their battles with swords or pikes, but with their wiles. They are formidable opponents. Do you remember my game?"

"Yes sir, the one where the woman is the most powerful piece."

"Do you believe the game's logic is sound now?"

Javik thought of his ache for Allana when he first saw her in fine women's clothes instead of her dirty buckskin dress, with her hair brushed and oiled instead of matted with burrs and twigs. He thought of his mother's power over him.

"Yes, sir, the game's logic is sound," he almost whispered.

"Good, Javik, good!" Tao Shan put an arm around Javik's shoulders and stopped walking.

"You have promised me one more year of training. In that year, I will teach you to be as wily as any woman, and as good a leader as any in our kingdom. At the end of that year, if Allana has not returned, I will recommend to Lord Browdat that he allow you to find her and help her in any way you can. Gorgos is many weeks journey from here, and her task is formidable. You have time to learn, Javik."

Javik looked at the wise old man beside him and remembered his teachings. He was right, as usual. What did Javik know of the affairs of men? In many ways, he was still a boy, and Allana would need a man beside her who could do more than act as a bodyguard.

"You are right, sir. When do you want me to start?"

"Tomorrow morning. You will begin with Bandor. He has many valuable lessons for you."

"I thought you were going to be my mentor, sir."

"I will see you every day after you finish with Bandor. When you complete his lessons, we will spend many hours together, Javik. I also want to see you after every hunt and every raid. I know it is difficult, but you must be patient. Above all, you must observe. Let nothing escape your vision. Study every man in your hunting group or raiding party, particularly the leaders. See how they react to each situation. I will be asking you to evaluate each one. Do you understand?"

"I think so, sir."

"Good! I will see you in the morning after breakfast. Until then, Javik."

The old man slapped his student on the shoulder and walked on toward his own longhouse as Javik stared after him. Tao Shan had mentioned nothing of weapons training or practice. It was hard for Javik to understand how this year of training could be valuable without improving his weapons skills. He turned to walk back toward the village.

He'd only gone a few steps when Grazhda stepped out of the forest and blocked the path.

"Hail warrior. As I told you, you've earned great honor in the war."

"What good is honor when Allana is not with me?" he asked.

"She's embarked on a great quest, and you will be reunited with her soon."

"I fear she'll be killed before I can find her."

Grazhda spat on the ground. "I protect her. Why should you worry? She paid for my counsel and protection with Grucheaux's sword."

Javik started at that announcement. "What? She gave you the sword? It was not her's to give. I want it back, if you please."

The old witch cackled at the request. "Which would you rather have, Allana's protection or a surplus sword? A fine blade already hangs at your side."

Javik frowned at the old hag. "What good is a sword to a witch?"

"That sword slew your father, and I owe him my life. It has great magical powers for one who knows how to use them. Be assured, young warrior, those powers will always be of benefit to you and Allana, but if I return the sword to you, those benefits will not be forthcoming."

"You drive a hard bargain, but you may keep the sword."

At that moment the grunt of a bear made Javik turn to look behind him. There was nothing there, and when he turned back to Grazhda, she was gone.

He continued on toward the village, and Berda and Karl met him as he entered the stockade gate.

"What did Tao Shan want?" Berda asked.

"Yes, what did he tell you?" Karl echoed.

"It was nothing. He only wants me to start with lessons from Bandor in the morning."

"Bandor?" Karl said. "What weapon does he teach?"

"No weapon, he has many stories of wars and heroes. His was the one class I had no trouble staying awake in. I only fear my weapons skills will suffer for all this classroom work."

"Well, we will just have to take that part of your education upon ourselves. Right, Berda?" Karl said.

"Yes, we will train against one another, and any bully who dares to cross us," Berda replied.

The three young warriors laughed at the thought of using each other as mentors, but their laughter died quickly as old Sasha approached on the run.

"There you are, master Javik. I've been looking all over the village for you. Lord Browdat commands you to return to the longhouse and join him on a hunt."

"We'll talk more tomorrow after my lessons," Javik said to his friends as he turned to follow Sasha. "Until then."

CHAPTER 12

The next morning, Javik arrived at Tao Shan's house early, but his old teacher, Bandor, was waiting for him in the sandy common area of the longhouse.

"Good morning, Javik. It's good to see you again. I'm glad Tao Shan convinced you to continue your studies. Did you fare well in the war?"

"Only a slight wound, sir." Javik showed him the scar on his right palm.

The old man sighed as he inspected the damage. "It is the first of many, Javik. The peoples of our lands will bear many worse scars before we learn to live without wars. Come with me."

He led Javik to a room he hadn't been allowed to use while a student training for Mauhad. Three walls were taken up with shelves holding hundreds of scrolls. Not even Buran, the law keeper, had so many.

Bandor lit a lamp and moved to one wall of shelves. "Sit down at the table, Javik. We will start with some reading."

Bandor placed a medium sized scroll in front of Javik. "Read this one over carefully. When you finish it, please write your evaluation of the king's actions on this scroll."

The old man indicated a blank scroll sitting next to an inkpot and a container of quill pens.

"When you've finished, bring your evaluation to the dining

hall. Tao Shan and I will discuss your work there." Bandor left the room without acknowledging Javik's quizzical look.

Javik unrolled the scroll and began to read. It was the history of king Elbus's campaign against the Sentii over two hundred years ago.

"What can I learn from a 200 year old war?" Javik snorted, but he read the history as requested.

The scroll told of how King Elbus was goaded into waging war on the Sentii by his chief General. The old King of Sentius was dying, and his sons were quarreling over the throne. The King's top General saw this as an opportunity to gain control of the rich Sentii province bordering Berglaundia and recommended an immediate attack. The King's counselors urged him to send in spies to determine the Sentii strength in the province and the reserves available in the bordering provinces, but the General urged haste. The General argued that spies would tip off the Sentii about the King's intentions. Surprise was essential for several reasons, but primarily for logistics purposes. If they struck now, before the fields were harvested, the Berglauni troops could subsist on Sentii grain and livestock. He could move swiftly without waiting on slow moving supply trains. He was confident the Sentii could not raise sufficient force to defeat him, providing they struck quickly. The king decided to approve the General's plan over the objections of his council.

When the army marched into Sentii territory, they found scorched earth. The Sentii had burned their crops rather than allow them to fall into enemy hands. The General also met no resistance as he marched into the heart of the province stretching out his supply lines. The weather was very hot for fall, and the march was arduous. The troops soon consumed their original rations, and there was little left in the countryside for the foraging teams. The men grew hungry and weary, while Sentii raiding parties picked off foragers at will. The General realized his plan had been compromised and was about to turn back in defeat when he was attacked from all sides by an overwhelming force of Sentii. He returned home with only a fraction of his original army, and the King was forced to negotiate a humiliating settlement.

Javik thought about the story for a long time. The General's plan seemed sound; he'd just encountered some bad luck. Who would think the Sentii would burn their own fields and herd their livestock out of the army's path? His only error was not turning back soon enough. Javik wrote his analysis and left the scroll library for the dining room.

Bandor and Tao Shan sat at the long table, now devoid of students, sipping mugs of qush. Tao Shan greeted his pupil.

"Ah, Javik. Will you join us in a mug?"

"Yes, sir. It would be a pleasure," Javik replied as he seated himself opposite Bandor.

Tao Shan called to a servant, and soon a mug of qush appeared before Javik. The cool liquid was refreshing to his throat after two hours in the dusty library.

"What lesson are you working on today, Javik?" Tao Shan asked.

"The war between King Elbus and the Sentii, sir."

"Ah, a good one. I will leave you and Bandor to discuss it. Come back in two days for another lesson." With that, the mentor left the table to Javik and Bandor.

"Have you written out your evaluation, Javik?" Bandor asked.

"Yes, sir. Here it is." Javik handed his scroll to the teacher who unrolled it and read quickly.

"I see, so you think Elbus's failure was more a matter of luck than poor planning, do you?"

"Who would think the Sentii would burn their own fields?" Javik said.

"Anyone who took the time to find out," Bandor replied. "You see, the King of Sentius was very old and quite sickly, and his three sons fought to divide the kingdom between them. The General incorrectly calculated that the internal strife would make the province easy pickings. He did not know it had already pledged its loyalty to Prince Hollum, the King's eldest son and the one most likely to succeed his father. The province stood to gain considerably with Hollum as king, but the people knew they would be little better than slaves under Elbus. When Hollum assured them they would receive grain from the royal storehouses if they burned their own fields, the choice was easy. By burning their crops, they gained the everlasting gratitude of Prince Hollum, who did become king on his father's death. Any spies sent into the province would have discovered this, and the council would have guessed the outcome easily. Elbus's general would have invaded with sufficient supplies to conduct the campaign without relying upon local crops, but it's more likely the King would have disapproved the invasion plans."

Javik pondered Bandor's explanation a while before a question occurred to him.

"Sir, if Prince Hollum made such a promise, he must have known about the planned invasion. How could he know that?"

"He had spies of his own. They saw the army assembling, but they also saw very few grain wagons in the baggage train. They reported this information back to Prince Hollum. What lesson is to be learned from this story, Javik?"

"I would say the lesson is to always use spies."

"Partly correct. Spies are one means of obtaining information, but not the only means. All information is important. There is no substitute for it. What are some other sources of information?"

Javik took a long swig from his mug and thought about the question. He remembered learning about other villages from his fellow students before Mauhad.

"A leader could find someone who used to live in the country he plans to attack. That person could provide him with valuable information."

"Good, Javik! What about these?" Bandor tapped the scroll between them on the table.

"Have you not learned much from scrolls today?"

"Yes, Sir, but this is an old tale of long ago."

"Not all scrolls tell of ancient times. Many are written to tell about countries, as they exist today. A leader should never neglect his library. Scrolls are expensive, but they can be an investment paying handsome dividends when the time comes."

"Master Tao Shan certainly has a large library," Javik commented.

"His library is available to any war leader of the Berglauni people. Many of his scrolls were gifts from war leaders while others were purchased with his share of the plunder from raids and wars."

"He gets a share even though he doesn't go to war?"

"The Berglauni are wise, Javik. Learn to follow the example of your fathers in supporting learned men. You will find they are worth more than all the scrolls in the world."

"I have much to learn, Sir. What is my next lesson?"

"That's enough for one day. Come back in two days, but remember Tao Shan's words, observe everything."

Javik left Tao Shan's long house and walked back to his village. It was going to be a long and difficult year.

CHAPTER 13

The alarm bell roused Javik from a sound sleep and dreams of Allana. He threw back the furs and shivered in the cold of the sleeping area. Browdat was already on his feet and nearly dressed while Dana fed wood to the remnants of the fire and blew it back to life. Over the clatter of the bell he could hear men tramping across the frozen puddles outside. He pulled on cold boots and buckled his sword belt around his waist. He did not forget Tao Shan's lesson to always put on a helmet even if he did nothing else.

"Come on, Javik!" Browdat yelled. "You're too slow!"

Javik had seen his father respond to the village alarm many times, and he felt strange being the one to dress and arm himself. He remembered pulling the warm furs closer around him and resting secure in the knowledge he was safe under Tolda's protection. Now it was Javik who must provide the protection while others slept. He pulled on a coat and slung his shield from one shoulder as he followed Browdat into the biting cold.

The snow that once blanketed the village in a clean, white coat was melted in most places, but the return of the deep cold that night froze the ground again. Where the snow remained, it was dark with soot from the cooking fires. Torches cast an orange glow on the frozen puddles as the men made their way to the common house, shouting encouragement to each other as they passed.

Javik followed Browdat into the meeting area, but sat back near the wall. He was a young warrior fresh from his first battles, and the more experienced men had precedence. Browdat took his seat at the table of the war leaders. Servants roused the big fire back to life, and the room was already warm enough for Javik to remove his coat. Goldar, the chief war leader of the village, rose to speak as the last stragglers came in.

"The Sentii have raided our horse corrals and stolen several dozen head of horses," Goldar announced.

His words were met with shouts of anger. Men demanded revenge and an immediate pursuit of the horse thieves, but Goldar called for silence.

"They must have come through one of the low passes. The high pass fortress would have stopped such a small party. The tracks indicate there were only a dozen, or so. Browdat will take his men and cut off the south pass. Mikka's group will take the waterfall pass, and my men will cover the north pass. If we hurry, we may catch them before they reach the desert. The first party to encounter the raiders will send messengers to the other groups. Good luck!"

Browdat bellowed for his men to assemble outside, while Mikka called for his people to meet at the fallen oak tree. Goldar's men gathered around the war leader in the meeting room. Javik thought his group, really Mikka's, had the easiest task. He was very familiar with the waterfall pass as it was the location of Allana's cave, and it was not far from the village. If the Sentii had taken that path, they would be well into the high desert by now. It would be an easy ride.

Javik raced back to Browdat's longhouse to select a saddle, then made his way through the bustle in the streets to the horse corrals. Fugnor greeted him.

"Well, it's warrior Javik now, is it. I have just the mount for you, young man." Fugnor led him to one of the corrals and pointed out a gray stallion. "That's Gunda. I broke him myself, and he's as swift as a mountain river. That's the one for you, Javik."

Gunda was more ghost than animal in the pale starlight, and Javik was not pleased with Fugnor's choice.

"He'll stand out like a polished shield in the blackest night. The enemy will see me a league off."

Fugnor laughed. "All the better once they've felt your blade. They'll run at the sight of him."

Javik saw it was no use arguing with the horse master and jumped into the corral with his rope. Gunda shied away knowing what a man with a rope meant, but Javik quickly looped the line around his neck and led the horse to the fence and his saddle. As he did so, he inspected the animal.

Gunda stood a bit smaller than Javik at his withers, but his musculature was good, at least from what Javik could see in the dim light. He patted the strong neck and spoke to the creature.

"So, Gunda, you are to be Javik's horse. I will do my best to see that no harm comes to you, but you must promise to obey me without balking."

Gunda snorted and seemed to nod his head in response. Fugnor handed Javik a carrot, and Gunda sensed the treat before Javik could move it to the horse's mouth. Gunda nosed past Javik's body and took the carrot in his teeth, but Javik held on.

"Not so fast, Gunda. There will be many more for you if you serve me well." Javik pushed the carrot into the eager mouth and held his hand next to Gunda's muzzle so the horse could get his scent. While the horse chewed the carrot, Javik saddled him and mounted. Gunda responded well to the reins as Javik rode him out the corral gate and on to the rendezvous point.

About thirty men were assembled there as Mikka gave his

orders.

"We will ride by the mountain path. That way, we will be above the Sentii if they are still in our territory. Once we know how many there are and where they are going, I will give you the battle plan. Are there any questions?"

No one spoke, and Mikka turned his horse. "Follow me!" he shouted as he broke into a gallop.

The route to the waterfall was easy, and the men had no trouble keeping up. There was no conversation. Only the sound of the horse's hooves and the jingle of harness broke the calm of the frosty night. The moon was a slender sliver crescent, but the stars gave enough light to see the pathway. It soon narrowed into a trail leading up the hills to the top of the falls. Once on top, Mikka signaled a halt and motioned for the men to dismount and assemble around him.

"Balda, Gulik and Teira will stay with the horses. I will take these men with me to block the path to the desert." Mikka indicated the partition of his men with his right arm. "The rest of you will go with Javik to flush the Sentii towards us, if they are there. Javik knows this country well. Javik, sweep to the south in a broad circle. If the Sentii are hiding out until daylight, you should find them. Once you do, send word to the other two parties. Your job is to make them move toward us. We will crush them between us as they flee from you. Does everyone understand their jobs?"

Nods greeted Mikka's request, but Javik was stunned. He was to lead men for the first time. Was he ready? Mikka said he knew this country, and he did, but was that enough? He decided to play the part to the best of his ability. He knew any hesitation or doubt on his part would only demoralize his men. As Tao Shan taught him, incorrect action is better than no action at all.

"This way, men." Javik signaled the direction of march. "We will go to the green rocks by way of the linden stream. Once there, we will form a line and march back through the forest. If the Sentii are there, we will find them. Anyone spotting the devils will give the call of the wolf. Is that clear?"

More nods met Javik's question.

"Good, silence is essential. No talking and watch for footfalls. Follow me." Javik led the men down the pathway.

At the green rocks, Javik signaled for the men to fan out. They formed a line with three meters between each man, and Javik signaled for them to begin marching. The group of men moved through the woods silently, black specters against the snow covered ground, but blending in with the equally black tree trunks at every opportunity. Javik trembled with fear. Not fear of the Sentii, but fear of his own inexperience. He prayed they would not find the enemy.

The party had only moved a few dozen meters when the snorting of several horses stopped them in their tracks. From the left end of the line, the howl of a lone wolf sounded. All eyes turned to Javik. He swallowed with great difficulty and used the hand signals of his people to indicate the line of approach, telling the men to stop before any attack. He sent out two runners who would return to the horses and ride to the other two parties of Bergalauni warriors.

The line moved forward slowly, taking advantage of any cover available. Javik smelled the horses before he saw them. He advanced slowly until the animals came into view. They were surrounded by armed men on horseback who seemed to be waiting for something. Their gaze was directed toward the pathway Javik knew led to the desert country. He signaled his men to hold position while he counted the enemy. Goldar thought there were only a dozen or so Sentii on the raid, but

Javik quickly counted fifteen, and he knew there were more on the other side of the horses. He dared not attack, but he must find some way to drive them toward Mikka. Suddenly, a plan came to him. He signaled for the men on either side to join him.

"Listen, there are too many of them for us to show ourselves," Javik whispered. "We must make them think we are the main party of warriors. Pass this down the line. Each man must tramp through the woods making as much noise as he can and shouting in as many voices as he can muster. If they think they're outnumbered, maybe they'll bolt down the path towards Mikka. Understand?"

One man nodded, but the other spoke. "And, what if they attack us?"

"Then we fight as best we can. When Mikka hears the noise, he will come to help us. Go, and Zhou be with us." The men scuttled off to pass the plan down the line. Soon the forest was ringing with shouts and the sound of many feet cracking twigs and dislodging stones. The Sentii horsemen turned toward the noise, and a cry from one who appeared to be in charge sent the group off at a gallop down the path they'd been observing. Javik knew they were headed straight for Mikka, and would soon break through his men unless Javik could bring help.

"Come, men! At a run! After them!" Javik broke into a run hoping his men were behind him. He dared not look back for fear he was alone. Soon, men appeared on either side of him with swords drawn and grim faces eager for a fight. They couldn't keep up with the horses, but they knew the mounted men would soon meet the other half of the vise and be forced to stop.

The sound of panicked horses and the battle cries of Mikka's men told Javik the fight was near. Several horses fled in panic back down the path nearly knocking over some of Javik's men in the process, but they pressed on until the shape of the Sentii raiders loomed before them. They fell into the fray with their own shouts of war.

Javik suddenly faced a smaller man with an axe. Moving his shield to deflect the expected blow, he lunged forward and felt his sword penetrate leather armor just as the axe clanged against his shield with a jarring force. The man fell at his feet, and Javik stepped back to select his next target.

A mounted man galloped toward Javik, but his men had no pikes or halberds. Javik braced himself to parry the arcing path of the rider's sword just as a man appeared beside him with a broadsword. The burly warrior swung the long, heavy weapon in a short arc landing the edge at the horse's knees. The bones splintered with a gush of blood as the animal cried out piteously and fell in a heap sending the rider tumbling over its head. Javik was on him in a flash and dispatched the Sentii with a sharp sword blow to the back of his neck.

More horses raced past the men – some with saddles and some without. Another Sentii appeared out of the melee to face Javik while the broadswordsman was occupied with an attack from his left. The Sentii lunged forward pushing his shield into Javik's own shield. Just as Tao Shan taught him, Javik turned his shield to an oblique angle deflecting the Sentii to Javik's left. The blow from Javik's sword cut the back of the man's legs, and he crumpled into a ball of pain screaming madly. Another sword dispatched the Sentii, and Javik looked up to see Mikka's face smiling back.

The fight was over just as dawn began to illuminate the battlefield. Only a few horses remained, standing beside their fallen riders. The largest dog Javik had ever seen also guarded one of the dead Sentii. It growled terribly at anyone who dared approach, and the men were giving it a wide berth.

"I've never seen a dog that big," Javik said with amazement in his voice.

Mikka looked up from cleaning his sword on a Sentii cape. "Nothing we can do about him until some archers get here. It's a Tellan war dog, and they die with their masters. He'll have to be killed."

"That seems a shame," Javik said. "He's such a magnificent animal."

"Nothing to do for it. There's no other way. He'll tear any man to pieces who dares approach that fallen war leader."

"I must get a better look at him," Javik said.

"Don't get too close, Javik. They're as quick as they are large," Mikka warned.

Javik walked toward the hostile animal. It eyed him suspiciously and began to growl as Javik penetrated its invisible perimeter. He stopped and looked at the dog with undisguised admiration. It was as tall as a man's chest, and a powerful body showed even under the thick, wooly, gray coat. That coat was stained in several places from cuts the dog probably suffered defending his master. The eyes were sharp and clear. They focused on Javik, but also kept watch for any other intruders. Javik took another step, and the huge dog bared long, white teeth in a hideous snarl.

There was no approaching this animal, that was sure, but Javik decided to try another tack. He laid down his sword and shield and removed his helmet. He even undid his belt and let it slide to the ground along with his dagger and sword scabbard. Then he remembered his sling.

Javik stepped back to allay the dog's fears a bit then seized the pouch from his sword belt. Selecting one of the soft stones, he stepped back a few paces and began to swing the leather weapon. The men around him sensed his tactic and murmured their approval.

The stone flew through the air hitting the huge dog squarely between its eyes. It stood for a moment with a dazed expression then fell to its knees before collapsing on the ground. A cheer went up from the men around Javik, and one warrior leaped forward, sword in hand, ready to dispatch the creature.

"No, don't!" Javik shouted. The stunned man only looked at Javik in surprise as the new warrior took the saddle rope from the dead Sentii's horse and approached the dog. He tied the animal's legs securely then cut part of another horse's reins for a muzzle.

"Why did you do that, Javik?" Mikka asked.

"I want to take this magnificent animal home with me," Javik replied.

A chorus of laughter and derision met the remark.

"Javik, that animal will soon sicken and die if it doesn't kill you first," Mikka said.

"I don't intend to let him kill me, but I'd like to try bending him to my service. He's so beautiful," Javik said as he stroked the coarse, gray fur. The animal's wounds were not serious, but they needed attention soon to prevent infection.

"Well, if you're sure you want to try this, there's only one way to get him back to the village." Mikka directed two men to cut a pole and rig it to carry the dog by its feet. They slung the pole between them and carried the animal back to the horses.

The smell of the dog panicked the horses for a moment, but they soon got used to it. The pole was slung between Javik's horse and Mikka's for the ride back to the village. By this time, the dog had recovered. It barked and growled viciously as it was carried to its new home.

"What will you use for a pen, Javik?" It was Naman, the warrior with the broadsword.

"I don't know. I will have to keep him tied up until I can build one, I guess."

"I have an old pen you could use. My son used to train hunting dogs, but he's moved to another village. They weren't as big as this monster, but I think it'll keep him in. It's yours if you want it."

"Thank you, Naman. We'll take him to your pen."

As they spoke, other parties of men arrived to join the group. Browdat bellowed his greeting.

"Javik, son. Are you all right?"

"Here father. I'm not harmed."

Browdat rode to his son's side and was greeted by a menacing growl from the huge dog.

"By Zhou! The Sentii are bringing bears along on their raids now," the big war leader said.

The men roared with laughter at the obvious jest.

"Just a large dog, father. I'm going to take him back to the village. I think I can turn him to serve me," Javik said.

"A bad idea, Javik. You'll wind up having to kill it, I'm afraid. These war dogs must die with their masters," Browdat said.

"I'll give it a try, sir. If I fail, the end will be the same for the dog in any case."

* * * * *

The village turned out to greet the returning men. There were no dead and only one or two wounded, but the dog was the center of attention. It growled terribly in spite of the muzzle and struggled against the ropes binding it to the pole. The children screamed in terror as it passed, and the men mumbled in wonder. The women only shook their heads at the folly of grown men.

Javik deposited the dog in Naman's pen but was at a loss as

to how he could release the thing without being torn to pieces. Naman made a suggestion.

"My son used to make a potion from stinkweed root to sedate his dogs when they were injured. I think I still have some." He entered his longhouse and soon returned with a small vial and some raw venison.

"He folded this in with the meat and fed it to the dog. It acted very quickly." Naman spoke as he poured a small amount of brown liquid into a depression in the meat. Carefully folding the slab over on itself, he handed it to Javik.

"He should take it from your hand," Naman said.

"If he doesn't take my hand with it," Javik quipped.

Javik moved to the dog's head and started to unwrap its muzzle. The animal jerked its head toward Javik and growled low in its chest. Javik held out his hand so the beast could get his scent and spoke in a soft voice.

"There, there, I know your master's dead, and you grieved for him while you defend his body. War is a hard master for all of us..." Javik hesitated. The dog must have a name, and that name might be a clue to gaining its confidence. He looked for a collar and found a wicked looking piece of spike-studded, thick leather. It was joined by a silver clasp ornately engraved with symbols of the Sentii language.

"Do you know what this says, Naman?" Javik asked.

"I'm afraid I know no Sentii, Javik, but I think Jundar knows a little."

"Go get him, Naman. I need to know this beast's name."

While Naman went in search of Jundar, Javik inspected the dog's wounds. His mother would probably know what to use on them. They didn't appear to be severe, but he knew nothing of dogs. His thoughts were interrupted by a new voice.

"He's marvelous, what's his name?"

Javik turned to see a man he knew only by sight. It was the man who kept the village's hunting dogs now that Naman's son was gone. He was not tall, but his physique was very athletic. His eyes were a soft brown color like his hair, and they radiated a kindness that was hard to miss. He was clean-shaven and wore his hair very short. His tunic and pants were stained with many shades of brown and black, and his boots were caked with mud and what Javik guessed must be dog excrement from the smell.

"I don't know. Naman's gone to find Jundar. Maybe he can translate this collar." Javik pointed to the item then offered his hand to the man as he stood up.

"My name is Javik of the house of Browdat. I've seen you many times, but I don't know your name."

"My name is Wollan. Where did you get this fine specimen?" He took Javik's hand in a strong grip.

"We killed his Sentii master, and I brought him here. I think I can turn him to my service."

"A difficult task. These kind are very loyal, and they're trained to respond to only one voice. You may have an even harder task since that voice was Sentian. He may only understand that tongue," Wollan said.

Naman returned with Jundar, and the dog strained at its bonds in response to new arrivals. Jundar greeted Wollan.

"Wollan, you're a good man to have around for this job," Jundar said.

"I hope we can do something with this dog, Jundar. I'd like to also have a female to breed them. We could use some war dogs in this village."

"I know the King has war dogs. Perhaps he'll let you breed this brute to one of his bitches?" Jundar said.

"Right now, I need to see if you can read his collar. We need a name for this snarling mass of fur," Javik said.

Jundar knelt well out of the dog's range and read the collar.

"It looks like mowr-daw as best I can make it out." Jundar rolled the words around in his mind for a moment before snapping his fingers in discovery. "Yes, that's it, Mordah, the Sentii word for death."

"Very appropriate," Javik mused. He leaned down toward the dog and placed the doped meat next to its nose. The animal sniffed at it and tried to stick its tongue through the leather strapping. Javik carefully unwrapped the thong, but Wollan moved beside him.

"Wait, Javik. Let me help you."

Wollan straddled the dog's shoulders and pinned its head between his legs. He held the huge jaws shut while Javik removed the makeshift muzzle.

"Dogs are hard biters, but they have weak muscles for opening their jaws. You see how easily I can keep the brute's mouth closed."

Javik pulled the thong away, and Wollan jumped away from the fierce head as he released his hold on the jaws. The animal growled low but immediately wolfed down the venison. It tried to rise, but the pole continued to hold him fast.

"Did you use the stinkweed potion?" Wollan asked Naman.

"Yes, my son left some here."

"Good, he'll be out soon, and we can take a look at those wounds," Wollan said.

The dog was soon sleeping soundly, and Wollan inspected each wound, applying various salves and ointments from a leather satchel at his belt.

"You can untie him now, Javik," Wollan said. As Javik released the ropes binding the animal to the pole, Wollan inspected each foot. He stood up and pronounced his satisfaction.

"He's in good shape, but you have a rough go trying to turn him. Be sure you're the one who feeds him each day, and speak to him as often as you can. He must learn your voice and our language. I will not go into his pen without you, so I'll let you know when his wounds need more attention. Naman, here, knows something about dogs, and he'll let me know if my services are required. All I ask in payment is that you allow me to breed him, if you ever turn him."

"I'll turn him," Javik said. "You may be assured of a stud, if you can find a bitch. How often should I feed him?"

"Only once a day, and make sure the meat is fresh. This fellow will consume several kilograms of meat a day. You'll be a busy hunter as long as you have him." Wollan laughed on seeing the perplexed look on Javik's face.

"I thank you, Wollan. Are you sure I can't pay you something for your services?" Javik asked.

"No, just remember our bargain. By the time he's yours, I'll have a bitch lined up. Now, we'd best be out of this pen before he comes around."

The men left the enclosure with Mordah still sleeping soundly.

CHAPTER 14

Allana and Ling were near the end of their supplies by the time they reached Ulum. The pass was knee deep in snow, but still open, and she was glad to be free of the bitter cold. Zargaia was not that far South of Berglaundia, but the temperature there was several degrees warmer. As the city came into view, Ling stopped their travels.

"This is where I leave you, Allana. I must take the horses back to Tao Shan, but he said you could keep the mule."

"Thank you for being my guard and companion on the journey, Ling." She leaned from her saddle and kissed him on the cheek.

"It's been a pleasure, Lady."

"Do you have enough money for inns on the way back?" she asked.

"Yes, Lady, Tao Shan provided some gold for that purpose. Being a man, I have no fear of the inns."

"Then goodbye, Ling, and tell Tao Shan that I'm grateful for his help."

"I will."

Allana dismounted and took her bed furs and saddle bags to the mule. She watched for a moment as Ling rode back toward Berglaundia. For a second time in her life she was alone.

She led the mule through the city gates and inquired about the market place from the guard. He directed her to the center of the city.

The market place was a welcome sight with its food stalls and wine merchants. She stopped to savor some warm roast chicken and a mug of fine wine before searching for Varuda.

Grazhda said she was to be found begging here, but Allana hadn't seen her as she entered the large plaza devoted to the merchants of Zargaia. She knew a little of the language here, having learned a bit while Grucheau's slave. She decided to try asking one of the merchants about the woman. An old man in a strange robe stood behind a table laden with furs, and she decided he might be a good choice.

"Excuse me, do you know a beggar named Varuda?" she asked in Zargaian first.

The man shook his head and raised his hands in a gesture indicating he didn't understand. She tried Sentii next.

"Do you know a beggar named Varuda?"

This time the man nodded vigorously and replied in the same language.

"Yes, she begs on the other side of the plaza near the gold merchant's stands." He indicated the way with one arm.

"Thank you." Allana reached into her purse and presented a silver coin to the man. He held his hands in front of his chest and pushed them toward her.

"I must not take your money, lady. It is forbidden unless you buy."

She looked at the furs and selected a fine red fox pelt. "How much for this one?"

"The coin is enough, madam. Thank you." He bowed low as she took the fur and moved on.

She found the gold merchants easily and followed the line of stalls to an area filled with dirty, misshapen humans in filthy rags extending wooden bowls to all who passed by and pleading with them in the native tongue. One sat slumped over with a hood covering her head and face. The arm holding the bowl was obviously a woman's. It was delicate and the fingers long and slender. It was surprisingly clean, and Allana stopped in front of her and threw a gold coin into her bowl.

"Are you Varuda?" she asked in Berglauni. To her surprise, the woman responded.

"Why do you seek her?" The woman kept her face hidden.

"I've come to stop her begging."

"Are you from the King?" The beggar cowered a bit as she replied.

"No, my name is Allana, and I've come to ask your help."

"Humph. What can a beggar do for one so fair as you?"

"You can teach me your trade."

The woman stiffened and sat erect. She pulled the hood from her face revealing a mass of scars and an unruly mop of red hair.

"This may be your fate if you follow my profession in Zargaia. Is this what you hope to achieve?"

Allana recoiled from the horribly disfigured face, but recovered quickly.

"I know your story. The witch Grazhda told me of your misfortune. If you will help me gain wealth and power, I will see that you never beg again though you live to be 100 winters."

"Are you some kind of Lord with unlimited gold?"

"No, I was once a slave, but Grazhda showed me my true destiny, and a wise mentor proved she was correct. I have barely enough gold to begin, and I know nothing of the profession you once pursued. I was told you were once the owner of the greatest bordello in Zargaia. Is that true?"

Varuda pulled the hood back to cover her face. "I once held sway over every great man in this kingdom, but now I beg. You will fare no better. Take the gold you have and go back home. Marry a rich, handsome warrior and live well under his protection. The road you seek to travel is fraught with peril."

"I've faced hardship before. I know how to survive." Allana stood more erect and spoke with an air or authority.

"Hah! How many men have you defeated in combat?" Varuda's voice held an edge honed by experience.

"If it would come to armed combat, I have warriors who would come to my aid, but I understand you know the way to defeat any man without ever touching a sword. That's what I need you for. You know who to bribe for protection and who to please for favors. The rabble will provide our gold, but you understand the politics of the profession. I have enough gold to make a start, but I need you to guide me through the maze of power in Zargaia."

"Humpf! How much gold have you?" Varuda almost laughed, knowing this stanger's idea of gold was undoubtedly too small.

"I have letters of credit with the Argani for 1,000 gold crowns."

Varuda threw back her hood and looked up at Allana with wide eyes above what passed for a smile among the mass of scars.

"Lady, you will have all the knowledge I possess for that sum."

"I will need a place to stay. Can you lead me to a good inn?"

"Inns are dens of thieves who will only take what gold you have and rape you in the bargain. I have a small room in a house not far from here. It's clean, and the landlord protects me as long as I service his needs." She laughed, and the sound was like a dozen silver bells chiming a hymn. "He covers my head with a towel when he does me."

"You need suffer that no more. I can pay him in gold."

"Gold? A few coppers will cover his rent. You can stay with me while I advise you on a proper location for your house of business. Once we have that, we can move in and purchase girls from the slave block." She stood, and Allana was surprised at her height. She was a head taller than Allana. She stood straight and erect belying her beggar pose. She pulled the hood back over her head and started to leave. The beggars on either side of her reached for her robe.

"Where are you going?" one asked.

"Stay with us, Varuda," another begged.

Varuda spoke to them in a soft voice. "Farewell my friends. Thanks to this lady, I will beg no more."

As they walked away the beggars shouted their pleas and pressed their bowls toward Allana. She dropped coins from her purse until only the gold coins were left.

Allana felt the strong tie among the poor wretches huddled over their begging bowls. "Aren't you sad to leave your brothers and sisters?" Allana asked.

"We protected each other as best we could, but it's a terrible life. I can't thank you enough for rescuing me from poverty."

"Take me to your home now. I will unload my mule and find somewhere to sell him."

"I know a man who'll give you a fair price, but come, it's this way."

She led Allana through a maze of back streets to a building with no windows. Allana tied her mule to a nearby post and removed her belongings and what was left of her provisions. Varuda helped her carry the load up to her apartment on the second floor.

The room contained little in the way of furniture, only a bed, one table, two chairs and a lamp stand. A threadbare carpet covered part of the floor. A water cask stood in one corner, and a small cabinet contained what few possessions Varuda owned and some stale bread. A large window opened to a narrow walkway surrounding a small atrium. There were no gardens, only a gnarled tree and a few scrubby bushes now devoid of leaves. A hand pump in the center of the atrium provided water for the tenants and their landlord. Allana could count three other apartments on this floor and surmised the building contained four more on the ground floor.

They dumped Allana's things on the floor, and Varuda spoke.

"Let's take your animal to my friend. He should bring a good price from the looks of him."

She led Allana and the mule to the edge of the city and to a pen containing several horses. A burly man with a coarse, black beard and bald head greeted her.

"Hello, Varuda. Who's the beautiful lady with you?"

"This is Allana, Brunne. She has a mule to sell. Allana, this is Brunne the blacksmith."

Brunne bowed to her and approached the mule. He looked it over with the eye of a practiced horse trader and turned to Allana.

"Seeing as you're a friend of Varuda, I'll give you 20 gold crowns for the animal."

Allana noticed Varuda standing behind the man and nodding vigorously.

"Done," Allana said.

Brunne went into his forge and pulled a leather curtain across the opening. In a few minutes he emerged with a small pouch. He handed it to Allana.

"You may count it, if you like," he said.

Again, Allana noticed Varuda shaking her head from side to side. She hefted the bag in her hand before speaking.

"I trust you Brunne, but if I find false coins in this bag, you will rue the day you cheated Allana."

The smith began to laugh heartily as he picked Allana up by the shoulders and held her feet off the ground. "Lady, I know Varuda's reputation, and I assume you are of the same profession. Why would I cheat one who can make my life pleasant? It's you who should thank me for protecting your kind. Should any man give you trouble, just call on Brunne." He set her down.

Allana blushed beet red. "I'm sorry. I didn't know about your relationship with Varuda."

"Don't bother your mind, lovely lady. Just let me know when and where you will be doing business. Good day."

The women returned to the apartment, and Varuda briefed Allana on Ulum and Zargaia.

"The kingdom is at peace thanks to King Kullan. He keeps the Magdan bandits warring with each other and thus, too busy to raid Zargaia. When they make peace with each other, he pays off the most powerful tribe to start the fighting all over again. Commerce is free of constraints here, but the tax is 10% of all sales. I found it more advantageous to pay an annual tribute to Kullan on his birthday. It's cheaper than the tax, and he calls off his tax collectors. Everyone comes to Ulum at least twice a year for the religious festivals. Both are excellent times to make money."

"I must eventually go to the island of Gorgos," Allana said. "What do you know of it?"

"I know you must pass through Magda and Ollon to get there. To avoid the bandits you must pay a strong caravan to let you travel with them through their lands. A woman alone, even with a strong bodyguard, will be easy prey for the brigands."

"What of Ollon?"

"A land ruled by a powerful sorceress but not war-like. Gorgos is part of the Ollon province of Tulla, ruled by Count Charlan. He's a womanizer who used to frequent my house from time to time. His wife is bi-sexual and also visited me quite often. I'm afraid he will demand your services in bed once he learns you're in business here."

Allana sat back in her chair and sighed in disgust. "Is there no man who will deal with a woman on a purely business basis? Why must they always be after our bodies?"

Varuda laughed and reached across the table to take Allana's hand. "Sweet child, that's their weakness. They'll do anything you wish if they think it will land them in your bed. You must learn to play one off against the others as Kullan does the bandits. You have much to learn, but I will be your mentor. Rest tonight. Tomorrow we will see if my old house is still for sale. The last I knew, it was still vacant. No one wanted to move into an old bordello."

"My stomach thinks I abandoned it in the mountain pass. May I suggest we find some food?"

"Certainly, I'm not used to regular meals, you must excuse me. I know a fine place to eat, if you have money. They used to let me beg outside their door because the owner was a good customer even though his wife was ignorant of his peccadilloes. He often fed me to keep me from telling her about him."

Allana picked up the sleeve of Varuda's robe and dropped it disdainfully. "I think we must find you some clothing more suitable to your new station also. I'm sure the fleas will find another home."

The women found clothes for Varuda in the marketplace, and the public baths provided the means of insuring fleas were a thing of the past. One of the attendants there also worked with Varuda's red hair, turning it from a tangled mass into a shining array of auburn splendor. With the new clothes and a hairdo, Allana almost overlooked her damaged face. She led Varuda to a large mirror.

"Look at you. You are a consort for kings."

Varuda studied her reflection then sat down and began to sob piteously. "Oh, Allana. I once was as you say, but now I'm not fit to be seen by anyone."

Allana sat next to her and embraced her new mentor. "We can remedy that also. In Sentius there was a man who made masks for people with scarred faces. Surely there is such a man here in Ulum?"

The bath attendant heard her and approached the pair.

"I know of someone who could fashion you a face to match your other grandeur, Lady," she said.

"Who is that?" Allana asked.

"Garnos has a small shop two streets over. His business is pottery, but he's also skilled in other materials. He is an artist in all he does. I know he'd be glad to help you."

"Then, we'll go to see him," Allana said, and she rose to leave.

Varuda grasped her arm. "Wait, this may be very expensive, and you'll need all the gold you have to revive the House of Orgama."

The bath attendant gasped at the name. "Lady, do you plan to re-open that house?"

Allana replied, "Yes, with Varuda's help. Why?"

"I came to Ulum to do massage in that house, but it was closed when I arrived. Please consider me when you are in business again."

"What is your name?" Varuda asked.

"I'm Marima, Lady. You can always find me here at the baths."

Allana produced a silver coin and handed it to Marima. "I will come to you again if we are successful, Marima. Until then, good fortune."

"The Lady Varuda may need this." Marima removed a silken scarf from her waist and tied it as a veil for Varuda.

Once more, Varuda inspected her image and declared herself suitable to return to the world of normal people.

CHAPTER 15

The next morning Varuda led Allana to her old place of business. The building sat on a secluded side street directly behind a large fountain. It stood two stories tall and was as wide at the street that dead-ended into it. Three windows on the second floor were flanked by statues of what Allana assumed to be goddesses, and the statue of a naked woman stood in the center of the fountain.

"Who is this?" Allana asked as she pointed to the statue in the fountain.

"That is Orgama, the goddess of love. The women you see on either side of the upper windows are her servants," Varuda replied.

"That was the name of your house, wasn't it?"

"Yes, I thought it appropriate since this was once a temple to her. She fell out of favor many years ago, and her temple fell into disrepair. I purchased it and was doing well until the bandits came. The man who minds it for me lives in that house." She pointed to a smaller dwelling to her right.

Allana knocked on the door, and a burly man with a curly brown beard answered.

"What do you want?" he asked Allana in a gruff voice.

He had no hair on top of his head, but he made up for that by letting his beard grow to hide his chest. His dark brown eyes radiated hostility to strangers, and his muscular build backed up the threat.

"Varuda and I are here to see the House of Orgama."

He looked past Allana at the veiled woman behind her. "Varuda?" he croaked.

"Yes, it's me, Hogor. This woman said she wanted to re-open the House of Orgama. Meet Allana of Beglaundia."

"Come in, come in, ladies." He held the door and indicated the inside with a sweep of his free arm. The women walked into what was, obviously, a man's home. It was very Spartan with only minimal furnishings, but clean and well kept. "Please sit down," Hogor indicated a divan next to a low table then clapped his hands. A servant appeared.

"Wine for our guests, Alvero."

"Yes, master." The young man bowed low and left as Hogor took a seat in a wooden chair opposite the women.

"I would certainly welcome the re-opening of the house, but it will take a good deal of gold to renovate it back to its former glory, I'm afraid."

"I have letters of credit to the Argani for 1,000 gold crowns," Allana said.

Hogor nodded his approval. "Enough for a start, but you will need another 1,000 by my estimate if you want to bring back your old clients."

"We will do what we can with Allana's gold, and earn the funds we need for the rest of the work," Varuda said.

Hogor smiled at Allana. "You will certainly draw a crowd, but I'm afraid Varuda's days as a money maker are gone." He passed his right hand past his face to indicate his meaning.

"We will use our gold to purchase slaves to do that work, Hogor," Varuda said.

"Then you'll have to make do with the house much as it is until they earn you enough to make it the envy of all lands bordering the great ocean," Hogor said.

"Show us the house," Allana said.

At that moment, Alvero reappeared with a brass pitcher and three silver mugs. He set the tray on the low table and poured a golden wine into the mugs before backing gracefully out of the room.

Hogor took one of the mugs and raised it in a toast. "First we must drink to the success the House of Orgama."

The ladies followed his lead and downed healthy draughts of the wine.

"Very good, as usual, Hogor. Where did this come from?" Varuda asked.

Hogor took another drink before responding. "From the vineyards of Tulla by way of the Magdan bandits."

"You do business with bandits?" Allana asked.

Hogor laughed. "You'll find they are a good source of excellent wine at a low price, lady. Since they take it at no cost to themselves, every copper they sell it for is pure profit."

Varuda spoke, "Hogor supplied all of the wine for my house in the old days. It's his business. He's the richest wine merchant in Ulum."

"I see, I'm sure we will want to continue dealing with you in the future, sir," Allana said.

After they finished the wine, Hogor lead them into the House of Orgama.

The great front door opened on an entryway featuring a long-dry fish pond in its center. Torn curtains shrouded the archway into a large open area surrounding what was once a swimming pool. Broken furniture lay scattered about, and rats scuttled out of their way as they walked to the center of the room. Allana sensed that the place was once decorated grandly even though little was left to only hint at its glorious past.

Varuda picked up a broken statuette. "You should have seen it then, Allana. It was a wonder to behold." She set the remainder of the figurine on a small table with the tenderness of one placing a child in its crib.

Allana placed her arm around Varuda's shoulders. "It will be the same again soon."

Varuda seemed to recover a bit. She shrugged off Allana's arm and turned to Hogor.

"How are the rooms?"

"Not much better, Come, I'll show you."

He led them up some stone stairs to a balcony overlooking the central room. Two rooms on each of the three side walls were small but large enough to accommodate one person with a guest. All the rooms were barren of any furniture.

"Nobody wanted the house, but everyone wanted your beds, Varuda," Hogor said.

The fourth side was one large apartment overlooking the street and the fountain outside.

Varuda passed her hand over a mural depicting the view from a seaside villa. "I loved this room," she said. "What a shame I had to sell most of my possessions to live."

She moved to a window and looked out at the empty street. "Look, Allana."

Allana moved to her side and gazed out the window. Varuda swept her arm across the scene. "This street was once filled with sedan chairs and carriages bringing the nobility of Zargaia to my house. Let's hope we will never see it this bare again."

The women left Hogor with instructions to re-furnish the house and hire guards to protect it along with enough gold to begin the process. The next order of business was to see the Argani.

They found Gallam easily and deposited the letters of credit. Allana drew out 200 gold crowns on Varuda's advice and the women moved on to the slave block.

On the way Varuda explained, "The auction is tomorrow morning, but we can look over the stock today. Let me choose the women, but if you object to any of my choices, let me know."

"I bow to your experience in these matters," Allana said.

"Also, I need to explain the way I pay them."

"Pay them? I thought we were buying slaves," Allana said.

"Slaves must be kept under close scrutiny, and that means guards and chains at night. The women will work willingly if they know there's something in it for them. I give them one third of their fee. The rest is ours, but it goes toward buying their freedom. The more they make, the quicker they're free."

"A good plan, but won't they leave us as soon as they earn their freedom?"

"Most will, but many stay on. They have a good life with us, and the work is done on your back in a bed." Varuda laughed at her own attempt at humor.

"Again, I defer to you in these matters. How many women can we buy with the gold we have?" Allana asked.

"I'd say three or four. We'll need twelve for full operation, but we don't have that much gold now. Besides, you seldom find more than one or two suitable women in any batch of slaves. Most people are looking for domestics or farm hands, and want substantial females. We need the more delicate type, though we can use one or two stouter girls. Some men prefer the plumper type."

"I've heard of women lying with other women. Would we accommodate that?'

"Certainly, but women don't pay as much as men. We'll

add that feature later on."

They arrived at the slave pens, and Varuda led Allana through the selection process. They picked out five women to bid on in case one was bid to a price beyond their means. They explained their plan to each woman, and only one turned them down.

That night they moved their belongings into the House of Orgama. Hogor provided a slave armed with a sword to serve as their bodyguard. He had no trouble recruiting volunteers for the duty once he hinted some female companionship might be part of the job.

In the morning the women and their guard ate breakfast in Hogor's house and then moved to the slave auction. Hogor stayed behind to supervise the renovation work. At noon they returned with three women in tow to find the house ready to begin business, though not much more than habitable at this point in time. The House of Orgama was once more in operation.

CHAPTER 16

Javik was due at Tao Shan's house early the next morning, and Bandor was ready with another scroll.

"Good morning, Javik. This is your lesson for today. When you've finished, Tao Shan and I will discuss this with you as last time. Any questions?"

"No, sir. Thank you."

Javik unrolled the scroll and was surprised to find it concerned the island of Gorgos. He read the material with a new zeal motivated by his love for Allana. It told of an elegant kingdom rich from the trade along the coast of the Great Sea. The line of its Queens stretched back for 500 years, and the island was recognized for its great university and the beauty of its women. Javik could vouch for the latter quality. The tales of its explorers were fascinating. Gorgon vessels had touched many unknown shores and returned with tales of strange animals and stranger peoples. Javik had to see this place now, even if it was only ruins populated by wild goats. He rolled up the scroll and took it to the dining room.

The smile on Tao Shan's face told Javik the old fox knew his assignment very well.

"Well, Javik, did you find this scroll interesting?" Tao Shan said.

"I certainly did. I never thought any kingdom could be great if a woman ruled it, but Gorgos definitely proves me wrong on that."

"Always remember my game, Javik." The old mentor pointed to a small table where the pieces were set up in order.

"Yes, sir, you game has many valuable lessons, but I'm not sure of the lesson in this scroll," Javik replied.

"The lesson is one of history, Javik," old Bandor inserted. "We understand you have..." the old man coughed and cleared his throat, "...some interest in the island."

"The woman I love is from that place, and she's gone back to it. I must go after her as soon as my obligation here is complete," Javik said as a red glow began to cover his face.

"I thought you might be pleased," Tao Shan said. "Bandor found this scroll among his own library's more obscure volumes after I told him of your interest. The history I have is written in Gorgon, but his has been translated. Your follow-up lesson today is one of geography. Come into my rooms, and I'll tell you more about Gorgos."

"I thank you, Bandor, for finding this scroll," Javik said bowing to the teacher.

"It is yours to keep, Javik. I had it copied so you could have it," Bandor said.

"I must pay you, sir. Copying is expensive." Javik reached for his purse.

"Tao Shan has taken care of that. I'll see you again in two days. Farewell, Javik."

Javik followed Tao Shan into his private rooms and sat in his usual chair as the mentor spread a map across a large table.

"Come here, Javik. I will show you Gorgos."

Javik moved to the table and studied the map. Berglaundia was a small area near the center. He could spot Sentius and Wallandia and a few other countries bordering his own land, but Tao Shan was pointing to the Great Sea to the west. A large island stood well to the South and a good distance from shore. Tao Shan's finger rested upon it.

"This is Gorgos. You can see it's a large island compared to the others on this map." Tao Shan picked up metal dividers and matched their width to a scale on the bottom of the map before walking them across the parchment from Gorgos to Berglaundia. "Over 1,000 kilometers distant, and across three lands. This one is Zargaia," Tao Shan pointed to one of the lands bordering Berglaundia. "They are our allies. Allana would have no trouble crossing their territory. West of Zargaia is Philisia, another seafaring people, but usually peaceful." He moved his hand to the country south of Zargaia. "This is Magda, the home of a fierce mountain people. They live by raiding their neighbors and these mountains provide a safe haven for them. They know the passes and guard them well; extracting tribute from all who use their roads over those passes to reach the sea. Allana would need all of her wits to pass these villains." Once more he moved his finger. "This is Tulla, a peaceful land of fishermen. They enjoy peace because their navy owns the sea and the mountains protect them from the landside. Here is where Allana might find some of her people. You've learned about Gorgos today. You will learn all we know of these other lands also."

"Sir, you're preparing me for my quest to find Allana," Javik said. The surprise in his voice made the old mentor smile.

"Yes, Javik. I know your heart will think of nothing else until you're on your way. I will try to be as brief as possible. But, you've seen more fighting since our last visit. Tell me about it."

Tao Shan sank into a comfortable chair and indicated its mate to Javik.

"Yes, it wasn't much of a fight. The Sentii were easily

defeated."

"Was it so easy? Our forces were badly scattered, as I understand it. Each band of pursuers was too small to attack the Sentii raiding party by itself."

"That's true, but Goldar had no choice. He had to cover all possible escape routes."

"Would it have done any good to cover all escape routes with forces too small to stop the Sentii?"

"No, but we didn't think the force was as large as it turned out to be. We were surprised."

"A good leader is never surprised, Javik. Goldar should have guessed the Sentii would have reinforcements hidden near the border to protect the raiding party from pursuers. It could have ended tragically."

"I must defend Goldar, sir. We had to know where the Sentii were."

"One or two scouts on swift horses could have done that job more quickly than parties of a dozen or so men. He could keep the bulk of his strength intact until he learned the location of the enemy. They were encumbered by extra horses to herd, and would not be making good time. It is almost never a good plan to split your command into smaller units. You should learn from Goldar's mistake."

"In any case, we defeated the Sentii and recovered our horses," Javik said.

"I understand you and Mikka were instrumental in that victory. Tell me of your actions."

"Mikka set up a blocking force on the trail to the pass and sent me to the south with a force he felt large enough to drive the Sentii to him. The raiders would be caught in the jaws of a vise and destroyed."

"A good plan, but there was a problem, wasn't there?" Tao

Shan said.

"Yes, the Sentii were too many for me to attack directly, and too many for Mikka to stop without assistance. I calculated that we must deceive the raiders into thinking a large force was coming up behind them. I sent my men back into the forest to sound like a large party moving carelessly through the trees. The Sentii believed the ruse and fled. We pursued as rapidly as we could and arrived in time to tip the battle in our favor."

Tao Shan smiled his satisfaction. "You did well, Javik. A tactic from the lessons of Master Ling, as I recall."

"Yes, sir. He gave us several good examples of deceptive tactics. I'm glad I remembered this one."

"I also understand you have an unusual trophy from that battle, a large dog?"

"Yes, I've never seen anything like him, sir. He's a magnificent animal."

"I wish you success with him, but don't be sad if you wind up having to kill him. These war dogs almost never take a new master after the original owner dies."

"I have no illusions, sir."

"Good, then we're finished for today. You may tend to your prize now."

* * * * *

Javik raced from Tao Shan's house to the pen beside Naman's longhouse. The barking from inside was almost deafening. Naman came out to meet him.

"Javik, for Zhou's sake get some meat for this beast. He's been driving me crazy since morning."

Javik nodded agreement and ran to Browdat's house. He found a fresh hog carcass hanging in the back of the house and cut off a large section with his dagger. Frieda caught him just as he was about to leave.

"Javik! What are you doing with that hog?"

"Lady Frieda, I was cutting some to feed my dog."

"I heard about that monster, but he doesn't rate a piece of our best boar. Here, come with me." Frieda took the pork from Javik and led him into the springhouse behind the hanging pig. She took down an older slab of venison and shoved it at Javik.

"This should be good enough for that thing. If you intend to keep feeding him, you must do much more hunting or buy some hogs of your own. Next time, ask me before you take any meat for it."

"I'm sorry, lady. I didn't think."

"Just be sure you ask in the future," Frieda said with a stern expression, which turned into a smile as Javik sped away to the pen.

Naman was waiting by the gate to the enclosure, and Mordah still barked like a demented demon. Javik moved to open the gate, but Naman stopped him.

"Use this smaller door, Javik." He indicated a small window in the wall of the pen.

Javik slid the window back, and Mordah rushed to the opening, still barking.

"Easy, Mordah," Javik said in a soft voice. He held the venison up so the dog could see it, and the barking stopped. Mordah stuck his head through the window as far as it would go and whimpered in anticipation of the meal.

"He'll have to back up a bit," Naman said. "He won't be able to get his head back through the window with that piece of venison in his jaws."

Javik considered the situation. He moved his hand above Mordah's nose and continued to speak. "Know me, Mordah. I will be your new master." The dog sniffed his hand, and Javik was not sure if he smelled Javik or the venison. He stroked the long muzzle and was rewarded with a vicious snap at his hand. Thanks to the window restricting the dog's movement, he was able to avoid a nasty bite.

"Throw the venison over the fence, Javik. That's the only way you'll get it to him," Naman said.

Javik threw the meat into the enclosure, and Mordah bounded after it as Javik watched through the window. The meat was gone in a few gulps, and the dog returned to the window for more.

"I thought that would be enough," Javik said as he scratched his head in amazement.

"It is. He'll eat all you give him. You have to keep these dogs lean and muscular. If you feed them too much, they'll grow fat and lazy."

Javik moved his hand closer to the muzzle protruding from the window. This time, Mordah allowed him to touch the coarse fur and stroke it for a moment before snapping again.

"You've made some progress, Javik, but this will be a slow go for a long time. You must be patient."

"I thank you for your help, Naman, and for your good advice. I'll be back tomorrow."

* * * * *

Javik worked with the huge dog every day, and hunted for his feed at every opportunity. Wollan dosed the animal again and inspected the wounds. They were healing nicely, and Javik was making slow headway in gaining Mordah's confidence. Wollan announced he had lined up a bitch for the breeding, but also said it was much too soon to consider any mating.

The studies with Bandor continued. Each scroll was an adventure in learning, and Javik was beginning to grasp the lesson more quickly with each one. Tao Shan continued his instructions on the lands between Berglaundia and Gorgos while critiquing Javik's responses to Bandor. There were no more raids, but Javik continued his weapons practice with Karl and Berda. The festival of spring was upon the village before Javik knew it. He decided to kill a deer for a sacrifice to Verna, the goddess of spring, and entered the forest to find a fine buck.

The first signs of spring were appearing. Small, green shoots popped through the leaf carpet on the forest floor, and tiny buds now graced the once barren and black branches of the trees. The smell of spring was in the air promising new life with each gentle rain. New, more melodic bird songs joined the raucous calls of the jays. Javik stopped to marvel at two squirrels chasing each other through the trees and felt a hand on his shoulder. He whirled with his hand on his dagger to find Grazhda by his side.

"Good day young warrior," the old hag cackled. She was so old nobody knew when she was ever young, and she lived by herself deep in the forest near a foreboding cave. She dressed in dark clothing with a wide leather belt around her waist. Several items hung from the belt including the skull of a large bird attached by means of a leather thong through the vacant eye sockets. She smelled of smoke and strange incense.

"Grazhda, you scared me to death," Javik panted.

The old woman stepped back and scanned Javik carefully. She moved closer and felt his arms and legs. "You've grown strong, Javik. Are you ready for your quest?"

Javik gave the woman a puzzled look. "What quest?"

"To find Allana, what other quest would I be speaking of, dolt?"

"I'm sorry, Grazhda. I didn't realize you knew about my love for her."

"Javik, Javik, when will you learn that I know all. I even know you seek a fine stag for Verna's offering."

"Yes, I do, but..."

"No buts, Javik. A stag is a simple matter. Study well with Tao Shan and learn of the path to your love." She reached into her pouch and produced a small wad of what looked like clay. "Soak this in your urine overnight, and then feed it to that monster you call a dog. He will be your servant forever after he tastes this." She handed the ball to Javik and pointed behind him. "Look! Your stag!"

Javik turned to see a fine six point buck not twenty meters away standing motionless between two trees – a perfect target. He took careful aim and loosed his arrow. It struck firmly in the buck's heart. The buck ran only a few meters before falling dead. It was too heavy for Javik to carry, so he decided to return to the village for help. He turned back to thank Grazhda, but she was gone.

The next morning he put the bolus inside a slab of Mordah's meat. The dog didn't seem to notice its presence. Grazhda hadn't said how long the potion would need to be effective, and Javik decided to wait until after the spring festival to attempt any further work with the huge dog.

* * * * *

The spring festival was much merrier this year. There was no threat of war, and Javik was not on trial for his life. Frieda had recovered somewhat from the loss of her son, and Dana was happy as a respected member of Browdat's household. Only the absence of Allana dampened his mood.

The ritual at Verna's grove was as spectacular as ever. The torch-lit procession in the hour before dawn grew steadily in length as each household added its members to the line. Javik shivered as the people gathered in the sacred grove, not so much from the pre-dawn air as from the sight of the goddess's statue in the torchlight. The wavering flames cast ever-changing shadows on the stone face causing the sightless eyes to take on an almost human quality. The chant of the priestesses pleaded eloquently for the sun as the sky turned pink in the east. A sudden gong sounded as the first rays penetrated the surrounding trees, and the villagers broke into their welcome for spring. The sweet, smoky smell of incense wafted across Verna's altar as the priests entered the grove swinging censers and chanting a reply to the priestesses.

Javik looked at his tree. It was now a sturdy sapling having grown from the bare staff he planted in the grove two years ago. The priestesses even put up a sign telling all who came there the tree was a gift from Javik, son of Tolda, and son of Browdat. It was now as thick as Javik's wrist with several branches spreading from the slender trunk – each one burdened with heavy buds ready to burst into new life at any moment. His stag was a welcome addition to the feast of the goddess, and this year, he had his own money to spend on whatever he liked. He intoned his part of the ceremony automatically until the gong sounded release for the villagers.

Karl joined Javik after the ritual.

"Well, Javik, a little more enjoyable than last year, eh?"

"Yes, sometimes I still mourn for Hella, she was so lovely," Javik said.

"But not as beautiful as Allana." Karl spoke as if his judgment were indisputable.

"I miss Allana even more, but as soon as I finish with Tao Shan's year of instruction, I will go to find her."

"You mean you'd leave our village and travel in unknown lands for her sake?" Karl was incredulous. Travel outside Berglaundia was no easy matter unless you had a sizeable army at your back.

"I'd cut my way through a thousand Sentii for her, Karl. I

have to have her for my own regardless of the cost or the hardship. My mind's made up."

The men were silent as they walked into the village square. The smells from the food vendor's stalls assaulted their hunger. The fresh, spicy scent of the sweet rolls, the smoky appeal of broiling meat even the acid tinge of the fruit stands beckoned to the hungry young men. The calls of the trinket vendors vied for their ears, each call claiming superiority and each vendor holding out samples of their wares for inspection. They seemed to be oblivious to all of this in spite of the rumbling in their stomachs and the sparkle of the baubles dazzling their eyes. Finally, Karl broke the spell.

"I will go with you, then."

Javik stopped and stared at his boyhood friend. "Karl, you would be a fine companion, indeed, but there's no need for you to face danger on my account."

"I don't want to go simply because I'm your friend. It's time I had some adventures of my own. I was looking at my father last night as we sat by our hearth. He is a good man, but he's never been farther than the capital. He wasn't even in the last war because he was too important here in the village. No, Javik, my soul burns for adventure."

"We may never come back, Karl," Javik warned.

"If that is my fate, so be it. Better to die a hero than live a dog." Karl smiled and snapped his fingers. "By the way, how is your dog?"

"I fed him a dose Grazhda gave me, and I hope it will do the job of turning him to me. Wollan says he needs to run free a lot for proper exercise. I can't wait to let him out. I'm getting tired of cleaning out his pen. That animal is a prodigious producer of waste."

"Karl, Javik!" It was Berda running to meet them from the

other side of the square.

"Berda, good to see you," Javik said.

"What news?" Karl asked.

"He's here, Javik! Margan is back," Berda almost shouted.

"Take me to him," Javik said. A broad smile spread across his face as he remembered how the deformed minstrel saved his life two years back.

Berda led the group to a small wagon. Margan was sitting on the tailgate strumming his lute and singing a song Javik had never heard before. He was too engrossed in his song to notice Javik's arrival.

Her wild, raven hair.
Her ruby red lips,
Her snow white skin,
She's captured his heart with her beauty.

The young warrior moaned,
As she bid him goodbye,
This great woman knows her duty.

In a far off land,
In the midst of the sea,
She searches for her destiny.

Young Javik must mourn,
The loss of his love,
Will they be reunited some morn?

With a flourish of chords he finished his song. The dozen, or so, people listening applauded him wildly while some threw money into his hat. One of the villagers pointed to Javik.

"The subject of your song arrives, minstrel."

Margan turned to see Javik smiling broadly and holding his arms open for an embrace. The minstrel leaped from his perch with an agility belying his humped back and raced into Javik's arms.

"Javik! It's good to see you. I have some wonderful news for you. Where can we talk?"

"Right here, these are my friends, and they may share any good news you have for me. This is Berda, and this is Karl."

Margan greeted the other young warriors before turning back to Javik.

"Javik, I saw Allana only last month. She's safe, and she asked me to bring you her greeting."

"Where is she, Margan?" Javik asked.

"She's in Zargaia, but she said she was moving on soon. She wants to get to Gorgos before winter."

"What is she doing there? She should be at the seacoast by now," Javik said.

Margan hesitated to answer. He swallowed hard and cleared his throat while looking away from Javik.

"Well?" Javik insisted.

"You won't like this, Javik," Margan hedged.

"Tell me, Margan!"

"She's running a house of loose women." Margan cringed a bit expecting Javik to lash out at him, but the new warrior only stared with open mouth and wide eyes.

"Wow!" Karl voiced the only reaction that came to mind.

"Why that?" Berda asked, since Javik had still not recovered enough to speak.

"As you might imagine, her beauty was quite an attraction to the men of Zargaia."

"Yes, go on," Karl said.

"She re-opened a house that was once the best brothel this side of the great ocean with the help of its previous owner, a woman named Varuda."

"Is she also beautiful?" Karl asked.

"She once was, but a Magdan bandit disfigured her face with acid. She now wears a curious mask to cover the scars. Allana rescued her from begging in the marketplace."

"A bordello, I can't believe it. It's just not like her. You must not tell anyone else about this, Margan, especially my mother. It would shame the whole village," Javik said.

"You may rely on my discretion," Margan answered.

"That goes for you two, also," Javik demanded.

"Our lips are sealed," Berda said, and Karl ran a finger across his lip to symbolize his agreement.

"I can't believe she sells her body" Javik said.

"She doesn't," Margan said. "She used the money Tao Shan gave her to buy several slave girls and set them up in her brothel to do the work. She only entices men into the house with her beauty. She's learned well from Varuda and has no trouble collecting expensive gifts. She's been overwhelmed with offers of marriage, but won't accept any of them. "

"A brilliant move, and worthy of her." Javik had recovered from his initial shock by now and praised his love.

"Brilliant?" Berda said. "What's brilliant about becoming a whore?"

"Don't you see, Berda? She's not a whore herself, she only owns them and profits from their work," Javik explained. "With so many offers of marriage from rich and powerful men, I wonder if she still loves me."

Margan broke in to dispel Javik's fears. "She loves you, Javik. She told me so herself. She wishes you would come after her, but she knows of your obligation to Tao Shan. She hopes to be established as Queen of Gorgos before she sends for you."

"Humph! That won't be too difficult. What does it take to rule a herd of goats?" Karl said.

"Queen of Gorgos." Javik said the words with a far-away look in his eyes. Somehow he knew Allana would do just as she said, and he would arrive on the island to find her in a royal palace attended by many servants. She was a formidable woman, indeed.

"Not yet," Margan said. "She must still pass through Magda, and that will be no easy chore. The Magdans are a fierce people who raid and pillage for enjoyment. They will not let so lovely a thing pass their borders unharmed."

"Then, I must go help her," Javik said with a resolve in his voice that frightened his companions.

"No, Javik," Margan said. "She told me you were not to come after her until you'd finished with Tao Shan. She said your training was more important to her cause than your concern for her. She will send word when she reaches Gorgos, you may go to her then."

Javik seemed to relax a bit at these words, but he still itched to be on his way. Karl noticed his agitation. "Come, let's have a mug together. I'm buying."

The offer of free qush overcame all other concerns. The young men sat down at a table and began a long night of drinking and swapping war stories.

CHAPTER 17

By this time, the House of Orgama was in full swing. Profits soared once the word of its reopening spread, and Allana and Varuda were becoming more powerful by the day as every noble in Zargaia and the lands beyond plied them with gold, jewels and land in hopes of bedding either one.

Varuda now wore a mask made of a fine material and painted to give her the beauty she once had. Customers paid a high price for her services and stood in line for the pleasure of trysting with a woman in a mask. Varuda was known far and wide as "The Marionette Whore". Allana did not offer her body to anyone but the most noble or powerful, and only then for huge sums of money and promises of political support once she made her move.

As the summer waxed hot, Ulum, the capital of Zargaia, bustled with activity. The Turreks were in town, and that meant prosperity for anyone dealing in wine, women and drugs. The fierce mountain men rarely came near the huge city. Though the border with Magda was quite porous, King Kullan maintained a solid ring of defensive posts around his key city to prevent any unwanted visits.

Magda, a loose confederation of robber tribes ruled by despotic warlords, loomed over Zargaia like a menacing, black storm cloud. King Kullan's father died trying to hold back that storm, convincing Kullan resistance was useless. The bandits were too mobile, and avoided any confrontation with superior forces. They terrorized the rural population into paying tribute in the form of grain or livestock by making grisly examples of anyone resisting their demands or providing intelligence to the king. Kullan played each of the chieftains off against the others in a skillful ballet of diplomacy. One of his rewards for cooperation was a chance to blow off steam in the capital city.

In Ulum, the bandits could enjoy good food, good wine and lovely women in relative security. They had little to fear from rival tribes and could sleep without one hand on their daggers. The people of the capital knew to stay off the streets during these vicious men's carousing, and the watch kept a loose lid on the boiling pot of male exuberance.

The Turreks were the worst of the lot. Most of the other bands showed them a deference born of being on the losing end of turf battles. Kullan kept these brigands sated with tribute not only to protect his own holdings, but also to encourage Turrek help in reigning in their competitors. As a result, the kingdom of Zargaia enjoyed a shaky peace on its western border.

One of the particularly favorite haunts of the Turrek chieftains was the House of Orgama and its beautiful mistress, Allana. Named for the Zargaia goddess of love, it was the best house of prostitution in the city. Because it was a favorite haunt of the rich and powerful men in the kingdom, it was also one of the most expensive houses in the country. Everything a man could imagine was on the menu, with the one exception of Allana, herself. She had even turned down the king's attentions, but he still held her in his highest regard and afforded her the protection of the crown.

On this particular visit, Vargon, the Turrek's current strong man, claimed the bawdy house as his sole property, only inviting his chief lieutenants to join him in the pursuit of sensual pleasures. He lay on a soft couch surrounded by scantily clad women pretending to admire his manly virtues. The couch sat next to a warm pool filled with naked women and three of Vargon's best captains cavorting gaily in preparation for love. Vargon was busy indulging his taste for fine wine, at the moment. Sex would come later. He held out his cup, and a redhead tilted a bronze pitcher to fill it. When the pitcher proved to contain only half a cup, Vargon snatched it from her hands and bellowed, "Allana! More wine!" holding up an empty pitcher for emphasis.

As the madam of the house appeared, a silence fell over the men in the room. She wore a filmy black gown slit in strategic locations to reveal just enough flesh to inflame the male lust urge. Her black hair was piled on top of her head and shined as if it were finely lacquered wood. She dripped silver at every place a woman should have jewelry, and she smiled with a self-confidence born of seeing men make fools of themselves over women in the past year. She snapped her fingers, and a slave appeared with an amphora of red wine.

"Are you enjoying yourself, Vargon?" Allana asked.

"I'd be doing better if you were beside me," the warrior said.

Allana sniffed her disgust. "You know I care for no man, Vargon. Now Sella here is a different story." She pulled a slender redhead closer to her and smiled down at the pale face. She used a ruse of Lesbianism to discourage the men she had no intention of bedding.

"Bah! What a waste of beauty. I could have you by force any time I wanted. You know that."

"And when would you sleep?" Allana nodded her head, and a dagger appeared at Vargon's throat.

"By Grun, where did that come from?" Vargon turned to see the lovely brunette who had just been massaging his back.

The brunette pulled back the dagger and slid it into a compartment in the couch the bandit rested upon.

"All the girls know where to find help when they need it," Allana said. "Besides, any attempt to force yourself on me would result in the King's greatest displeasure."

"Hah! You think Kullan would dare oppose me?" Vargon bragged.

"You are not the only warlord he pays tribute to," Allana replied.

"Yes, but I'm the most powerful. Besides, I'd never really force myself upon you. If I had you, I'd want it to be your decision. That way I would have the full measure of your romantic skills. I'll bet you could drive a man wild."

"I've had men, Vargon. I found them to be as hairy as goats while not smelling nearly as nice."

The other men roared in laughter, but Vargon raised a hand to silence them.

"For you, Allana, I'd shave my body and bathe in all the perfumes of the far lands."

"Ooooh!" Allana faked admiration. She moved to the bandit chief and rubbed her hand on his wooly chest. "I'd love to see you as smooth as Marna, here." She indicated the brunette with a nod.

Vargon sat up quickly. His eyes focused intently on Allana. "How much gold would you want in addition to my hair?"

"Oh, I wouldn't want much gold. Let's say only an amount equal to the weight of your hair. My real desire is something you can easily grant."

"Name it!" Vargon shouted.

"Safe passage through Magda for me and my party this summer." Allana smiled sensually at the chief of thieves.

"Done!" Vargon cried. "Bring on your razors!"

The girls around the brigand began to giggle almost uncontrollably. Two of them ran to fetch the creams, perfumes and razors needed to change the rough warrior into a smooth god.

"I'll await you in my bedroom. Varuda knows the way." Allana left the room to the cheers of Vargon's men.

"The first order of business, sir, is a bath." Varuda spoke with a sense of authority brought on by the chief's eagerness for her mistress. She led him to a large, brass tub and nodded for two of the other women to undress him while two more poured hot water into the tub. When Vargon stood nude before her, she pointed to the tub.

The warrior tested the water with one hand. "It's too hot. Cool it down."

"It must be that hot to remove your foul stench. Get in," Varuda insisted.

The chieftain slowly put one foot in the tub and howled with the shock of the near scalding temperature.

His lieutenants gathered around to watch the spectacle and jeered at their leader in devilish delight.

Vargon stepped into the tub and began to rub his overheated lower legs. "Can't I have some cool water?" he begged.

Varuda signaled and another woman brought an amphora of cool water for the bath.

"Ahhh! Thank you." Vargon settled gingerly into the tub as the hot water woman returned and dumped in another steaming pitcher. Vargon howled with surprise, and his men doubled over in laughter.

"Now we will wash some of the scum from your carcass," Varuda said. Her voice was tinged with laughter, but she managed to keep from laughing out loud at the plight of the vicious warlord.

Two women went to work with sponges and a perfumed soap. They scrubbed the parts above the water line then lifted Vargon to his feet and continued until all of his body was covered in soapy foam. At that moment, two women appeared with pitchers and poured warm water over their victim. Several more women of the rinse brigade followed until Vargon stood calf deep in filthy water.

"That was delightful," he said. "I'll have to do that more often."

"We still have to clean your legs," Varuda said. "Step out of the tub and onto the pan."

She indicated a shallow brass pan, and Vargon obliged her request. Two women went to work on his legs while another placed a heavy robe over his shoulders.

"You must stay warm for the razors," Varuda explained.

The next stop was a padded table. Two women helped Vargon lie on his stomach, and another, brawnier woman began to spread oil on his back and legs while a fourth cut his hair catching the black, curly locks in a bowl. Once his back was thoroughly oiled, more women shaved Vargon's back, neck and legs until no trace of hair remained, then they rolled him over and repeated the treatment on his front half including, against his protests, his pubic hair. All this time his lieutenants roared with laughter and shouted obscene taunts at their leader. Finally, he was pronounced done and stood bald and naked before them all.

"This has been very humiliating," Vargon said as his rage seethed inside his smooth, soft chest. "Your mistress had better make it worth my suffering."

"We are not finished yet, Lord." Varuda moved closer to the man and sniffed at his body as other women toweled him off. "You still need help."

She snapped her fingers and three women brought up small vials of perfume. They poured the vials over his body and massaged the lotions into his skin. Varuda sniffed the air.

"Ahhh, much better. Follow me, Lord." She led the bandit through a hallway to heavy door guarded by two husky men with war axes. A knock on the door brought a soft response from within.

"Is he ready, Varuda?"

"He is ready, Lady."

"Then bid him enter."

The two guards opened the double doors to reveal a dimly lit room. Flimsy curtains billowed from large, open windows. The spring air was cool, but held the hint of warmer weather to come. Allana lay completely naked on a huge bed in the middle of the room surrounded by silk pillows and furs. Vargon ran to her side.

"Softly, Lord," Allana almost whispered. "This night must last you a lifetime. Don't rush it along."

Vargon slid down on the bed beside her. "I have gone through hell for you. Make me think it was worth every moment."

"Relax, and enjoy," Allana purred as she gently pushed him down beside her.

* * * * *

Later that night, as Vargon lay sound asleep, Allana left the bed and dressed. She moved through a door to a brightly lit room with a rough table and several chairs. A well-dressed man sat at the end of the table. His hair and beard were neatly trimmed and oiled expertly. His clothes were obviously expensive, and a heavy gold chain of office hung from his shoulders. He rose as Allana approached and bent to kiss her extended hand.

"Good evening, Lady," he said in a husky voice. "How fares our victim?"

"Good evening, Rennick. He is sufficiently humbled and fully satiated. I think he will agree to whatever terms you wish to present later today. I've put him in an excellent mood. He'll be hungry for more of my favors even though I've told him there will be no more. Use this as an inducement to obtain a favorable position. King Kullan should have no trouble with this bandit."

"I bow to your superior means of persuasion, Lady." The man made a mock bow, and Allana smiled in amusement.

"Just tell the King that I expect my usual fee for this service."

"It will be delivered as soon as our meeting with Vargon is concluded on amicable terms. Until then." Rennick bowed again and left the room.

Allana sat at the table for a moment disgusted with herself over the role she was forced to assume in this land. She'd learned well from the Sentii, but she didn't relish putting the lessons into practice. She'd managed to avoid making love to any of the Zargaian nobles up to now, but her evening with Vargon, no matter how demeaning to the warlord, would only goad the King's counselors into more aggressive pursuit of her body. She would have to leave soon, but she now had her safe passage through Magda. On the other side of the mountains was Tulla, but she would arrive there with enough gold and prestige to make her own way. After only a few months in Zargaia, her fortunes had improved a hundred fold. If only Javik were here to help her and share her success.

CHAPTER 18

Javik approached the pen door with trepidation. It had been two days since Javik fed the dog Grazhda's potion, but Wollan was not yet sure it was safe to enter the pen. Javik placed more confidence in the witch's magic, but a tinge of fear still colored his confidence.

"Be ready with your bow, Karl. If Mordah attacks me, you'll have to kill him," Javik said.

Karl was positioned on top of Naman's longhouse with a good field of fire into the pen and ready to shoot if the dog should leap at his friend. Naman was behind Javik with his broadsword ready to slay the beast should Karl's arrow miss.

"Ready, Naman?" Javik asked.

"Aye," the swordsman flexed his two handed grip on the long blade and braced himself for any charge from the huge dog.

Javik checked the window. Mordah knew something was up. He was eyeing Karl with suspicion but glanced back at the gate from time to time. Javik opened the gate.

Mordah stood for a moment looking directly at Javik and growling softly, but he made no move toward his new master. Javik walked slowly toward the dog holding a slab of venison in his left hand while extending his right toward the animal palm down. He was helpless should Mordah charge him. He'd left his dagger outside the pen in case the dog could sense the weapon. He spoke softly as he closed the gap to the beast.

"Mordah, I am Javik. You know my scent. Smell me. See, I've brought you good meat, but I also bring you my love and affection. Know me better."

Mordah stopped growling and sniffed the air. Javik could see the taut muscles under the gray fur and feel the apprehension radiating from the beast, but he also seemed to sense an acceptance, no matter how grudgingly it was given. He was close enough now to touch Mordah and extended the venison toward his muzzle. The big dog snapped up the meat and lay down with the huge portion between its front paws. Javik knelt beside him and started to reach out toward the dog.

"Don't do that, Javik. Not while he's eating," Naman shouted in a husky whisper.

Javik pulled back his hand and waited as the dog gulped down his meal. To everyone's surprise, Mordah licked his lips, rose from his stomach and padded to Javik's left side before lying down again panting contentedly.

"You've done it, Javik," Naman chortled. "He's yours now. Pet him."

From the longhouse roof, Karl added his congratulations. "Good job, Javik."

Javik felt the coarse wool of the dog's head and scratched it behind the ears as Wollan instructed him. Mordah looked up at his new master with a soft expression in the formerly hard, black eyes. Javik continued to pet the monster for a long time until Karl joined the group watching from the pen door.

Several villagers gathered every time Javik fed his dog. They were probably hoping to see the beast tear him limb from limb, but they applauded as Javik rose to leave the enclosure. Javik bowed to acknowledge their appreciation but stopped short when he heard a collective inrush of breath. He turned to see Mordah standing to his left and slightly behind him. As Javik walked forward, the dog followed, tongue lolling out of his massive jaws. The villagers dispersed rapidly.

Naman offered his hand to Javik but drew back at the sound of Mordah's deep growl.

"Sorry, Mordah," Naman said as laid the broadsword on the ground before extending his hand to Javik again.

"That's amazing," Javik said. "He knew you were armed."

"Aye, that dog will never let anyone near you with a drawn weapon. He's your protector now."

Wollan came running up to the group, but stopped several paces away and walked slowly toward Javik.

"Javik, I heard the dog is yours now. Congratulations!" He slowly extended his hand to Javik as Mordah watched intently.

"I could never have done it without your help, Wollan. Look, his wounds are nearly healed."

Wollan approached the dog carefully extending his hand palm down to the beast's muzzle. Mordah sniffed and turned back to watching the other men as Wollan inspected the scars.

"Yes, he's done well. He needs exercise now. Take him hunting, Javik. He'll bring down a deer for you," Wollan said.

"A deer?" Javik questioned.

"Oh yes, you'll see. May I go with you?" Wollan asked.

"Certainly, we'll go in the morning. Should I put him back in the pen?" Javik asked.

"No, he's safe enough now. Just warn your household about him. He won't hesitate to attack anyone he considers a threat to you. Don't expect him to stay outside either. He'll sleep at your feet and curl behind your chair while you eat. I'll make arrangements for a bitch very soon. I can't wait to breed him."

"I think he'll probably enjoy that too," Karl said, and the group broke into laughter.

* * * * *

Bandor was not pleased to see Mordah come in with his pupil, but Javik explained the dog quickly, and the old man seemed to relax a bit.

"Today, Javik, we have a new kind of lesson. I'm going to give you a problem requiring a speech from a war leader, and you will compose one suitable to the occasion. Tao Shan and I will hear your speech and critique it. Do you understand?"

"Yes, sir. What is the problem?"

"It's all here in this scroll. Read it and compose your speech. We will be in the dining room when you are ready." Bandor left Javik to his studies.

The scroll told of a trying time in a distant kingdom called Yubra. The King of Yubra decided to invade the neighboring country of Bythaidia, because his sister had a legitimate claim to the throne on the death of her uncle. The campaign went well until the armies reached the capital. Perzius, the capital city, was very rich, but its walls were thick and very strong. The king lay siege to the city and waited. After more than a year, his men were becoming discouraged. They had mined the walls in four places, but the defenders managed to close the breaches with temporary fortifications each time. The king's advisors estimated the city could hold out for another six months, and his military commanders cautioned him to end the siege soon or face mass desertions. They must either penetrate one of the breaches or break the siege and return home. What should the king do?

Javik thought about the problem a long time. Maybe it would be best to end the siege. Storming the walls would cost many lives, and if they failed, it might mean death even for the king himself. If the enemy successfully defended four breaches, they must be strong warriors indeed. Was the prize worth the cost? He took the quill pen and wrote out his speech.

Tao Shan and Bandor were busy studying a map when Javik entered the dining room. Tao Shan looked up first.

"Ah, Javik. Do you have a speech?"

"Yes, sir. I do."

"Fine, fine!" Tao Shan clapped his hands, and a half dozen of his servants joined the group.

Javik was taken aback a bit, but recovered quickly. Tao Shan noticed his discomfort.

"A good speech needs an audience, Javik. These fellows have heard many speeches before. They'll give you good advice on yours. Go ahead."

The servants took chairs around the long table, and Javik took a position at the head end. He unrolled his scroll and began to read. Tao Shan stopped him at once.

"No, Javik. Never read a speech. It must come from your heart."

"But, sir. I need to see my speech to know what to say."

"Didn't you write it, Javik?"

"Yes, sir, but..."

"No buts, give your speech without reading it."

Javik swallowed hard as he tried to remember what he'd written on the parchment. All he could recall was the opening and the fact that he was going to call off the siege. He began, hoping to do as well off the top of his head as he had after hours of thinking about the problem.

"Countrymen! I have good news. Tomorrow we return to our home and families." He paused expecting a cheer, but only heard grumbles from the servants. He went on.

"It has been a long siege, and we are all weary of war. This city has claimed too many of our comrades, and no matter how large its treasury, it's not worth another of your lives. Let us have peace."

Javik looked at his audience and saw only glum faces.

"Is that it?" Tao Shan asked.

"Yes, sir. I thought this response would please the people."

Tao Shan turned to the servants around him. "Well, people, what did you think?"

One of the cooks raised his hand.

"Yes, Bylum," Tao Shan recognized him.

"Well, sir, I fought with King Hagan at Mippilia. We were in front of that city for two years. If the King had given that kind of speech, we'd have had a new king overnight."

Another hand rose.

"Lugan," Tao Shan said.

"Aye, no matter how many men we lost, I'd want to get my hands on the treasure and kill enough of the enemy to avenge our losses. I agree with Bylum."

"Me too."

"Aye, he's right."

"Depose the king."

The other servants joined in.

"Well, Javik, your solution doesn't seem to be too popular," Tao Shan said. "What say you to that?"

"Sir, I'm amazed. I've seen war now, and I know how horrible it is. I'm surprised that any man would want to continue when he could go home with his king's blessing."

Tao Shan turned to his servants. "That's all for now. We'll try again tomorrow after Javik has a chance to revise his approach. Thank you all."

The servants returned to their duties, and Tao Shan turned to Javik.

"You see, Javik, men hate to die in vain. A king should never begin a war he does not intend to see through to the end.

Giving up without being defeated is worse than defeat itself. A king may suffer defeat honorably, but to quit the field with forces capable of victory is the most terrible shame."

"I never thought of it that way, sir."

Bandor broke in. "Men are complex things, Javik. They hate war, and they will constantly complain about the food, the weather, their tents, the losses and many other things, but they don't want to quit. In their hearts, they love victory more than life. A leader must learn to correct the things he can remedy and ignore the complaints over things he can't change. He must be above the petty bickering of his troops and set an example of courage and fortitude for all to follow. Bravery must be rewarded generously and cowardice punished severely. He must always place an image of victory before his men as a goal worthy of their blood. A good king could lead his armies into the deepest pits of the underworld and back again with the treasure of the demons. Read this scroll now. It is the actual speech of the king you read about earlier. When you've finished, we will speak some more."

Bandor handed Javik another scroll, and the young warrior returned to his study room. He opened the scroll and read.

"Warriors of Yubra, I have decided that we must leave this place soon. We must return to our villages and our families. We must, once again, till our fields and tend to our livestock. We must caress our children and give our wives the love they've missed for so long. What a happy thought, to be home again. And, after we plant our crops, milk our cows, love our wives and bounce our children on our knees, we will share mugs of qush with our friends. We will sit in the common houses and drink with the old men. How many times have we all listened to them tell of forgotten wars and heard them endlessly recount their tales of victory? Then, we will tell them of the walls of Perzius."   The king paused here to gage the mood of his men, and the scroll said he heard only silence.

"What? No tales of glory for us? What shall we tell them? Shall we tell of our orderly retreat? Shall we describe how we failed? Will our brothers who died against these walls have died in vain?" The scroll described how the king paused again here and was greeted with shouts of opposition.

"Well, what shall we do?"   The scroll told of the men shouting, "Storm the breach once more."

"Then, we attack now. We will attack knowing that the spirits of our old men and all who died here attack with us. Who back home will dare to tell of their old victories when they've heard how we stormed the walls of Perzius? On men! On to victory!"

The scroll recounted the battle and the terrible losses suffered by the king's forces, but it also told of the valor at the breach, and the ultimate victory won by sheer grit. The king's sister was crowned queen, and the land prospered under her reign.

Javik sat back in awe of the king's speech. He'd hit the warriors where they lived. No matter how discouraged or how overwhelming the task before them, returning in defeat was worse than death on the walls. He'd painted them a picture they couldn't stand to see come to life. Javik rolled up the scroll and returned to the dining room. Only Bandor was there now, and Javik sat down opposite the old teacher.

"You have read the king's speech, Javik?"

"Yes, sir. It was quite impressive."

"And, what lessons have you learned from it?"

"I see that men may be motivated to do more than they think they're capable of, if the right words are used."

"Very good. How do you think you learn the right words?"

"You will teach me?" Javik looked at the old man with a quizzical expression.

"I can only teach you so much, Javik. Finding the way to men's souls comes only from years of experience. I can give you many examples like the one you just read, but you may never face an identical situation. You must learn how other leaders solved their problems and keep those lessons in your mind as you study the actions of the men around you. When the time comes for you to lead, you will grow from each experience. You will make mistakes, and sometimes those mistakes will cost men's lives, but you must not dwell on your mistakes any longer than is necessary to extract the lessons they hold for you ."

"But, sir. How can you forget the death of anyone?" Javik was even more puzzled.

"I didn't tell you to forget, Javik. I only told you not to dwell on the deaths. You will never forget the death of your father, but I'm sure you don't think of him every moment of your day." Bandor looked at the young warrior to prompt and answer.

"No, I don't. I must go on with my life, though he will always have a place in my heart."

"You will find a leader must have a large heart, Javik. Many people will claim a spot there before you are old." Bandor smiled at Javik and placed a firm hand on his shoulder.

At that moment, Tao Shan entered the room carrying a rolled up map.

"Ah, I see you've read the king's speech. Did he learn the lesson, Bandor?"

"Aye, he's learned it well. I think he's ready for you now." Bandor turned to Javik. "I will see you in two days, Javik. Until then."

Javik rose and bowed to his teacher. "I look forward to it, sir."

Bandor left the room, and Tao Shan spread the map on the table.

"Now, Javik. Come look at the first land you will have to cross to find Allana."

CHAPTER 19

Javik walked back to the village in deep thought. Being a leader was such an onerous task. Maybe he should just follow and be content with his lot? He was so engrossed, he didn't notice Polla emerge from the forest on his left until Mordah's growl shook him from his personal fog.

"Polla, I didn't see you there," he said as he placed a hand on Mordah to restrain the big dog.

"I'm glad you noticed before that monster tore me to pieces," she said.

Javik knew the young woman only slightly. She was one of the girls every boy in the village dreamed of. Tall for a Berglauni, her head was only slightly below Javik's. Shining blonde hair framed a narrow face, but her eyes were her most striking feature - they sparkled like light blue gems. Even in the shapeless dress typical of his people, her figure was evident as the soft wind blew the fabric against her slim form. She carried a basket filled with mushrooms.

"Mordah wouldn't attack you unless you threatened me."

Polla reached out to pet the animal, but Javik stopped her.

"I don't know how he'd react to you touching him. I wouldn't want him to harm you."

"Is he that dangerous? He looks so loveable." Her voice held that note of affection women always express for furry creatures.

"It's just that I haven't had him out of his pen that long, and I'm not sure of him yet. Are you going back to the village?" Javik rubbed Mordah's coat behind the ears to relieve his own nervous tension.

"Yes, may I walk with you and your dog?"

"Certainly." Javik gulped and felt overly warm even in the chill air of early spring.

"What's his name?" Polla asked.

"Oh, his name is Mordah." Javik fought hard to keep from stammering.

"What a peculiar name. Does it have a meaning?"

"It means 'death' in Sentii."

"Death?" Polla grimaced as she spoke the name.

"He's a war dog, and trained to defend his master should the warrior fall in battle."

"Are you expecting an attack?" Polla laughed as she said the words.

"No, of course not." Javik laughed nervously in response. "Wollan advised me to keep the dog with me as much as possible until I'm sure he's truly mine."

"Truly yours? Didn't you buy him?"

"No, I took him in battle during the last Sentii raid. His master was killed, and Mordah defended his body. Mikka said we'd have to kill him, but I wanted him, so I knocked him out with a soft stone from my sling. Wollan helped me heal his wounds and advised me about his training, but I think the special bolus Grazhda gave me was the thing that finally turned him to me."

Polla stopped walking and looked at Javik in shock. "You've met Grazhda?"

"Twice, in person. Three times, if you count my dream."

"Tell me about her. I've never met anyone who actually

spoke to her."

"She's as old as everyone says she is, and just as wily. She can sneak up on you before you're aware of anything, and she vanishes in an instant. I don't know how she does it."

"What did she say to you?"

"She told me I would do great things and one day be a king. She told me what staff to cut for Verna's ceremony last year, and it lived. She said she helped me defeat Grucheau, and this year, she told me to follow Allana."

Polla's expression took on a dour mood, but she caught herself quickly and resumed her usual sparkle. "That's wonderful. I've never known anyone who was blessed by Grazhda, mostly she curses people who drive her off their land."

"She said my father saved her life once, and that's why she's helping me."

"Lucky you. She made my father's cow go dry, and we had to butcher her and buy another one."

The village stockade was now visible on the other side of the newly plowed fields, and Javik was almost sad to see the end of their time together. He struggled to think of some excuse to see her again, but she solved his problem.

"Javik, I saw a bear today while I was gathering mushrooms. Could I ask you and your dog to protect me tomorrow when I go out again?"

Javik grew even more nervous. Several hours alone with Polla would test his resolve to the limit. His store of subjects to discuss with a woman was nearly exhausted, and he didn't want to appear an oaf, but something deep inside him urged him to accept.

"Why, ah, yes. I'll have to check back at our longhouse, but I don't think Lord Browdat has any chores for me tomorrow.

What time would you like to go?"

"I'll come for you after breakfast. Don't sleep late, or you'll miss me. I must be in the forest early to catch the newly formed stems. They're the most delicious ones."

"I never sleep late. I'll be looking for you."

They passed through the gate, and Polla waved to Javik as she ran off toward the other side of the village.

"Until tomorrow, Javik," she called over her shoulder.

That evening at dinner, Browdat reacted to the presence of Mordah in the room.

"Javik, I hope that dog is properly trained. It doesn't seem like that long ago he was ready to tear you apart."

"He seems to obey my commands, sir. Wollan told me I should have him beside me as much as possible," Javik replied.

Frieda broke in. "That animal eats enough to feed half a village."

Browdat gave his adopted son a critical glance, and Javik felt the need to insert an explanation.

"I hunt to feed him, sir. He takes no food from our table."

"Good, I also assume you're hunting for our table also," Browdat said.

"Yes, sir. Between my lessons with Tao Shan and hunting, I have little time left for weapons practice with Karl and Berda."

"How goes it with Tao Shan?" Browdat asked.

"I'm learning all about the lands between here and the great sea, and..."

"Why those lands?" Browdat broke in.

"I want to find Allana, and her island kingdom lies beyond those lands, sir."

"You must forget her, Javik. It's foolish to think of traveling through those lands without an army at your back. Zargaia is friendly enough, but you'd be killed for the boots on your feet in Magda. I could never allow it, Javik." Browdat frowned his disapproval of Javik's suggestion.

"Lord, he loves the woman dearly," Dana said.

"He can learn to love one of our village girls," the big war leader bellowed. "Zhou knows we have enough of them. It seems all women drop today are females when we need more sons."

Javik sat silent. He had no intention of quarreling with his adopted father at this point. It would be many months before he was finished with Tao Shan, and he would make his decision then. The fates might have some surprises in store for him in the meantime.

"Tao Shan is also teaching me how to speak to men." Javik changed the subject.

"Good! Good!" Browdat roared. "A leader must be able to inspire his warriors." He leaned closer to Javik and almost whispered, "And, seduce the women."

"I heard that," Frieda scolded. "Stop filling the boy's head with such trash, husband."

"He's not a boy any more, woman! Besides, it's time he knew about such things. Someone should educate him." Browdat stared at Dana with an expectant look.

"His father should be his teacher in that regard, sir." Dana looked down at the table as she spoke.

"Not that I couldn't give him some excellent advice, but..." Browdat said. He started to go on, but Frieda interrupted.

"Hah! You could certainly advise him on how to save time."

Javik noticed the servants suppressing their snickers.

Dana intervened. "Lord, I would gladly tell my son all I know, but I think the thrower of the spear makes a better instructor than one of his victims."

At this, neither Frieda nor the servants could hold back their laughter. Browdat turned beet red and rose from his chair. He pounded a large fist on the table.

"By Zhou, I'll have order in my own house. Enough of this."

Only the war leader's heavy breathing broke the resulting silence. Dana rose and bowed to Browdat. "I'm sorry, sir. I only meant the words in jest."

Browdat settled back into his chair, and his expression softened somewhat. "Lady Dana, you did not offend me. It was these stupid oafs who don't know their place." His arm swept across the row of servants standing along the far wall as his expression changed from resignation to mild anger.

Frieda spoke. "Well, if the lad wants good advice he'll go to old Nielen."

"And, how would you know about the quality of Nielen's advice?" Browdat said with a suspicious look at his wife.

"Well, I've never taken advantage of his services myself, but if the gossip in the marketplace is to be believed, he is the best lover in Berglaundia," Frieda said.

"I've heard the same tales myself, Lord," Dana added.

"The man is more than ten years my senior. What prowess can he have with the fair sex?" Browdat asked.

"All I know, Lord, is what the other women say," Dana replied.

"Well, we'll see to your education in these matters in any case, son. I don't suppose Tao Shan has covered this subject?" Browdat asked with a note of hope in his voice.

"No, sir. He said this is something our parents must teach us."

"Damn!" Browdat said between clenched teeth. "We'll speak more of this later, Javik. Right now, I need more qush." He pounded his mug on the table for emphasis.

That night, Javik thought about women. He knew the basics

of the process, but he also knew women expected more than that. The other boys in the village and those at Tao Shan's house all had stories about women, and some of them even sounded plausible. He vowed to see old Neilen as soon as possible.

* * * * *

The next morning, Javik stood outside his longhouse after breakfast and studied the sky. It was overcast a dull gray, and the smell of rain permeated the air. The rumble of thunder in the distance told him it would not be a good day to hunt mushrooms. He glanced down at Mordah, lying at his feet. The thunder had not disturbed the animal. He was about to take his shield and boar spear back to the longhouse armory when Polla approached, basket on her arm.

"Good morning, Javik. A fine day for mushrooms." Her voice held a lilt of happiness that was hard to mistake.

"I'm afraid it's going to rain, Polla. Maybe we should go mushroom hunting on another day?"

"Nonsense, this is the best time for them. If we wait another day, the best ones will be gone. Besides, this kind of weather brings them out in abundance. We'll have a full basket before the rain begins. Come along!" Polla took Javik's arm and pulled him toward the village gate. He had no choice but to follow with Mordah loping along behind them.

"You look so manly with your shield and spear. I understand you were quite a hero in the war and during the last Sentii raid."

Javik blushed. Polla still held his arm, and her touch was like fire.

"I only did what any other man would do."

"That's not what my father says. He's very proud of you, and wishes I were a son."

"Why would he wish that? He has two fine sons."

"Men are like that. They always want sons, but we'd be in a fine pickle if they got their wish. Can you imagine an all-male world?" Polla laughed brightly.

Javik marveled at her, she was so carefree and vibrant. Life was a festival to her, and he wished he could share her joy. Without Allana, something seemed to be missing in his life. He kept up a good humor, but deep inside him there was an empty space only she could complete. Polla's laughter almost filled that void, and it frightened him.

"It would be a lonely place." Javik looked off into the forest as he spoke, still thinking of Allana.

They walked in silence for a while before they entered the forest. Polla's hand never left his arm, but he was beginning to get used to the touch. He was surprised that Mordah had no objection to Polla's grip on his sword arm, but the huge dog seemed to sense no danger in the woman's presence.

"This way, Javik." Polla tugged on his arm as she turned off to her right, and the sensation sent his blood coursing more swiftly through his body. She led him deep into the wild tangle of brush and young saplings to a clearing near some large rocks. Polla stopped.

"You stand guard, Javik, while I gather the mushrooms. I don't want to be surprised by any bears."

"You'll be safe with me and Mordah." Javik doubted her tale about seeing a bear. The she-bears had long been out of their dens by now. Still, they had cubs to defend, and could be touchy about anyone near them. Perhaps it was wise for Polla to want some protection.

The girl hummed a sensual love song as she stooped to gather the delicious fungi. Javik knew the words, and they made him very uncomfortable. A sudden clap of thunder evoked a scream from Polla, and Javik turned to see her cowering against a boulder.

"It was only thunder, Polla. You're in no danger." Javik snorted his disgust at the cowardice of women.

"I know, but that means lightning is near, and I'm afraid of lightning."

As she spoke, Javik felt the cold droplets of rain on his skin and heard the patter of the spring shower on the new leaves.

"We'd better get back before it starts raining too hard," Javik said.

"No need. I know a small cabin near this place. We can stay there until the rain stops. Follow me, Javik."

The girl led him through the woods along a seldom-used trail as the rain began to fall in earnest. Javik tried to shelter Polla with his shield, but did little good due to their brisk pace. Mordah seemed to relish the rain. Before they reached the shack, they were both soaked to the skin. Polla opened the creaky door, and Javik followed her inside. Mordah followed them in and shook his shaggy coat with a vengeance that soaked them even more before he settled down across the doorway.

There was not much to the place. There were no windows, and the only light came from the smoke hole in the ceiling. Rain sparkled in the shaft of dull light and fell on the ashes of an old fire. Javik noticed some wood stacked in one corner of the single room.

"I'll build us a fire. I'm afraid these wet clothes will give us a bad sickness if we don't find warmth."

He found kindling and some wood shavings for tinder beside the wood. Whoever owned this shack was well prepared for an emergency. In no time he had a small blaze going. He turned his back to the fire and let the heat drive the cold, wet feeling from his clothes.

"Come close to the fire, Polla. You'll need to dry your clothes."

"They dry better this way, Javik," she said.

He turned as a flash of lightning revealed a naked Polla holding her dress on a stick. She placed the stick in a hole in the floor and stood before Javik smiling broadly in the firelight.

"Polla, I, I ..." he stammered.

"Why don't you get your wet clothes off too, Javik?" She moved toward him and began to unlace his tunic.

"Polla, I...you..."

"Don't speak, Javik." She held a slender finger to his lips. "We have no need for words now."

* * * * *

The fire was dying, but the patter of rain on the wooden roof was warmth in a different form. Polla lay in Javik's arms asleep, and he relived the experience. How wonderful to feel her soft skin, to know the touch of her lips on his, to see her body glow in the firelight. She was so kind, so gracious in dealing with his clumsy pawing. Those few moments taught him more than a year with Tao Shan. Now he knew what it was to have a woman, and he would never rest until he and Allana shared this happiness.

A twinge of guilt swept over him as he thought of the raven-haired girl so opposite to Polla. Allana was fair, while Polla was dark skinned. Polla's hair shone like gold where Allana's was polished ebony. He fantasized about making love to Allana, but he couldn't see her body clearly. Polla broke the dream by stirring beside him.

"Thank you, Javik. You are a good lover," she cooed.

"I should thank you for bearing with my inexperience."

"This was your first time, wasn't it?"

"Yes, and I couldn't have had a better teacher."

Polla nestled her head into his chest.

"I love to be a man's first lover. I don't know why I should feel that way, but I do. There's something so innocent and so fresh about it. I could never marry, Javik. I'm afraid I'd grow tired of my husband in a short while."

Javik stroked her hair. "He would have to make each time a new experience. I think a man might be able to learn how to do that."

"If you succeeded, you'd be the first, Javik. I've found that all men become boring after two or three encounters."

"I never knew you had so many lovers. I've heard the other boy's tales, but I put no stock in them."

"That's why I only take young men or older boys. Nobody believes their boasting, and my reputation is safe."

"What if you become pregnant?"

Polla laughed. "I take precautions, and I also have other means of dealing with that situation."

"But, how can you know when a man will take you?"

Again, Polla laughed merrily. "Javik, you are so innocent. It's part of your charm. Do you think I was not prepared for today?"

"Well, I..."

"Javik, I've wanted you for a long time, and I've planned this day for over a week."

Javik felt used, but quickly pushed the thought from his mind. Polla was an answer to his prayers. He didn't want to face Allana as a novice when he knew she was very experienced, even if it was experience she'd rather forget. He turned to face Polla.

"Polla, will you teach me how to make love to a woman?"

The girl pushed herself up to a sitting position and stared at

Javik for a moment before answering.

"Yes, Javik. I'll teach you what a woman wants, but you must not listen to any man on this subject. Men only know what they want, and it's not the same thing. Could you do that?"

"Yes, Polla, yes I could."

Javik seemed too eager to Polla. She thought of his motivation for making such a request, and it hit her squarely. He would use her to learn how to please another woman.

"Who is it you want to learn for, Javik?" Her voice turned cold, and her eyes held a new hardness.

Javik suddenly understood a lot more about women, and carefully weighed his answer.

"Perhaps for you. Maybe I see you as a challenge. If I were to marry you, I'd be forced to find a new pleasure each time, and I couldn't do that unless I knew what made you happy."

"It couldn't have anything to do with that dark haired bitch you found last year, could it?"

"Allana? She's gone back to her people in a far land by the great sea. I'll probably never see her again."

Polla fell back down beside Javik and kissed him gently. "Then meet your new mentor, Javik."

CHAPTER 20

Spring gave way to summer, and Javik's ignorance of women gave way to Polla's teaching. He felt a bit shameful to be accepting such pleasant lessons, but Polla seemed to be enjoying them just as much as he was. In spite of that, he knew he would feel guilty when the time came to leave her behind and seek Allana.

Things on the dog front were progressing much better. Wollan was proving to be an excellent teacher, and all he asked in payment was the use of Mordah as a stud to the three huge bitches of his breed the dog trainer managed to borrow from the King's kennels. The King had pick of the litters, but the rest belonged to Wollan. Javik's dog sparked considerable interest in the village, and the offers for the pups grew in value each day in anticipation of the first bunch.

Javik and Wollan were now engaged in teaching Mordah the Berglauni words for his commands. Javik and Mordah met the trainer inside Wollan's compound.

"What will Mordah learn today?" Javik asked.

"Well, he knows basic obedience in Berglauni. Now, we must teach him the commands he will use in war. "Here," Wollan said, handing Javik a heavy leather leash, "put this on him."

"Aren't we going to use the choke chain?" Javik asked.

"Not for this work. We don't want to discourage him in this phase, we want to encourage him. Take these too."

He gave Javik a bag of diced meat, and Mordah knew by scent it contained food. The huge dog sat in front of Javik and whined piteously as he stared at the bag.

"When he does what you want him to do, give him a treat and tell him he's a good dog. Pet him a lot when he's right, and scold him when he's wrong. He knows what to do, he just doesn't know the right word for it yet. This won't take long."

"Would it be any help to learn the Sentii words for his commands?" Javik asked as he watched Wollan don a padded suit.

"No, we need to get him used to your voice and our language. I only hope he will forget the Sentii commands," Wollan answered.

"Why's that?"

"Well, suppose you're engaged in combat with some Sentii, and one of them commands your dog to kill. What will he do?" Wollan asked.

"Hmmm, a good thought. I would hope he'd kill someone other than me."

"But, he might kill one of our men."

"True, true, but I hope we won't be seeing the Sentii for a while. At least until we have him trained as a Berglauni dog."

"I need to put on the training suit now. I'll be right back." Wollan went into his longhouse and returned wearing a curious costume. He stood before Javik and Mordah looking more like a drab snowman than a dog trainer. He waddled to the center of the compound and turned to face Javik.

"Now, Javik. What command would you like to give as an attack command?"

"How about 'attack'?"

"Too easy for another person to guess. You must use a word no one will associate with the action but Mordah."

Javik thought for a moment then snapped his fingers. "I know, Grucheau."

"Why Grucheau?"

"He was Allana's master, and I killed him. I still hate the name."

"Good choice, Grucheau it is. Now an 'on guard' command."

"Well, how about 'watch'?"

"Good. We'll start with that. I'll approach the dog while you hold him on the leash. Give him the 'watch' command and hold on to the leash. Reward him every time he doesn't let me move, but don't let him attack. Got it?"

"Yes, are you ready?"

"Give him the command."

Javik shouted, "watch" and pointed to Wollan, but Mordah only looked at his master with a curious expression. Wollan moved toward the dog, and Mordah's attitude changed. He growled at the trainer and started toward him, but Javik held the leash firmly and repeated, "watch" several times. Finally the strain on the leash relaxed, and Wollan stopped advancing.

"Reward him now, Javik."

"Good dog, good boy." Javik produced a lump of meat and Mordah gobbled it down.

Wollan started to move away, and Mordah barked and lunged to block his path almost pulling Javik to the ground. Wollan stopped and told Javik to produce another reward. This training went on for several more minutes before Wollan pronounced success.

"I knew he would learn quickly, Javik. All he needed to know was the correct word. Now we will try an attack."

Wollan moved to a table and picked up a slender stick with thorns on one end. He returned to the center of the compound.

"Now Javik, I will intimidate him into attacking me. You must hold him until you give the command to attack. Is that clear?"

"I'm afraid he'll harm you."

"I'm padded, and he knows the heel command. Don't worry." Wollan approached the dog and began to prick it on the nose with the stick. At first, Mordah only snorted and shook his head, but soon he growled and lunged. It took all of Javik's strength to hold on.

"Give him the command, but don't let him have too much leash," Wollan said.

"Grucheau!" Javik called, and he let Mordah have enough leash to reach Wollan.

The trainer held out one arm to the dog, and the beast took it in his massive jaws.

"Give him heel now, Javik." Wollan's voice was calm in spite of the death grip of the dog's jaws on his arm.

"Heel, Mordah!"

The dog released his grip and returned to Javik's side.

"Are you hurt, Wollan?" Javik called.

"I'm fine. I have wooden planks in these sleeves to protect me, but Mordah cracked one of them. I heard it break a bit when he clamped down on my arm. Your dog is quite powerful. We'll try it again. This time we'll start from the 'watch' command."

They repeated this training only four more times before Mordah was performing on cue. Javik's bag of treats was almost exhausted, but he was pleased with the monster's progress.

"That's enough for now, Javik." Wollan moved to a far corner of the compound and removed the suit. He was sweating profusely from the exertion and the tension. He knew

Mordah was capable of killing him even with the suit's protection.

"He learned quickly," Javik remarked as the trainer rejoined them and petted Mordah.

"He's an intelligent dog. He knew what we wanted, he only had to learn new commands for his actions."

"I'm surprised he's letting you pet him after that," Javik said.

"He knows my scent by now, but the padded suit fools him. I've smeared it with cow dung to throw him off my scent while I'm in it."

"I thought you were quite fragrant, but I just assumed you hadn't bathed recently." Javik said.

"Bring him back in two days, and we'll reinforce these commands," Wollan said.

"How are the bitches doing?" Javik asked.

"They should drop their litters in the next week, or so. I'll let you know as soon as they're born."

Javik walked back to Browdat's house pleased with Mordah's progress. He was also pleased with his progress in learning the ways of love. Polla was a patient teacher, but Javik was sure she was becoming tired of him. She didn't seem to approach their sessions in the small shack with as much zeal lately. He hadn't seen her in several days now, and perhaps she thought it was time he graduated.

Karl joined him as he walked past the common house.

"Good afternoon, Javik. How goes the training?"

Javik had to think a moment before responding. His first response would have described his sessions with Polla, but he knew Karl wasn't asking about that.

"He's learning fast. Wollan says it's because he knows what we want, but he doesn't know the commands in Berglauni."

"Has the Lady Frieda accepted him yet?" Karl was well aware of the woman's dislike for the animal.

"She tolerates him, but she'd rather have him penned up outside. I can't seem to do that to him. He enjoys being near me so much." Javik patted the dog on its neck and ruffled its fur. Mordah responded with a shake and an affectionate look at his master.

"I wish I had a dog like that."

"Wollan said the puppies will come next week. Perhaps you could buy one from him?"

"I don't have much money yet. I'm afraid they'd cost too much."

"Maybe I can talk him into giving you one. After all, the services of this prime specimen should be worth one puppy besides the training he gives me."

"I'd appreciate it if you'd ask him, Javik. By the way, are you going to join the boar hunt tomorrow?"

"I can't. I have a lesson with Tao Shan tomorrow."

"Too bad. We could probably use your dog."

"Wollan has some excellent boar hounds. I don't think Mordah likes to hunt."

"Not for hunting, to protect me in case I stumble upon a boar unknowingly."

Javik laughed at his friend's sincerity and clapped him on the back.

"No boar would be a match for your expertise with a spear, Karl. Have a good hunt tomorrow."

Javik turned into his house and bid Karl goodbye. His mother met him just inside the door.

"Javik, we must speak," Dana said.

"Certainly, Mother."

"Not here, in my room." She led him to her small apartment

and closed the door.

"Sit down, Son." Dana indicated the one chair in the room, and Javik took it while Dana continued to stand.

"What is it, Mother?" Javik knew her expression from previous sessions in his mother's doghouse and dreaded the coming conversation. He couldn't remember making any mistakes with her lately, but he would soon find out the cause of her serious manner.

"I understand you are seeing Polla."

Javik wondered if she knew all that transpired between him and the girl, but decided to keep the secret as long as possible.

"Yes, Mother. I've helped her gather mushrooms and berries."

"And, what else?"

"Nothing, Mother. All we've done is talk."

"Javik, I know the look of a sexually satisfied man. You aren't a boy anymore. Your walk is different, and your attitude toward the women of this house has changed. I even sense a new tone in our conversations since you've been seeing her."

Javik knew further protest was useless. Women seemed to have some kind of sixth sense about these things. He decided to make a clean breast of it.

"Yes, Mother. We've been intimate together for several weeks now."

"I thought so. Have you had sexual relations with her?"

Javik blushed. It was difficult for him, hearing these words from his mother. He hung his head as he answered.

"Yes, Mother."

"Javik, Javik. I knew you wouldn't be a boy forever, but I was hoping you would explore these strange waters with your wife. Now we have a problem."

"What problem, Mother?"

"Polla is with child, and I fear it might be yours."

Javik sat back in his chair stunned by the news. The child could be his, but how could anyone be sure? He remembered Polla telling him not to worry, and thought his mother should know about this.

"I admit being intimate with Polla, but she told me not to worry about her getting a child. She said she had ways of dealing with the problem."

"That's what brought the matter to my attention. Polla tried to abort her baby by taking a poison. She nearly died, and her parents are frantic. They will try to force her to name her lover."

"She could name me, that's certain, but there are many stories about Polla and other boys from our village. She even admitted to me she'd had many lovers."

"Polla's reputation is well known, but if she names a particular man, that man will be judged to be the father."

"What will it mean if she names me?"

"You will marry her. You can't let her live in shame and without the protection of a man. How would she live?"

Javik hung his head and sighed. "I trusted her, Mother. She said she would teach me how to make a woman happy, and she told me not to think about her becoming pregnant. What a fool I was."

"You are not the first man to face this problem, and you will not be the last. We can only wait to see if she names anyone as the father. You should be thinking about what course of action you will pursue if she names you. Until then, go on as usual. We'll speak no more of this until that time, son."

Dana walked to Javik and held his head against her body. "I love you, and I know you'll do the right thing."

Javik was devastated. His world was collapsing around

him. Polla was from a good family, and Browdat would insist he marry her. It would spoil all his plans for finding Allana. He would consult with Tao Shan, perhaps the mentor had a way out of this quicksand.

The next day, Javik sat through his lesson with Bandor and gave a speech to the servants. This time they cheered his words. Tao Shan took him aside afterwards.

"Today, I want to show you a very closely guarded secret of my people, Javik. Come with me."

Javik followed his mentor into his private quarters with Mordah at his heels. His attention was immediately drawn to a hand cannon resting on the table. It was a metal tube half a meter long attached to a stout pole about two meters long. A peculiar mechanism occupied one side of the tube near the pole. Tao Shan picked up the weapon and handed it to Javik.

"Do you know what this is?" he asked.

"Yes, sir. It's a hand cannon. Noka showed it to me when I first came to your house."

"Have you ever seen one outside of my house?"

"No, sir. I've heard of them, but I've never seen one anywhere else."

"They are not widely used. They aren't very accurate, and it takes a long time to load and fire it. A good archer or crossbowman is of more value in battle these days, but the time will come when these weapons will rule the field of honor. My countrymen were at this stage before I left." Tao Shan pointed to the weapon. "I'm sure they have much more advanced models now. Would you like to see it fired?"

Javik's face brightened up considerably. All thought of Polla faded in light of seeing the mysterious weapon in action.

"Yes, sir. I would."

"Follow me, but you'd better leave Mordah here." Tao Shan

shouldered a belt with several pouches attached and took the hand cannon. He led Javik out to the archery range.

Javik watched as he poured black powder into the tube and rammed a wad of moss in after it. Next he dropped several metal balls in the tube and added another wad. He stood facing the targets and poured a bit more of the powder into the mechanism.

"This will make a loud noise, Javik. Don't be frightened."

Javik nodded his assurance, and Tao Shan pulled back on a lever part of the mechanism. From one of the pouches on the belt he produced a rope-like material. Carefully resting the hand cannon on the ground, he struck his flint and steel at the end of the rope. The spark produced a faint glow, which he blew into a solid ember. Retrieving the hand cannon, he threaded the rope into the lever and turned to Javik.

"When the fuse hits the powder in the pan, the weapon will fire with a loud bang. Watch the targets."

The mentor braced the pole against the ground and pointed the metal tube at the archery targets. Javik watched in awe as the rope snapped against the pan. A bright flash of light was followed by the sound of summer thunder. In an instant the metal balls splattered against the canvas targets hitting not only the one in front of Tao Shan but also the one on either side of it. A cloud of white smoke hung in the air, and the smell was like an old campfire gone out.

"Great Zhou!" Javik whispered. He suddenly realized that any men standing in the path of the weapon would have been hit with lethal force.

"A formidable weapon, indeed, is it not?" Tao Shan asked.

"It is, sir. How could any army stand against those things?"

"Very easily. The initial shock power is formidable, but one shot is not enough to stop a charge. The opponent's cavalry of their archers would slaughter me before I could reload. There are tactics to help prevent that, but they require large numbers of these things, and they're quite expensive."

"Is this the secret you spoke of?" Javik asked.

"No, the secret is the black powder, but I wanted you to see its power before I showed you how to make it. Come back inside."

The pair returned to Tao Shan's room to find a whimpering Mordah.

"The noise frightened him, sir, though he's not afraid of thunder."

"It takes a long time hearing the sound of the hand cannon for dogs to become accustomed to it. He would learn quickly, I'm sure. Now to the powder."

Tao Shan took three canisters from a shelf and opened them for Javik's inspection.

"This one is ground charcoal. See how fine it is."

Javik picked up a pinch of the black powder and felt its silky smoothness. "It is fine, indeed," Javik said.

"This one is sulphur. You're familiar with that, I know."

Javik looked at the yellow powder and nodded. "We use that to ward off the biting bugs of the forest."

"Yes, but it's also a basic ingredient of black powder. The next you may not be familiar with, it's saltpeter."

Javik looked at the white powder and felt its consistency. "No, sir, I've never seen this before."

"Ah, but you've tasted it."

Javik looked at the old man in amazement. He touched a bit of the powder to his tongue and made a face. "I know I've never tasted anything this vile."

Tao Shan laughed. "Every time you drank water in this house as a student you tasted saltpeter. I have my servants mix it in to keep you boys' lustful urges under control. It's hard to taste in the quantities we use."

"And the powder is a mixture of these three things?"

"Yes, but the real secret is in the proportions. Start with the saltpeter." Tao Shan picked up a small cup and scooped out a level measure of the white powder. He used his knife to be sure the cup was level before dumping it into another canister. He repeated the process many times.

"Fifteen saltpeter starts the mix. Next comes the sulphur." Tao Shan measured two scoops of the sulphur. "Remember, fifteen saltpeter, then two sulphur."

Javik nodded.

"Now we add three charcoal." As he worked he reminded Javik of the proportions. "Two, three and fifteen. There's an easy way to remember it. Two plus three is five, and five times three is fifteen."

"I see, it is an easy formula to remember." Javik smiled at his newfound knowledge.

"I give you this secret now, even though you have no hand cannon, because the powder has many other uses. It's good for starting fires on a wet day, and it can be used to destroy buildings, if they aren't too sturdy. It takes a lot of the powder to do this kind of work, but it's easy to make. All you do is mix the ingredients together."

Javik rubbed his chin. "I know where to find charcoal, and sulphur is usually available, but this saltpeter is new to me. Where can I find it?"

"You can make it, but it's a long process. The best place to find it is in caves. Have you ever noticed the white residue on cave walls?"

"Yes, sir."

"That's saltpeter. You can scrape it off easily. Also, look for old stables or dung piles. Under the old manure piles you can often find a great deal of saltpeter, if the conditions are right."

"I'm honored that you chose me to share this secret," Javik said.

"You must realize the importance of this knowledge, Javik. It is a serious matter to my people. We've kept it to ourselves for hundreds of years, and until a few generations back, no one outside our country possessed the knowledge. Now, some other men know the secret, and the knowledge is beginning to spread. I fear all nations will soon be using hand cannons instead of crossbows."

"I will keep your secret, sir."

"I know you will, but I sensed something was bothering you when you came in. Was Bandor's lesson too difficult today?"

"No, sir. It's another matter, and I want your advice please."

"Sit down and tell me about it."

The two took facing chairs as Mordah shifted to a position at Javik's feet.

"I may have impregnated a woman, sir."

Tao Shan reacted with a slight start, but quickly resumed control.

"This is a serious matter, indeed, Javik. Who is the woman?"

"Polla of our village."

"Do you love her?"

"No, sir, I only love Allana."

Tao Shan's face took on a puzzled expression.

"Then, why did you lay with her?"

"She seduced me, at first, but then, I asked her to teach me how to please women, and she agreed. She said she was taking precautions, and that she had ways of dealing with a baby, should it come, but she lied."

"Has she named you as the father?"

"Not yet, my mother says her parents are pressing her for the name, but she has refused to name anyone, so far."

"Hmmm, has she had other lovers?"

"She tells me she's had several, and I've heard tales from other boys, now men, but I don't know if she's had any besides me recently."

"You say she told you she had means for dealing with a pregnancy. Did she tell you what those means were?"

"No, sir, but my mother said she tried to take poison."

"If that's the case, she would be far enough along to miss one or two of her cycles. How long have you been 'seeing' her?" Tao Shan used the more courteous term for sex.

"Over the last three weeks, maybe six or seven times. I've lost count."

Tao Shan smiled remembering his younger days. "I doubt you're the father, Javik, but you're a good catch for any woman. Son of Browdat, fine looking man, good prospects, any woman in the village would love to have you. She may use this child to gain the position of being your wife."

"But, sir, that would be dishonorable."

Tao Shan laughed out loud. "Javik, Javik, you have much to learn about women."

CHAPTER 21

Javik left Tao Shan's house and walked back toward the village with a plodding step. All he could think of was the loss of Allana should Polla name him as the father of her child. He would have to marry her, it was the only honorable thing to do. A low growl from Mordah brought him to full alert as Polla stepped from the forest.

"Polla, what are you doing here?" Javik asked.

"Is your dog safe?" she asked before advancing any further.

"Yes, he knows you by now."

The girl moved to Javik's side and Mordah sniffed her dress before looking up at her with a friendly expression. Polla scratched the animal behind its ears before she spoke.

"Javik, I am with child."

"My mother told me. She said you tried to take poison."

"It was not poison, only a potion to make me lose the baby. I went to the cabin to take it, but it made me very sick. I'd never used it before, and I was afraid I was going to die. I managed to make my way home before I fainted on our longhouse doorstep."

"But you still have the baby?"

"Yes, my mother knew the antidote for my potion, and she gave it to me in time to save the child, though I wish she had not."

"No more than I. What will you do now?"

"My father wants to know whose baby it is, but I've refused to tell him."

"Are you certain of the father?"

"It's you, Javik. I know because you are the only man I've lain with in the last two months. I've only missed one cycle, but I'm sure I have a child inside me."

Javik hung his head even lower and sighed in resignation.

"Then I will marry you, Polla."

"I don't want you that way, Javik. I could easily come to love you, and I know our life together would be wonderful, but I also know you love another."

"I do, but I must do the honorable thing for you in spite of that love."

"Do you love me, Javik?"

He looked at the golden hair and tanned face. Every man in the village desired her, and many claimed to have had her before. He knew the stories about her, but he truly believed she'd changed her ways since lying with him. Now, she could be his with a single word. Many tears dimmed those gem-like eyes, yet they still captivated his heart. If it were not for Allana, he would jump at the chance to have her as a wife in spite of her reputation. He smiled at her and shook his head.

"I wish I could say I do, but it doesn't matter. I will take you as my wife and give you all the honor you deserve."

Polla dropped to the ground and began to sob piteously. "Oh, Javik. Can't you see? I want love, not honor."

Javik knelt beside her and folded her into his arms.

"Don't cry, Polla. My mother often told me that love would come, in time. Allana is far away. I must deal with the here and now. You may name me as the father of your child, and I will admit to it."

Polla continued to cry with her face turned away from Javik.

"Javik, you are such an honorable bastard! I don't want to name you as father under these circumstances. I'd rather jump in the river and drown."

He turned her to face him and lifted her chin.

"That would be a great loss to the beauty of this world and I would never know my son."

"We don't know it's a son," Polla said.

"If it's my child, it must be a son." He placed one hand on her stomach as he held her chin in the other hand. "I can feel his manhood, Polla. Don't you think the world could use the product of two such formidable people?"

She smiled for the first time, and nodded her head as she dried her eyes with her sleeve.

"Then it's settled. We will marry as soon as possible."

"You must demand a dowry, Javik. We will need money to start our own hearth, and my father has enough to insure we'll be comfortable."

"I'll speak with my mother and Lord Browdat about it. I know nothing of these matters. Come, put on a cheerful face. We will walk into the village arm in arm and quell all the gossip with a single kiss."

As the couple walked through the village to Polla's house, groups of women gathered and began to whisper as they passed. Javik stopped in front of Polla's door where two groups of gossips could see them clearly. He enfolded Polla in his arms and kissed her tenderly.

That evening, Javik told his mother of his decision.

"Mother, I've told Polla I will marry her."

Dana looked at her son with a mixture of surprise and pride. "You're doing the right thing, son. I know you love Allana, but I would be ashamed if you spurned Polla."

"Well, perhaps it's best. Allana is far away, and I'm not sure she even wants me anymore. I know Polla loves me, but I will always dream of Allana."

At supper, Browdat was overjoyed at the news.

"By Zhou, you've made a good choice, son. Polla is one of the most beautiful women in our village, and her father can offer a fat dowry. I'll speak to him first thing tomorrow."

Dana knew she must warn the war leader of the beehive awaiting him at Polla's house, but she decided to do it in private. Browdat was probably the only one in the village unaware of the girl's condition, but it would all be right now since there was a willing husband for the expectant mother.

Browdat called for more qush and raised a toast. "To the marriage. May Javik and Polla have many sons."

The family and servants joined in the toast, and Frieda drank along with the rest. She set her mug on the table and muttered, "Well, they have a head start, anyway."

"What was that, woman?" Browdat asked.

"Everyone knows but you, husband. Polla carries someone's child, and now we know whose it is."

Browdat sat stunned for a moment before collecting his thoughts. "Well, that's even more reason to celebrate. Not only has Javik made his first conquest, he's also done the manly thing in marrying the girl - two reasons to be proud of him. Another toast."

The qush flowed freely the rest of the night.

The next day, Browdat walked to the house of Challa, Polla's father. The servant he sent to arrange the meeting advised his master that Challa was in a foul mood over the matter and Browdat should tread lightly, but the big war leader was never one to approach a problem with any degree of subtlety. He did have the good sense to put on his best manners and make sure there were no food scraps in his beard.

Challa met him at the door and saluted the war leader in a suitable manner.

"Hail Lord Browdat. Welcome to my humble house," Challa said.

"You house honors me, Challa," Browdat replied. "I've come to arrange the marriage of your daughter, Polla, to my son, Javik."

"Come in, Lord. We have much to discuss." Challa led Browdat to one of the sleeping rooms of the longhouse and sat him down at a table brought into the room for their use. Challa's wife entered behind them carrying mugs of qush and a tray of snacks. She bowed to Browdat and left the room, closing the door behind her.

"Well, Browdat, my daughter says your son is the father of the child she bears, and I must believe her."

"A union between our houses is a good thing, Challa. Your family gains much prestige through this marriage." Browdat sat back in his chair and sampled the cold venison.

Challa fumed but maintained his composure. "My house is not a warrior house, as yours is. I am a farmer, and a seller of grain, but I'll wager my treasury is as rich as yours, and my name is as respected as yours."

Browdat fussed a bit before answering. "Well, I, ah, didn't mean to imply your house was not honorable. I only meant we would both gain through this nuptial contract."

"I know you've come to negotiate a dowry for your son, but I believe my house is due some consideration in light of the reasons for this hasty union."

"Well, when a man has daughters, he must realize the hazards associated with female children. She is not the first, nor will she be the last, to be forced into a marriage. The circumstances should have no bearing on the size of the dowry."

"But they have a great deal to do with the status of the marriage. It will be recorded in the law books as a forced union. Javik will be able to divorce Polla any time after the baby is born." Challa stared at the war leader with a glimmer of hatred in his eyes even though his voice was even and calm.

Browdat thought about that aspect of the marriage for a moment, then his face brightened up and he smiled broadly at his future relative by marriage.

"Not if Javik swears Polla was a virgin when he lay with her the first time."

Challa sat back in his chair and eyed Browdat with suspicion.

"I've heard your son is a very honorable man. Why would he lie?"

Browdat leaned on the table and began to number his points on his fingers.

"First, he values your daughter's honor as much as his own. Why else would he admit he's the father? Second, he needs money for a great quest he plans to embark upon sometime in the future. Your dowry will give him the nest egg he needs, and you and I will help him invest it well. In a year, or two, he'll have what he needs. Third, I'll beat him senseless if he doesn't."

Browdat smiled even more impishly at Challa, and Javik's future father-in-law stroked his chin pensively.

"How much?" Challa asked.

Browdat sat back in his chair and tented his fingers while he pretended to think.

"Shall we say, three hundred gold crowns?"

"Three hundred!" Challa thundered. Browdat only raised his eyebrows in response, while Challa pursed his lips and furrowed his brow in consternation. "Two hundred!" he said holding up two fingers.

Browdat cocked his head to one side and shrugged his shoulders. "Two hundred and an equal share with your sons when they inherit."

Challa began to sputter. "But, that's likely to be over four hundred crowns besides the dowry – impossible."

Browdat sighed. "Oh well, I told you Javik was determined upon a great quest in the near future. He won't want to leave a wife and child at home with no support. All he has to do is assume responsibility for the child and repay half the dowry, and he can divorce her without prejudice. Maybe that's the best way, two hundred it is." He stood and offered his hand to Challa.

Challa bit his lip and frowned. "Very well, three hundred, but no share in my son's inheritance."

"Done!" Browdat shouted. "Let's drink to it." He raised his mug to Challa.

"I'll drink to your good intentions, Browdat, but the deal will not be sealed until Javik makes the appropriate statement before Buran, our law keeper."

"Consider it done," Browdat smiled then drained his mug.

CHAPTER 22

Browdat returned home to an expectant crowd of family and servants.

"Well?" Frieda assailed him. "What kind of a dowry did you manage to get?"

"Quiet, wife. I need to speak with Javik alone. You'll have to await his decision before I can speak more. Lady Dana, you may stay with us. The rest of you, out!" The order was delivered with such force and authority that not even Frieda dared linger. Soon the room contained only Browdat, Javik and Dana.

"Sit down, we must discuss the situation calmly," Browdat said.

When Javik and Dana were seated, he continued. "I have an offer of three hundred gold crowns for a dowry, but there is a condition."

Dana inhaled sharply at the news. "That is a generous dowry. What is the condition?"

"It is for Javik to decide this, Lady Dana, but I trust you will share my advice to him once he hears the condition."

"Go ahead," Dana said.

"Challa will pay this amount providing you swear Polla was a virgin when you first entered her, Javik. If you will not, he only offers two hundred crowns."

Javik looked to his adoptive father and then to his mother. He thought for a while before answering.

"But, Father, the whole village knows she had many lovers before me, and I assure you, she was no novice at sex. I'd be lying."

Browdat exhaled sharply and rolled his eyes back in his head. "What does it matter, son? This is a question of the woman's honor, not yours."

"Lord," Dana broke in. "If Javik swears to this, the marriage will not be recorded as forced."

"What's that, Mother?" Javik asked.

"If the marriage is recorded as forced, you would be able to divorce Polla after her child is born. You'd have to adopt the child and return half of her dowry, but you could be free of her with no dishonor on your part." Dana looked at her son with a mixture of hope and trepidation. She wanted him to be free to find Allana, but she also wanted to save Polla's honor, if possible.

"That doesn't sound fair, Mother," Javik said.

Browdat broke in. "It's a man's world, Javik. Our laws are made to protect our men. We are the ones who till the fields, tend the livestock and fight the wars. We deserve all the respect the law allows, but this is a matter of three hundred crowns in your pocket."

Dana spoke up before Javik could answer. "The laws are truly made by men and for men, but you must make the decision based on your own conscience. You know well that money can never buy honor. You have it in your power to mend a woman's life. I know you love Allana, but she may never return, and even if you find her, she may not want to marry you or return here. I know you will do the right thing."

Dana sat back with her hands folded in her lap and smiled at her son.

Javik's head was reeling. He hadn't been aware of the forced marriage provisions. They would be an ideal way for him to have all he wanted. Even giving back half the smaller dowry would leave him with one hundred crowns to finance his journey to find Allana. The problem was Polla's honor. He'd admitted to being the father of her child, and he thought that was enough, but now, he had the opportunity to do even more to save her image in the village.

"If I swear to what you want, Father, will the gossip about Polla stop?" Javik asked.

"You can never stop gossip, Javik, but as a spoiled virgin and the wife of a son of the house of Browdat, she will command enough respect to stop people from listening to it," Dana said.

Javik's face took on a firm expression, and his eyes assumed that steely cast Browdat had come to know very well. "Then I'll swear to it."

Browdat slumped in his chair exhausted, and Dana beamed at her boy, now a man.

* * * * *

The wedding plans progressed rapidly out of necessity. A proper contract was drawn up between Challa and Browdat after Javik signed the papers attesting to Polla's virginity. He felt uncomfortable doing it, and he thought he heard several men laughing behind his back as he walked through the village, but he was sure he'd done the right thing.

At last the big day came, and half the village assembled before the great statue of Zhou, the god of the Berglauni. Browdat was dressed in his finest armor, and Dana was radiant in a soft blue gown and wore a gold tiara in her hair. Even the Lady Frieda was lovely in spite of her ample frame and unruly, drab brown hair. Challa wore an expensive robe with a heavy gold chain across his shoulders while his wife absolutely stole the show in a filmy white dress embroidered with gold ivy leaves.

The priest intoned an invocation in the ancient language of the Berglauni while acolytes swung censers of burning incense around the statue of the god. At the sound of a gong, he turned to the people.

"Bring forth the bride and groom!" he commanded.

Mikka entered from the priest's left carrying the sword of Aelin the Red and followed by Javik in polished armor. From the priest's right, one of Polla's brothers carried a rather large broadsword as Polla trailed behind him in a magnificent gown of pale blue satin. The color matched her eyes and set off the blaze of her golden hair. The bride and groom each carried a small sculpture.

The parties stopped in front of the priest with the two sword bearers facing each other. The priest spoke again.

"If any man here would dispute this marriage, let him speak now."

Silence was his only answer. He continued.

"The house of Browdat and the house of Challa are to be united here today. Do these houses agree to the marriage?"

Mikka turned his sword point down and rested the point on the ground. Polla's brother did likewise, and a cheer arose from the crowd. They had not expected trouble, but there was always the possibility one house would object and the two swordsmen would decide the question. The men walked to the rear of the assembled group, and the priest continued.

"There being no objections, I now ask you, Javik, do you take this woman, Polla as your wife of your own free will and with no coercion whatever from any man?"

Javik was being coerced, but he knew this was not the time to object.

"I do," Javik replied.

The priest turned to Polla. "Do you, Polla, take this man,

Javik, to be your husband of your own free will and with no coercion whatever from any man?"

Polla had already decided being pregnant was not coercion and spoke, "I do, gladly."

The priest spoke to the crowd. "Here before Zhou and this company, the two houses have agreed to this union and Javik and Polla have declared their desire to marry. A valid contract has been sealed, and there are no objections from this village." He turned to Javik and Polla. "What symbols have you brought to Zhou to seal your vows of marriage?"

Javik stepped forward and handed his sculpture to the priest. The holy man set in on a flat stone at the base of the god's statue and turned to Polla who handed him her sculpture. The priest returned to the stone and placed Polla's piece next to Javik's before turning back to the new couple.

"Javik, do you promise to provide for Polla, to protect and defend her from all dangers and to remain true to her only, so long as you both shall live?"

Javik looked at Polla before answering, but his mind was focused on Allana. Forgive me, Allana, he thought, then said, "I do."

"Polla, do you promise to obey Javik in all things, to keep his hearth, bear his children and remain true to him only, so long as you both shall live?"

Polla couldn't look at Javik. She focused on the ground in front of the priest as she said, "I do."

The priest turned back to the statue. "Oh great Zhou, this man and this woman have sworn their fealty to each other. We now ask you for your blessing on this union."

The holy man began a soft incantation as he gently pushed the two sculptures toward each other. The pieces were made as two parts of a whole and meshed easily, but the assembled crowd breathed a collective sigh of relief. It was an old ritual, and no one could remember when the pieces didn't fit, but the legend said that if Zhou objected to the union, the priest would not be able to make the sculptures come together. He turned back to the crowd.

"Zhou has given his blessing. Let the celebration begin!"

The crowd cheered, and most of the people left for the common house where a lavish feast and barrels of qush awaited. Javik turned and offered his arm to Polla. She linked her arm with his, and they walked the few steps to the waiting parents. Challa extended his hand.

"Welcome to our family, Javik," Challa said.

"I'm honored to be the one to join our great houses," Javik responded.

Challa's wife embraced her daughter then Javik. She was crying so hard, it was impossible for her to speak.

Dana was next to greet the couple. "I'm proud of you today, my son," she said as tears rolled down her cheeks. She embraced her boy then turned to Polla. "I'm glad my son chose you, Polla. I will always be your friend."

Polla embraced Dana and whispered in her ear, "I know your son loves another, lady, but I will try to make him happy."

Browdat was beaming as he held his arms open to welcome Polla. "You are a worthy addition to our house, Polla. I know you will make my son very happy."

Polla survived the bear hug of the gruff war leader with a smile and said, "Lord Browdat, your son honors me with his love."

Brothers, sisters, aunts and uncles and various cousins offered their congratulations before the entire party joined the celebration in the common house. The qush was already flowing freely, and the musicians played a merry tune as the villagers enjoyed the dozens of dishes spread out on long tables. The smell of roast meat and spiced pastry mingled in the air with the perspiration of the dancers. The summer was now in full swing, and even in the cool of the sunset, the room was very warm.

Javik and Polla were passed from one well-wisher to another barely having time between for a cup of wine for Polla and a mug of qush for Javik. Berda finally found his way to the new couple.

"I wish both of you all the happiness in the world," Berda said as he embraced Javik.

"Thank you, Berda," Javik replied as his friend moved from him to Polla.

"Polla, I know you will make Javik a good wife."

Polla let Javik's friend kiss her on the cheek before replying, "I will do my best, Berda."

"Javik, may I dance with your bride?" The request took Javik by surprise. He'd never thought of Berda as a dancer before.

"Why, certainly, Berda." Javik placed Polla's hand in Berda's, and the pair took the floor.

The song was an old dance tune of the Berglauni people. Everyone knew the dance, but most couples only pranced around the floor in a stately embrace. Berda took Polla to the center of the room and began by leading her through several twirls. Polla seemed to understand what he wanted to do and flowed smoothly through the steps. They separated and each began to do their own steps. Berda dropped into a squat and extended each leg, in turn. Javik wondered how he could maintain his balance, but he moved as if he were suspended by ropes. Polla stepped in a circle around him. Her long dress drug on the floor hiding her feet, and she used such tiny steps that she seemed to be floating along. Berda leaped in the air and touched the toes of his boots before landing, then lifted Polla high above his head and turned in a circle several times before putting her down. All this time, Polla assumed the position of a bird flying through the air.

They were beautiful together, and the rest of the guests stopped dancing to watch them and began clapping in time to the music. The pair did several steps facing each other but with Polla moving in the opposite direction of Berda. Whistles and shouts of encouragement filled the air, and Javik wondered if he was doomed to learn these steps so he could be the one with her at future festivals. The smile on Polla's face told him she was enjoying the dance very much. They began dancing together again just as the musicians stopped playing.

Polla fell into Berda's arms exhausted as the crowd applauded wildly. They bowed in recognition of the praise, and Berda returned Polla to her husband.

"Thank you, Javik. Your wife is an excellent dancer," Berda panted.

"I didn't know you could dance that well," Polla said between gasps.

"Nor I," Javik added.

"I've been taking lessons from Margan. He knows all the steps to every kind of dance, though he has trouble doing many of them," Berda said.

"Where did you learn?" Javik asked Polla.

"My mother and I danced many times when I was younger. She taught me all she knew, but I haven't used any of her training for a long time. It all came back with Berda's good leading."

Karl joined them and slapped Berda on the back. "Wonderful! You two are the hit of the evening. May I kiss the bride?"

"Certainly," Javik said, but he was a bit late with his permission as Polla was already presenting her cheek to Javik's friend.

"It's your turn now, husband," Polla said as she dragged Javik to the dance floor.

The musicians began a slower tempo song, and Javik was glad that Tao Shan's instruction had included a few lessons in dance. Polla was like a feather in his arms, as he led her through the steps he knew. She seemed to be in her own world as they moved around the floor.

"What are you thinking?" Javik asked.

Polla closed her eyes and smiled even more broadly. "About us, Javik. I'm so happy right now. Please don't let it stop."

"The evening must end sometime."

"No, I want this to go on forever. Our life must be one long dance together."

Javik thought about a life with Polla, but he kept seeing Allana instead. Would he ever be able to forget her? He would do his best to make Polla happy, but he doubted he would ever give up hope of being with the wonderful wild girl again. He held Polla closer and whispered, "I will try to give you all the happiness you deserve."

Polla opened her eyes and looked at her new husband with a softness he hadn't seen before.

"I know I'm not first in your heart now, Javik, but I will do my best to earn that position."

Across the room, Browdat sat at the family table drinking qush and accepting the congratulations of his friends. Tao Shan approached him carrying a small chest.

"Congratulations, Lord Browdat. I've brought you a gift to mark the occasion of your son's wedding." He laid the chest on the table.

"It's Javik and Polla who should get gifts today. Zhou knows they'll need everything to set up a new hearth."

"I thought you might need this since you'll soon be a grandfather again. Open it."

Browdat lifted the lid of the chest and pulled out two gold knobs attached to waxy plugs.

"What are these?" Browdat asked.

"Ear stoppers. When the baby cries too loudly, you can shut it out by simply inserting the soft end into your ears. Like this." Tao Shan placed one of the plugs in the big war leader's left ear.

"Hah! I'll make good use of these when my wife wants to scold me for something." He placed the other plug in his right ear and smiled at the mentor.

"I heard that," Frieda said as she turned from her conversation with a seldom seen cousin. "You'll know well enough when I want to be heard, old man."

Browdat pretended to ignore her; though he knew full well she was speaking. He continued to smile up at Tao Shan and shrugged his shoulders.

Frieda grabbed a large wooden spoon from a bowl of gravy and smacked her husband across the back of his neck sending gravy spattering everywhere. Browdat howled and removed the earplugs. "What was that all about, woman?"

"Just to let you know I have other means of getting your attention."

The people around the table roared with laughter.

Dana smiled, but a firm hand on her shoulder drew her attention away from the comic scene. She turned to see Goldar standing beside her.

"Lady Dana, let me congratulate you on your son's wedding."

"Thank you Goldar, his father would have been proud to see

this day."

"Aye, Tolda would be dancing with you until the dawn."

"I can still dance, sir, if anyone would ask me," Dana smiled up at him.

"Then, consider this an invitation." Goldar extended his hand to help Dana to her feet and led her to the floor.

"How fares your wife these days?" Dana asked as they danced.

"No better. She's very ill. The healer doesn't know how she was able to survive the winter. We fear the summer heat may spell her doom."

"I'm sorry. You've been together a long time," Dana said.

"Twelve winters now. I won't know what to do without her should she leave me."

"You will have no trouble finding another woman."

"Aye, but not another Lyda."

They danced on in silence.

The evening wore on, and the crowd diminished. Challa finally silenced the musicians and took the center of the floor.

"My friends, the time has come for the newlyweds to leave us. Who will help me escort them to their bridal bower?"

A cheer arose from those still left, and several men raced to lift Javik and Polla on their shoulders. To the strains of a bawdy ballad, they carried the bride and groom to the special tent in a nearby forest clearing. Javik bid the crowd goodnight, and they departed. He carried Polla into the candle-lit tent and closed the flap. As the noise of the guests faded into the distance, the gentle voice of Margan and the soft notes of his lute replaced it as he serenaded the couple with old love songs.

Javik laid Polla on the pile of skins and fell down beside her. The wedding night held no new adventures for these newlyweds.

CHAPTER 23

Rennick groaned as Allana kneaded the muscles in his neck.

"Relax, Rennick. Your neck is a mass of knotted flesh."

"That's what comes of advising the king. I bear all of his troubles in my neck. Ahhh, that's better."

Allana moved from his neck to his shoulders moving her hands expertly across the chamberlain's anatomy as Marima taught her. He was not a warrior, and the muscles beneath his skin were as soft as a child's. The scent of the oil rose like incense from his warmth, and the aroma almost tempted her into coupling, even with this inferior species, but she quickly pushed the thought from her mind.

"Tell me of Tulla," she asked.

"There's not much to tell. Darrin, the King, is a weak man who rules in name only. The real power lies with his queen, Nonia."

"At least they have power in the proper hands," Allana quipped as she slapped Rennick on the behind. "Roll over."

Rennick complied revealing his lustful arousal.

"Forget it, Rennick," Allana said as she flicked a finger at a strategic location.

"Ouch!" Rennick reacted to the mild shock and watched his ardor dwindle.

"What about this Queen?"

"She's reputed to be a sorceress, a great witch. They say she controls the King through her magic, and his counsel fears to cross her. Even the Turreks keep out of her territory."

Allana was now working on his arms. They were spindly, and she remembered Javik's powerful arms. She often dreamed of his caress.

"Then, I must make an ally of this witch if I'm to spend any time in Tulla," Allana said.

"That would be easy for you," Rennick replied.

"How so?"

"Her only opposition is the King's chamberlain, a man named Oliga. She respects him because of his magical prowess. It's said that if they ever decided to fight it out with magic, there'd be nothing left of Tulla when they were finished. Legend says that this Oliga has never had a woman, and his magic powers would be lost forever if he did."

"So much magic. The people of Tulla must be ignorant, indeed, to believe in such nonsense."

"You can scoff at it here, but all who enter her realm come back with tales of her powers. The people there fear her more than the raiders who plunder the seacoast."

Allana had progressed to Rennick's legs, which were every bit as weak as his arms. Only this man's skill at diplomacy kept him alive.

"You and I know all magic is deception," Allana said with a tone of disdain.

"Yes, but if people believe in magic, it is effective nonetheless. Facts are poor cousins to perceptions."

Allana knew he was right. She had seen Sentii magicians actually make people sick by casting spells because the targets considered themselves doomed by the words alone. The charlatans often had no need for the poisons they kept in abundant supply.

"And you think I could seduce this magician?"

"You could seduce the gods themselves, Allana."

Allana only smiled. If this man had resisted women up to this time, it was unlikely she could succeed with feminine wiles alone. No, a far more devious plan was needed. She slapped Rennick on the thigh.

"You're finished - time for your steam bath. Who would you like to have waiting when you come out?"

"I think I'll take Varuda. I don't feel like losing all of my hair to have you."

Allana laughed. "Then you know about Vargon."

"His wig and false beard were not very convincing at his last audience with the king. If I thought there was any hope, though, I'd gladly go through with it."

"No chance, Rennick, even though the cost to you would be less than half the price Vargon paid. Varuda will be waiting for you."

Allana wiped the fragrant oil from her hands and strode to her private room stopping briefly to inform Varuda she was needed to service Rennick. She sat on her divan and stared at the distant mountains. When the summer ended, she would leave this place and find her people in Tulla. King Kullan would provide her escort to the lands of the Turreks, and Vargon had promised her safe passage over his mountains to Tulla, but she had no ally in that land. From Rennick's information, it appeared there were two choices. She could ally herself with the queen or side with Oliga the chamberlain. She needed more information. Her mind wandered to thoughts of Javik. If he were here, she would fear nothing.

Mellina broke her train of thought. "Mistress, a man has

come seeking to see you. He says he is from Gorgos."

Allana broke quickly from her musings about Javik. "Who is he? Did he give a name or any hint of his business?"

"No, mistress, two of Vargon's warriors brought him. They only said you would be happy to see him."

"Send him in, but have my guards watch him closely." Allana checked her image in the mirror and assumed a regal pose as Mellina ushered the man in followed closely by the two guards. He was an old man with silver hair and a white beard. The weight of his years caused him to slump, and he walked with a pronounced limp, but Allana could sense the remains of a once-noble warrior about him. He was dressed in simple clothes and wore no weapon of any kind, but he carried a leather bag under one arm. He knelt before Allana.

"I have been told there is one here who bears the sign of the serpents." The old man's voice was more of a gasp, and he seemed to have trouble drawing his breath.

Allana turned to the guards. "You may leave us. This crazy old man is no threat to me."

The guards saluted and left the room. Allana turned to the old man.

"And what do you know of such marks, old man?" Allana asked.

The old man rose to his feet and stared at Allana. "My name is Barinosh, and as a younger man, I served the royal house of Gorgos."

"What has that to do with me?" Allana asked knowing the answer, but she continued to pretend ignorance in case this man was a fraud.

"The lord of the Turreks captured my partner and me two days ago. We are pearl merchants from Harrish, a port on the coast of Tulla. We were traveling to Ulum to sell our pearls because we heard the king was willing to pay well for good quality pearls. Everyone advised us to pay the price and travel through Magda with a caravan, but we did not have enough gold to spare. We thought we could evade the Turrek bandits by traveling at night, but they caught us and demanded half our pearls for safe passage through their lands. We couldn't do this because we needed all of our profits to repay our creditors back home. We decided it was better to die rather than return to Tulla and face life in debtor's prison. When we refused to pay, they laughed at us and tied us to trees. I don't want to sicken you by saying how they killed my partner."

"I know the Turreks," Allana said with a tone of disgust in her voice. "How did you survive?"

"They were ready to kill me also when one of them noticed the tattoo on my arm." He bared his right arm and showed Allana the image of two red snakes consuming each other. The snakes surrounded a seashell of some kind unfamiliar to Allana.

"And how did that save you?"

"When they saw the tattoo, they brought me to their master, a large man named Vargon. He asked me what it meant, and I told him it marked me as a sea warrior in the service of the royal house of Gorgos. He questioned me about the fate of that house, but I could only tell him about the stories I'd heard concerning that tragic family. When I told him there were some who believed a princess of Gorgos had been saved from the Voldunee, he asked me how such a person could be identified. I told him of the royal mark, and then, he sent me to you. He asked me to tell you that he would be king of Gorgos."

"Everyone knows the house of Gorgos was destroyed completely. How did you survive?"

"When the house of Gorgos fell, I was away on a voyage. My ship returned to find only devastation and my people slaughtered by the Voldunee. I served with the fleet of Tulla until I was too old to go to sea any more then I went into partnership with the pearl merchant."

"And you never found any more of your people?"

"Only a few, lady. I learned there are remnants of my people across the sea, but they are greatly scattered. Can you tell me why the bandit king spared my life and sent me to you?"

"I can, old man. The sign you bear, I also bear, but not on my arm, and my sign has no shell."

The old man's eyes glowed more brightly, and he seemed to straighten his back considerably. In a moment, he lost twenty years of toil and strain. "I beg your pardon, lady, but is the mark on your rump?"

"And if it were?" Allana said.

The old man fell to his knee before her and bowed his head. "Your majesty," he whispered.

"Rise Barinosh. I want no one to know the meaning of my tattoo. You must never address me that way again. Do you understand?"

"Yes, your ma..., I mean Lady."

"Where are your pearls now?"

"Most of them are safe, Lady. We took the precaution of hiding the majority of our stock in a statue of Godon, the sea god of Tulla. I begged the bandit chief to let me keep the statue as a sacred totem, and he relented. The statue is in this bag. May I?"

Allana nodded, and Barinosh opened his bag to reveal a plaster idol shaped like a large fish but with the head and shoulders of a man. He handed the figure to Allana.

"What is the value of the pearls inside this statue?" Allana asked.

"We hoped to get 5,000 crowns for the lot, but the bandit

chief took over 1,000 crowns worth."

"And, how large is your debt?"

"A little over 4,000 crowns, Lady."

"What did you plan to do with the money if you'd sold all the pearls?"

"Our pearling boat was lost in a storm. We needed to buy a new boat, but the creditors would not advance the money until we paid our old debts. I fear my partner was much too liberal with our funds at the gambling tables, and in the market at Harrish the pearls were not worth enough to pay the creditors. That's why we were coming to Ulum."

"I see. How would you like to have a new partner, Barinosh?"

"Who, Lady?"

"Me. I will help you sell your pearls to the king. Their sale should provide the money you need to pay off your partner's debts. I will pay for a new boat from my own funds and provide any other gold you need to equip it for a pearling voyage. Do you accept?"

"Gladly, Lady, but what about your people? If they knew you were alive, they'd gather around you. I could sail to the other lands and bring them back to our beloved island. Gorgos could live again."

"In time, Barinosh, in time. First, we must build our wealth, and then we must secure the protection of a powerful kingdom, like Tulla, to keep us safe while we re-build Gorgos. When the time is ripe, we will declare our independence."

"I pray I will live to see that day, maj... Lady."

"You will, Barinosh. I promise you, you will."

CHAPTER 24

Javik never knew there was so much work involved in setting up a new hearth. By noon, his back ached from carrying heavy bundles between Browdat's longhouse and his new home, and Dana indicated there was just as much more to carry before dinner.

The long houses of the Berglauni held as many as four hearths. The individual living areas were arranged two on either side of a common room. Cooking was done in the common area, and meals were taken there as well. A center hallway ran the length of the building dividing two rooms on each side per family hearth. The four room family areas could be closed off from the common room and the other family hearth by solid doors. If these doors were closed, the families could gain access through outside doors between the two rooms on one side of the hallway. The common room also had an outside entrance, which served as the main entrance for the longhouse.

The common room held two cooking areas, both venting their smoke through holes in the roof. Each hearth had a fire holder in the center of its area, again, venting through the roof. Families often shared meals with the women combining to create a more lavish feast than any one family had time or resources to prepare. The men hunted together and shared the task of plowing, planting, tending and harvesting the crops and caring for any livestock.

Javik had managed to find hearth space in a warrior longhouse. The other families were headed by experienced warriors who, though wary of admitting a novice, were glad to have a son of Browdat as one of the households. These men purchased most of the meat they did not hunt, but the women kept chickens and geese and planted gardens for fresh vegetables. The women also drew water from the village wells and gathered cooking firewood. The men felled larger trees and cut them up for the fires used to heat the building in winter.

The longhouses were wood construction, but the roofs were covered with sod to help insulate the living areas in the hot summer. The walls were faced with a mud brick for the same purpose. Each room included a large window that could be opened in the summer and walled up with mud brick in the winter.

Dana was to live with Javik and Polla. One of the rooms would be hers. Another room was for Javik and Polla. The third room would house the baby after it arrived, while the fourth room was for storage. Javik's weapons and armor were placed in that room along with all the items Polla and Dana required from time to time. Javik, with Karl's help, built shelves in the storage room that were quickly filled with crocks, jars, boxes and bags by the women.

A necessity for every family was a secret space to hold the family gold. Browdat convinced Javik to let Challa and he invest the bulk of Polla's dowry, but there was still a sizeable amount of money to hide. Karl came to the rescue with the gift of a statuette of Zhou for the family shrine. The carving held a secret compartment in its stone base. The hiding place could only be revealed through clever manipulation of several parts of the idol in the correct sequence.

They settled into a routine quickly, and life became a rather dull business for Javik. Only his lessons with Tao Shan and Bandor provided any break in the monotony. He was glad when the fall came and hunting season arrived. Polla's stomach had grown considerably by this time, and their evenings in bed together had ceased to be anything more than an opportunity to rest.

Javik was very happy to see Karl enter the common room that evening.

"Javik, we're planning a boar hunt tomorrow. Will you join us?" Karl sat down at one of the tables and helped himself to some leftover chicken stew.

"You don't know how much I've been wishing you'd come in and ask me that question," Javik responded. "Of course, I'll join you. If I'm not out front at dawn, come wake me."

"I don't think Polla would take kindly to me charging into your bedroom before dawn."

"Then I'll sleep in the common room tonight. I have to get out of this house, Karl."

"Then it's settled. I'll come for you at dawn. Pass the qush please."

The next morning, Javik was up well before dawn. Polla still slept, but Dana roused herself to heat some porridge for her son.

"I hope you have good hunting today. I'd love some wild boar. I get so tired of the bland taste of the village pigs."

"Karl knows how to find boar, and Wollan's hounds are good at cornering them. We should all have plenty of meat to show for this hunt," Javik said.

At that moment Karl entered the longhouse.

"Good morning. Do I smell porridge?"

"You do Karl. Have a bowl," Dana said as she spooned him up a portion.

Karl dove into the hearty mix with gusto. "Where's your wife, Javik?"

"She's still sleeping. The baby wears her out so. I'll be glad when it comes so we can get back to normal."

Dana laughed. "There's no such thing as normal after a baby arrives. I know from good experience with you. I got no sleep for a month except in fitful naps when you weren't bawling your head off."

"I can't believe I was any trouble at all," Javik said trying to be convincing.

"Trust me, you were a trial sent from the underworld until you were three years old."

A horn sounded in the fields outside the stockade wall, and Javik heard the barking of Wollan's hounds as they passed outside the longhouse.

"Time to go, Karl," Javik said as he downed a cup of hot bark tea.

Karl stuffed his jaws full of porridge and mumbled an unintelligible thanks to Dana before heading off behind Javik.

"Good hunting!" Dana called after them.

Five other men were waiting as Karl and Javik joined the group. Wollan was already sending his dogs off in search of scent. Today's hunt would be on foot as Mikka had seen several boars very near the village in the last few days. They loved to raid the garbage pits at night, but it was too dangerous to hunt them in darkness.

Each hunter carried a stout spear with a broad point, and some had quivers and bows slung across their backs. In addition to their spears, Javik and Karl carried short swords specially forged for dealing with the powerful animals. They strode off into the forest following the sound of the dogs.

They had not gone far when Javik noticed a movement off to

his right.

"Karl," he whispered. "There's something in the bush over there. It might be a boar."

"The dogs would have scented it. It must be something else."

"It could have doubled back to fool the hounds. I'm going to have a look."

"Be careful, the brush is thick there, and you don't want to be surprised."

"I'll be on the lookout for him," Javik said as he slid silently through the drying underbrush.

The sound became more pronounced as he approached a small clearing. It was a snuffling noise punctuated by a soft grunting sound from time to time. It had to be a boar. He inched to the border of the clearing and lifted his head enough to see beyond the foliage. He was surprised to see Grazhda standing beside a large boar. The boar was busily rooting out some form of tuber and paid no attention to the witch.

"Come out, Javik," she called to him. "I have your boar here."

Javik moved cautiously with his spear at the ready. He knew Grazhda was a powerful witch, but he didn't trust the boar at all.

"Strike when you wish, young warrior. I've made sure this fellow is sufficiently distracted to allow for an easy kill."

Javik thought he'd better get the hardest job over first. He lunged with the spear and drove it deeply into the animal's chest. The spear point turned easily as it passed through the ribs and into the heart. The animal squealed piteously and struggled to free itself of the spear, but Javik only drove it out the other side and pinned the beast to the earth. It took several seconds for it to die.

"Thank you, Grazhda. Once more, I owe you for my good fortune. Will you have some of this boar?"

"I will, but first, I wish to scold you. Why did you marry that slut, Polla?"

"Her baby was mine, and it was the honorable thing to do."

"Bah! You could have just left to search for Allana and let her find another of her lovers to serve as father. Zhou knows she has a wide choice there."

"I couldn't do that." Javik looked at the ground as he answered. He did not want to admit he'd considered just that course of action.

"Well, it will be of no consequence come spring. I've come to tell you that Allana may find considerable trouble this fall. She will need you as soon as you can get to her."

"I can't go anywhere until the child is born."

"Truly said, but you must not delay once the babe is here and safe." Grazhda knelt down and pulled a knife and a leather bag from inside her flowing garment. She opened up the boar and removed its liver and kidneys placing them in the bag. Next, she removed its testicles and added them to her store. "You've a good aim. You've ruined the heart, but I have enough for my needs. Remember my words, Javik. Don't delay in going to Allana."

Karl came crashing through the bush, and Javik turned to see it was he and not another boar. As he turned back, Grazhda was gone.

"Javik, the dogs have cornered a boar not far from here, and..." He stopped and stared at the dead boar. "You found one all by yourself."

"No, only with Grazhda's help."

"Grazhda? I saw no one as I came up."

"She was here, Karl, and she told me Allana would need me

soon."

"You're married. Forget about Allana. Browdat would never let you go after her now. You must support your family."

"I know, I know, but I still dream of her."

The bounty from the hunt was hung in the springhouses, and each longhouse shared in the results of the hunt. Javik loved roast boar, and Dana explained to Polla how to make his favorite dishes to go along with the main course. Between the two women, they created a feast, and Javik dove into it with gusto.

"This is delicious," he said as he washed down a helping of the roast boar with some wine. Then he noticed Polla was only picking at her food. "What's wrong? Don't you like it?"

"It's not that, husband. My appetite has not been good lately."

"Probably the baby," Dana said. "I lost my appetite with Javik, too. It will pass."

"I hope so, Lady. I'm so sick in the mornings I can't stand even the smell of food."

"Don't worry. Next you will be asking Javik to find you strawberries out of season or you'll develop a burning hunger for stewed rabbit. It's all part of being with child."

Polla only held her protruding stomach with both hands and sighed. "I'm so ugly. Will I ever be beautiful again?"

"Look at my mother," Javik said. "She survived having a child fairly well, don't you think?"

"Certainly, but I also see many of the other village women who were lovely before they had children and now can hardly walk through a door."

"You just need some exercise," Javik said as he rose from the table. "Come walk with me, wife."

He extended his hand to her, and Polla smiled up at him.

She took his hand, and Javik led her out into the cool twilight of autumn. The sun was behind the trees, but the sky still glowed a bright orange giving the already colorful leaves a new patina of gold. The smells of the cooking from the other houses assaulted their noses, and Polla urged Javik on past the stockade wall to escape any possible bouts of nausea.

The fields were barren now, and the harvest festival would soon take place. The crops had been good, and there was much to celebrate.

"We will have a fine festival this year," Javik said.

"Yes, Zhou has been good to us. I just wish the time would fly faster. Your son becomes more of a burden each day."

"He's our son, not just mine."

"I'm sorry, but I can't help but think of my life before he came along. I was so gay, and life was a constant festival. Now, I'm just like my mother. Look at my hands, Javik."

Polla held her hands out for inspection, and even in the dying light, Javik could see the change. Once they had been smooth and slender, but now they were red and coarse.

"You've just been working too hard setting up our hearth. Give them time to heal."

"But they won't heal. They'll be like this the rest of my life."

Javik took her hands in his and brought them to his lips.

"They are still the only hands I long to kiss. They're still beautiful to me."

Polla pulled her hands away. "You're very kind, and I can't even repay your kindness as I would like."

"Don't worry about that. We will catch up after the child is born."

"No we won't. I've seen the burden a child brings to other families. We will be no different. The child will rule our lives. Your lessons with Tao Shan will be over by then, and you will spend more time being a father than a warrior. A son must be mentored."

"You're right. He will be my first duty. I have to give him the same opportunity my father gave me. He must be a warrior."

"War, war, war. Is that all you men ever think of?"

The light was nearly gone now, and the chill of the night air became more pronounced. Polla shivered as she embraced herself seeking warmth. Javik noticed her and put his arm around her.

"No, we often think of the woman we love," Javik said as he lifted her chin to kiss her.

Polla pulled away. "You don't need to remind me. I know you think of her. I've heard you say her name at night."

For the first time, anger spread across Javik's face. "I was speaking of you. You're my wife now, not Allana."

They walked back to the longhouse in silence with Javik cursing himself for agreeing to marry Polla, and she wishing the poison had done its work more quickly.

CHAPTER 25

Barinosh was jubilant. He strode toward Allana with a spring in his step belying his years. Behind him, two of the king's guards carried a chest slung between them on a heavy pole. They leaned against the pull of the load, and Allana knew the chest was full of gold.

"Mistress, the King has paid us well for the pearls," he said with a devilish gleam in his eye.

The guards placed the chest in front of Allana and bowed as they left the room.

"See our treasure!" Barinosh knelt and opened the chest revealing stacks of gold coins.

"You've done well. How much is it?"

"4,000 gold crowns. It is enough to pay my debts, but I will still need your help for a new boat.

"You have that. Now we must put these funds in a safe place."

"I hope you have a secure hiding place, Lady."

Allana laughed. "I don't hide my gold. I give it to the Arganii."

"I know of the Arganii. They hold most of my partner's debt."

"Then we can settle that part in a few moments." Allana clapped her hands, and her two guards appeared. "Go to Gallam, the Arganii and tell him I have business for him today."

The guards saluted and left the room.

"Have you counted this money?" Allana asked Barinosh.

"No, Lady. Shouldn't I trust the king?"

Allana laughed. "No wonder your partner gambled away all the money. You are much too trusting." Again, she clapped and Varuda appeared.

"Varuda, bring in three of the girls who can count to 100. We have a counting job to do." She pointed at the chest, and Varuda sucked in her breath.

"I've never seen so much gold in one place before."

"Come back with the girls, and tell them there's a gold crown in it for each one."

Varuda soon returned with three wide-eyed women, and they began to count the coins into stacks of ten and grouping them into clusters of 100. The count was exact, and Allana handed out the rewards as promised from her own purse after the coins were safely stacked back in the chest.

"Rennick does his job well," Allana said as she closed the lid on the chest. "I thought I could rely on his honesty with me."

"An old sailor had much to learn about politics, Lady." Barinosh sat back in his chair and admired the woman who was now his partner. The business would prosper under her guidance, if they could reach Harrish with their funds intact. There were many hazards between Ulum and that seaport town he called home.

At that moment, one of the guards entered and bowed to Allana. "Gallam awaits your arrival, Mistress."

"Good! Take this chest to him. We will be right behind you," Allana said.

"But Mistress, who will carry you?" the guard said.

"I will walk. It's not far. Barinosh will be my protection."

The guard gave the old man a quizzical look but saluted and

left to bring in the other guard and a pole for the chest.

"I'm honored you have such confidence in my fighting abilities, Lady," Barinosh said.

"You have a sword now, and I trust even a naval commander learned something of its use."

"I once was an excellent swordsman, but my skills are rusty with disuse."

"Just glare fiercely at everyone as we walk, and no one will dare challenge you."

The guards returned, and the party was soon off to the house of Gallam.

The old Arganii met them at the door with a broad smile. He was old and stooped, but he had never been tall. Now only about 160 centimeters in height, Allana doubted he ever measured over 163. His silver hair and long, white beard framed a dark complexion and thick, pale lips. His deep black eyes glowed with expectation of profit.

"Welcome, Lady Allana. My house is yours," he said bowing as low as his age allowed.

"Greetings, Gallam. I'd say it's more like my house is yours from the fees you charge.'

"Lady, a man must live," Gallam protested. "As you see, I have few luxuries." He swept his arm around the sparsely decorated room.

Allana knew he was one of the richest men in the kingdom, but he maintained this image of near poverty as a façade. She got right to the point.

"I have a new partner. Meet Barinosh of Harrish." The men exchanged greetings.

"What business are you entering now, Lady?" Gallam asked.

"I'm now in the pearl business, and I will soon be moving to the seacoast. This gold is our capital, and I fear for its safety traveling through Turrek country. We will deposit it with you for the usual fee."

Gallam licked his lips. "And how much gold are we speaking of?"

"4,000 crowns." Allana instructed the guards to place the chest on a table and open it.

Gallam looked inside the chest and his eyes took on a new luster. "Indeed, a fine sum." He motioned to his assistant who summoned help from the next room, and they began to count the coins.

"We also have some debts to settle with some of your people in Harrish. Give him your list, Barinosh."

The old man handed a scroll to the Arganii. "These are my old partner's debts."

Gallam studied the list and nodded at each name and amount.

"I know these people well, but the sum is a few crowns larger that I expect this chest contains. Where is the difference, not to mention my fee?" Gallam asked.

"You may make up the difference plus your fee from my account. I want you to prepare the letters of credit to these bankers and another for my use. I will need a letter for half of my account at the end of this month."

Gallam looked surprised. "You are leaving Ulum?"

"I go to Harrish to take charge of our pearl business. Varuda will take over the House of Orgama. She will buy me out over time and deposit the money with you. As I need funds, I'll contact you in the usual manner."

"We will all be sorry to see you leave, Lady," Gallam smiled his most obsequious smile.

"You mean you will miss my money. I know your heart, Gallam, but I still love to be fawned over." She leaned over and kissed the old man on his forehead.

"Master, the count is sound," one of Gallam's assistants broke the mood.

"The letters of credit will be ready tomorrow," Gallam said.

"I will send Varuda for them. Farewell, Gallam. Your services have been as helpful to me as they have been profitable for you."

"Thank you, Lady." The old man bowed low and ushered the party to the door.

On the way back to the House of Orgama, Barinosh said, "I never trust those Arganii. Are you certain this one is honest?"

"I'd put my very life in his hands," Allana said.

"They're always charging some kind of fee on each transaction. I think it's disgusting. How much of the 4,000 will he take?"

"Only 40 crowns, just one hundredth of the amount."

"Still, a good sum in any man's purse. I hate to see you paying that, Lady."

"We can't carry that much gold plus my funds through both Magda and Tulla without a large guard, and that would be much more expensive and less reliable. Even with Vargon's promise of safe conduct, it would be too much of a temptation."

"Who would know we carried that much?" Barinosh asked.

"Hah! Everyone in Zargaia and half of Magda by the time we departed. There are no secrets in this world when it comes to money."

The preparations for the trip to Harrish took another week. Allana's baggage filled two carts, and two more were fitted to carry she and her party in comfort during the journey. The last day came, and Allana handed Varuda a ring of keys.

"The House of Orgama is yours now. May it bring you even more wealth."

"Allana, you've been a blessing from the gods for me. How can I ever thank you for this?"

"Just make the payments on time, and pray I remember all you've taught me about dealing with men."

"I will pay promptly, you can count on that, and you've become quite a formidable lady since we first met. I just hope I can continue to attract the high class customers when you're not here to draw them in."

"I'm sure you will have no trouble in that regard, goodbye friend." Allana embraced Varuda and tears ran down both their cheeks. Allana turned quickly and fled to her wagon. If she stayed any longer, she'd never leave.

* * * * *

The road was good far into the mountain lair of the Turreks. The King's guard detachment left the caravan there and returned to the city. Allana was on her own now, trusting only in Vargon's promise of safe conduct. The next caravan over the mountains was not due to leave for a week, and she didn't want to wait.

The climb became steeper by the hour. Barinosh rode in front of the wagons to lead the way and scout for any rockslides or washouts. At the summit of the pass, the land leveled out into a plateau between two lines of mountains, and the party stopped for a rest and a meal. As the cook was lighting her fire, Barinosh rode up on a well-lathered horse.

"Lady, you are betrayed," he shouted as he dismounted. It was only then that Allana noticed the blood on his sword.

"What is it?" she asked.

"A large party of Turrek bandits is right behind me. They're too many for us to fight. I was jumped by three of them waiting in ambush farther up the trail, but I managed to fight them off. Then I saw the rest of the band close behind them. We are lost."

"Not as long as they're Vargon's men." Allana snorted in disgust. "I can still handle that rascal."

A horn sounded followed by the sound of a hundred horses and the fierce cries of the Turrek bandits. Soon the little camp was surrounded by a motley group of men dressed in furs and leather and holding a mixture of weapons. One who appeared to be the leader rode toward Allana, and she recognized him from the band's last visit to Ulum.

"Lady Allana, I bring you greetings from Vargon," he said.

"I know you, Tumak. What is the meaning of this assault?"

"Lady, it is we who have been assaulted. Two of my men lay dead on the trail and a third will need good care for a month, if he lives. Your old man is much more formidable than he looks."

"If you attack from ambush, you must expect to be assaulted," Barinosh said.

"What does Vargon want?" Allana asked.

"He offers you his hospitality this evening. I am your escort to his stronghold. He fears there may be other brigands on the loose in these parts, and sent us to protect you."

Allana knew there was no good in this offer. She remembered Barinosh's words after his session with Vargon. The bandit said he would be king of Gorgos, and this was part of his plan. She studied the situation, and saw no way out. The Turreks were too strong for her meager force; she had no choice but to accept Vargon's invitation.

"We were about to have a meal, Tumak. Why don't you and your men refresh yourselves also? We will follow you to Vargon after that."

"Agreed," Tumak said. He turned and gave commands to his men who dismounted and pulled rations from their saddlebags, but stayed fixed in their ring surrounding the camp.

After the meal, they escorted Allana's caravan to Vargon's stronghold.

Allana had heard tales of the place, but the sight was even more impressive than the stories. As they rounded the edge of a tall cliff, it came into view. The cliff curved around a large lake fed by a waterfall spouting from under a fortified stone bridge a hundred meters above the water. On either side of the bridge, tall stone towers rose another twenty meters and melded into the mountains on either side.   It had the appearance of a man-made dam, but it did not impede the flow of the water over the falls. A causeway jutted out into the lake and ended just before the cliff face on the left where another structure guarded a drawbridge. The assault on this fortress broke the back of the Zargaian army led by Kullan's father many years ago. Allana thought Kullan wise for dealing with Vargon instead of fighting him.

As the group approached, the drawbridge was lowered revealing a road cut into the very heart of the mountain itself. They wound steadily up to the high valley above the falls and stopped at a village before another stone wall.

"We leave the horses and wagons here," Tumak commanded.

Men arrived from the village to take care of the horses and carry Allana's baggage into the fortress. Once inside the wall, Allana noticed the place was little more than a collection of caves carved into the side of the mountain. Below them, the river tumbled over the cliff.   The bridge they had seen approaching the fortress connected this complex with what appeared to be a similar one on the other side. They stopped in front of one rather large cave.

"These are your quarters, Lady," Tumak said.   "You may refresh yourselves here. Vargon will see you soon." He bowed and left the rooms, but four guards posted themselves outside the cave entrance.

The cave was divided into several rooms by crude stone walls. Candles provided the only light away from the entrance, and crude rugs covered the stone floors. It had a cold, dank feeling, and the only heat was a small fire in the center of the entry. Allana assigned the rooms and directed the unloading of the baggage. Turrek women brought in water and linens along with some fruit and a coarse brown soap.

Several hours later, Tumak returned to lead them to Vargon. Allana and Barinosh entered a very large cave illuminated by torches. A huge fireplace roared at the back of the room, and the floors were covered with slabs of marble in various colors. Vargon sat on a gold and jewel encrusted throne on one side of the fireplace. Allana noticed that his hair and beard had grown back even more curly than the original with a slight auburn tinge to the raven color.

The room was filled with men and women dressed in what passed for fine clothes among the Turrek. They did little trading, preferring to steal what they needed from passing travelers. What that didn't supply, they secured by plundering the villages and cities of the bordering kingdoms. There was little comparison with the court of Zargaia, but Allana supposed she was seeing the best available to these people.

"Welcome, Allana!" Vargon roared as they approached his throne.

Allana and Barinosh knelt before the bandit chief, but Allana was hard pressed to suppress her anger. She knew a cool head was needed here more than anything else.

"You honor us with your hospitality, Lord," Allana replied.

"Rise, come join me, we have much to talk about." Vargon offered his hand to Allana who took it and rose to her feet. He turned to the assembled court. "We will be meeting in private for a time. Amuse yourselves until our return."

Barinosh started to follow, but Allana indicated he should remain behind. She let Vargon lead her into a chamber behind the throne. It was a meeting room with a large table and several chairs. Allana was relieved when she saw no bed or couch.

"Sit down, Allana. I see my messenger found you."

"If you mean Barinosh, he did find me."

"Yes, the old man. I never got his name, but I recognized his tattoo." Vargon smiled an oily smile at Allana and patted his own behind.

"Now you know what many men know about me. What do you want, Vargon?"

The bandit chief leaned across the table and put his face close to hers. "You know what I want. One taste of a banquet is never enough."

"I told you then, it would never happen again. You promised me safe passage in return for that night, but here I am, a prisoner in your caves. Why should I have you again? I'd rather die first."

"I could arrange that," Vargon hissed.

"Would that satisfy your lusts?"

The bandit swept his hand toward her, but she set her jaw even harder. He stopped the blow short and a smile spread across his face.

"Allana, why do we argue? My purpose for bringing you here was quite honorable. I want you to be my wife."

"Your wife? I'm not a she-bear to live in a cave like this." She swept her hand across the room.

"I would build you a palace on Gorgos," he said.

The remark stopped her short. He really meant his comment about being king of Gorgos.

"An empty boast. What do you propose to do, ask Queen Nonia to give us the island as a wedding gift? Tulla now claims Gorgos."

"Nonia may not rule much longer. Oliga seeks allies in his bid to overthrow the king. When I found out your true nature, I offered him the full support of the Turrek in exchange for the island with me as king. When I am king, I'll need a queen, and what better queen than the true ruler of the island kingdom."

"You're foolish, Vargon. Gorgos is nothing but ruins and wild goats. Only a few fishermen live there now. Barinosh knows the island well, ask him."

"What else would I expect you to say? You don't fool me, either one of you. I've heard the stories of the riches to be found on Gorgos, and Oliga told me he has a map revealing the hiding places of that treasure. Your people were very clever, but not clever enough. The island will be mine along with all its gold, but the real treasure is you. I offer you a throne in exchange for union with me. Our children will be rulers by blood and not conquest. You can gather your people to you and the glory of your throne will be restored."

Vargon painted an enticing picture, but Allana knew she would be queen in name only. She hadn't endured years of slavery to the Sentii to become a slave to this Turrek bandit. She considered her options. Vargon would not let her leave without marrying him, but she might be able to stall him long enough to get word to Javik. She laughed inwardly at her own folly. Javik was a boy. What good would he do against this monster? No, she had no hope outside herself. Barinosh was too old to help and King Kullan could not challenge Vargon even for her sake. She had to think up a plan.

CHAPTER 26

Polla's belly grew larger each day, and her disposition soured more in direct proportion. Javik could do nothing to please her, and she stayed in bed as long as anyone would let her. Dana ran the hearth and did the cooking and washing while Polla only sulked over mugs of wine. Even Polla's mother tried to scold her into behaving as a wife should, but it was to no avail.

Javik was beginning to think about divorce, but he knew his honor would never tolerate such an action. He spoke with Dana about the problem, but she only told him pregnant women were moody and irritable creatures requiring a good deal of patience on their husband's part. He did a lot of hunting and weapons practice now that his formal lessons with Tao Shan were finished. The routine of the village was beginning to wear on his nerves when the rider arrived.

He wore the King's livery and carried no weapons of any kind. The villagers gaped as he galloped past, and they followed behind as fast as they could run. This type of messenger meant something of great importance. The rider stopped his well-lathered horse before the common house and called for the village leader. Soon, Tahsla and Goldar appeared.

"What news?" Tahsla asked.

"The King sends his greetings, and he bids your village respond to this levy." He handed a scroll to the village elder.

Tahsla unrolled the scroll and read while Goldar looked over his shoulder. The old man heaved a heavy sigh as he handed the parchment to the war leader. "This is more in your line of responsibility, Goldar."

Goldar's expression changed from anticipation to regret. He'd already read enough of the document to get its gist. He rolled it up and faced the assembled crowd.

"This levy requires us to furnish fifty men to the fortress at the high pass to Sentius. The King fears an attack by the Sentii within the month. We must report to the fortress within one week. I'll need every crossbowman and archer we have plus some good swordsmen and pike men. Pass the word that we will assemble here at sunset."

The crowd dispersed, and Goldar handed the scroll back to the messenger.

"I assume you have other villages to warn?" Goldar asked.

"Yes, sir. I will need a fresh horse."

Goldar turned to find Fugnor, but the horse handler was already by his side.

"I'll take care of him, Goldar. Come with me, lad." Fugnor led the rider and his horse toward the corrals.

"Who will you take as sergeants?" Tahsla asked Goldar.

"Mikka, for sure, and I think Javik. I'll have to think about the other two."

"Good choices. I'll tell both of them about the meeting."

"Thank you. I'll inform the others after I've made my choices. The only problem may be Javik's wife. He might be gone when it's time for her to deliver."

"The Lady Dana lives with them. She will take good care of Polla," Tahsla said.

"He's a lucky man to have two fine women at his hearth. I'll understand if he doesn't want to go, but try to get him to come."

"I'll do my best. This is a fight he should be in." Tahsla left for Javik's hearth.

Javik welcomed the chance to be away from Polla. He didn't care how long it would be, he was tired of the boredom of family life. He agreed readily.

Polla took the news badly. "Javik, you could be snowed in up there the rest of the winter. What will I do when our child comes?"

"You'll do what all women do. You'll go to the delivery house and have our son."

"Who will help me with the child after it is born?"

"My mother will help you until you can care for the child yourself."

"Lady Dana is busy with the cooking and the other chores of the hearth. She'll make me care for our child alone."

"You don't think my mother would put any undue burden on you, do you? She knows about caring for a new child. You're being foolish."

Polla fell onto the bed of furs and began to cry. "You don't care what happens to me anymore, Javik. You don't love me anymore."

Javik knelt beside her and whispered, "I never did love you, Polla. I gave our child a name and a father. I hoped that love would come, but you haven't done much to help it along these last few months. I have to go to this fight, but I also want to go. I can't stand your constant crying and complaining any more. I'll come back to you, and I'll do my duty as a father and husband, but don't expect my love unless you're ready to act like a wife when I get back. Think about that while I'm gone."

With that, he left the room and sat down at the table in the common area of the longhouse. Dana joined him.

"Is there to be war?" she asked.

"I don't know, Mother. The King only anticipates a Sentii attack. If we fortify the passes, we may prevent a war."

"I know you have to go, son. Don't worry about Polla while you're gone. I'll take good care of her, and the child when it comes."

"I could be there the rest of the winter if we have a big snow in the pass."

"Just take care of yourself. The Lady Frieda and I will manage here very well. Think only of your son and how proud you will be to see him when you come home."

"Thank you, Mother. I know my son will be in good hands with you."

That evening, over one hundred men gathered at the common house. Goldar and Mikka interviewed the men while Javik and Berda looked on to learn the procedure. Bodor, an old friend of Zuban's, was to be the fourth sergeant, but he was off on a hunt until the next day. It took all evening to narrow the group down to forty-eight men, twelve for each sergeant. Finally, Goldar rose and addressed the assembled men.

"We will leave for the high pass in two days. Put your affairs in order between now and then. You must be ready by sunrise on the third day. We will assemble here. All crossbowmen will report to Bodor. He's not here, but I think most of you know him." Nods greeted Goldar's statement along with some bitter murmurs.

"Archers will report to Berda." Goldar indicated Berda should stand up, and the young warrior put on a good front for the older men he was to command. "I know he is young, but he's one of the finest archers in the village." The undercurrent of grunts and moans was not encouraging for the fledgling leader.

"Wall pike men will report to Javik." Javik stood and held

up his arm in acknowledgement. "You all heard of his valor in the war with Wallandia." Murmurs of agreement flowed through the men.

"Swordsmen will be under Mikka." Applause met this announcement. Mikka was a proven leader, having led men in many previous raids and two wars.

"You all know what to bring along. Bring as much food as you can carry. We'll have to stock the fortress well as we may be snowed in. We'll take some wagons and livestock also and hunt some on the way. Long live the King!"

"Long live the King!" the assembled warriors shouted in response.

The meeting broke up, and Browdat met Javik.

"I'm proud of you, Son. A sergeant at your age is wonderful. I was ten years older before I had my first command."

"Thank you, sir. I hope I can bring glory to our house."

"I know you will, and don't worry about your family while you're gone. I'll see that they're taken care of."

"You should be going too, sir," Javik said.

"No, Son, I'm not good at defending fortresses. You can't use a horse and lance on battlements. Learn this aspect of warfare well. I'm sure Tao Shan gave you some excellent training, but there's nothing like being there. We'll all be anxiously awaiting your return." He slapped his son on the back and went his way.

The departure day came, and Polla hung on her husband as he tried to leave.

"Don't leave me alone, Javik. I'll die if you're not here." She cried piteously as she sat on the dirt floor of the longhouse clinging to Javik's knees.

"Nonsense, woman! You have my Mother, your family and

the entire household of Lord Browdat to help you. I have to go now." He pried her away from his legs and stepped quickly out of her reach. She fell on the floor sobbing, and Dana knelt beside her.

"Go, Son. It'll be all right. Just go."

Javik left. He was sad to be leaving Polla in such a miserable condition, but glad to be getting away from her for a while. Perhaps once the baby was here, she'd change for the better. He prayed for a lot of snow in the high pass during the coming winter. Mordah trotted along at his heels.

The pre-dawn was bone-chilling cold. Javik shivered a bit as he carried his shield and baggage to the assembly point. The smoke from the cooking fires hung heavily near the ground, and the smell of breakfast made him wish he'd eaten more before saying goodbye. He dropped his baggage at one of the carts and proceeded to the corrals to saddle Gunda. The apple in his hand would tell the horse his master was there.

Mordah put his front paws on the top fence rail and panted in anticipation of seeing the horse. He and Gunda had become fast friends, thanks to Wollan's training.

The horses' breath rose from the group of animals like little clouds as they milled about the corral. Other men were busy saddling their mounts, and Javik called to Gunda. The little gray snorted his recognition and pranced to the fence knowing a treat waited. Javik held out the apple, and watched in amusement as the creature wolfed it down then nuzzled his shoulder for another.

"Not now, Gunda," Javik soothed as he patted the horse's forehead. "We have miles to go today in this bitter cold, I fear. No warm barn for you today, friend."

Gunda snorted as if he understood every word and objected to the journey. He turned to Mordah who began to lick the horse's nose.

Javik saddled his horse and attached his bedroll and shield to the saddle before mounting. He spread his large cloak over Gunda's rump to offer some small shield against the cold.

The party was finally assembled, and Goldar gave the command to advance. A stream of horsemen and wagons plodded off over the frozen trail and through the bare, black trees. There were no songs to shorten the time. It was much too cold to sing.

* * * * *

The trip to the fortress took most of a day. The column arrived just before sunset, and Goldar sounded his horn to alert the guards on the gate wall. The heavy wooden bridge dropped across the protective ditch, and the iron portcullis lifted to welcome the reinforcements. In normal times, the roadway through the fortress would be open to allow free flow of traffic across the pass, but the threat of invasion changed all that.

Javik looked at the ditch as they rode across it. It was filled with sharpened sticks and the smell of human waste assaulted his nostrils. Anyone falling upon those points would suffer the kind of infection that was nearly always fatal. He assumed the other side of the fortress held a similar ditch.

The great stone structure was very impressive. It spread between the mountains on either side and rose a good 20 meters into the air. Three towers guarded the walls on this side, and Javik could see the tops of four more on the other wall. It stood like a gray, brooding monster guarding the entrance to Berglaundia.

The small force rode into a courtyard in the center of the fortress where several men in full battle dress stood waiting. Goldar signaled a halt and dismounted. The oldest of the men embraced the war leader eagerly.

"You are a welcome sight, Goldar," the older man said. "We have only a minimal garrison here until the King's levies arrive. You're the first. How many did you bring?"

"A little over fifty men, Samack, but I can bring more if the need arises. I wanted to leave enough able men at our village to defend it in case of a breakthrough by the Sentii."

"A wise precaution. The low pass may not hold if they concentrate their forces there. Come with me, and we will discuss the defensive plans while you warm up. Targon will show your men to their quarters, and his men will attend to the horses."

Goldar left the group in the command of the sergeants and walked into a large building with Samak.

"This way to the stables," Targon called as he walked away. The men dismounted and led their horses after him.

Once Gunda was fed and in a stall, Javik led his men into the barracks Targon assigned to them. It was one huge room with many bunk beds stacked two high. Each man quickly staked out a claim to his bed and hung his things from the rows of pegs on the wall behind the beds. The next stop was the roaring fire at one end of the room. The griping began immediately.

"I wonder when we eat around here," one man said.

"I ain't lookin' forward to duty on that wall in this weather," another added.

Javik remembered Tao Shan's teachings. Men will always complain. Take action only on the things that really matter.

"I'll look into the food situation," Javik said. "You men can take it easy until further notice."

A chorus of semi-affirmative grunts was his only response as he left the barracks area in search of the kitchens. He soon found the dining hall where several women were setting up for the evening meal.

"How long until dinner?" he asked a portly woman with red hair tied up on top of her head.

"The little bell will ring when it's ready," she answered.

"Little bell?" Javik asked.

"Aye, the big bell only rings if there's an attack. The little bell rings for lunch and dinner. Breakfast is whatever's available in the mornin' when you get up. That's first come, first served."

"Thank you, I'm sure the food is excellent," Javik remembered Tao Shan telling him to always compliment the cooks because it usually paid dividends.

The woman broke into merry laughter. "Did you hear this one, Gilda? He says he's sure the food's excellent."

The other women joined her in laughing at the remark, and one added, "Well, it won't kill ya, but you ain't gonna get fat here as long as old Samack's in charge o' the victuals."

Javik decided he'd better hold any further compliments until after he'd tried the food. He returned to the barracks and informed his men of the arrangements just as Goldar appeared.

"I need all sergeants now for a briefing. Follow me."

Javik, Berda, and the other sergeants fell in behind the war leader. He led them to a room higher up in the fortress where a large map occupied most of one wall.

"Sit down, men. Samack will fill you in," Goldar said.

The men found chairs, and Samack used an arrow to point to different regions on the map as he explained the situation.

"Our spies say the Sentii have amassed a large force at each of the passes into Berglaundia. The King feels that they will only attack one of the three, but they want to keep us guessing until the last minute. If they attack here, it must be soon, before the snows close this pass for the winter." He tapped the map at the other high pass. "This pass will also be closed if we get any snow, and I expect a storm any day now. The most likely point of attack is the low pass, here," another tap of the arrow on the map. "The King has sent most of our forces to defend that pass, but the fortress there will not be at full strength for two full days yet. If that is to be the point of attack, we will send our reinforcements there as soon as we get word. Any questions so far?"

"Yes, sir," Mikka said. "How many more men are we expecting here? We could not hold this pass with what I've seen so far."

"Two more contingents will be arriving before tomorrow night. They will bring us up to three hundred men. I could hold these walls against twenty times that many for the rest of the winter, if needs be. Any more questions on that?"

Silence met his question.

"Good. Now the duties here are simple. We will have six watches of four hours each once everyone is here. Until then, we will continue six hour watches. Each contingent will serve one watch on and one watch off. Is there a watch you want your men to have, Goldar?"

"We will take the second day watch and the second night watch since we are the first ones here." Goldar jumped on the chance for a good watch.

"You have it. The watch bell will ring every six hours to start and end your watches. You know how to man the walls, I take it?" Samack said.

"Yes, sir. I'll instruct my sergeants."

"Good. Any questions?" Samack turned to the assembled men and looked for hands.

Javik stood up. "Sir, if the Sentii plan to attack here, how much warning would we have?"

"And you are?" Samack asked.

"I am Javik, son of Tolda and son of Browdat, sir."

"I knew your father, young Javik. I only hope you are as fierce a warrior as he was. Welcome to our castle."

"Thank you, sir."

"Well, we hope to have a day's warning, if our spy is not found out before then. Without his information, we'd only have a few hours from the lookouts in our high towers. That is, if it's a large force moving along the road. A small force moving through the trees could be upon us almost without warning."

"Thank you, sir," Javik said.

"Do you have any catapults or rock throwers in your towers?" Mikka asked.

"The towers facing Sentius have two of each, four total. We also have ports for hot oil and scalding water."

"What is the water supply here?" Berda asked.

"We have three springs from deep in the mountains. Water is no problem. Once the snows come, we'll have plenty for the melting."

Nervous laughter responded to the chief's words.

"Anything more?" Samack asked.

The men were silent.

"They're yours to post, Goldar. Show them their positions before dinner. They will assume the watch at midnight."

Goldar led his sergeants to the walls and assigned each man the stations they would be responsible for. Javik's pikes were placed along the walls with a swordsman and crossbowman between each one. The archers were divided among the four towers on the Sentii side. They would also serve as helpers for the catapult crews when those machines were in action. The sound of a small bell signaled welcome relief from the cold and the prospect of a hot meal.

Javik briefed his men on their duties before the meal and

joined the rest of the garrison in the dining hall. The woman had not lied about the meals. The food was well prepared, but there wasn't much of it. The men complained immediately.

"These rations couldn't keep my dog alive.

At that moment Javik appeared in the dining room carrying a large chunk of raw venison. As the men watched he threw it to Mordah. The huge dog moved to it and began to devour his dinner.

"What's that?" one man said. "That dog eats better than we do."

"Yeah, Javik, I'll bark for you if it means I get that much to eat. The dog's big enough to carry my pike and man the walls in my place."

Jeers and laughter spread across the room, and Javik signaled for silence.

"I hunt to feed my dog, but if the food gets short here, he'll be the first to starve. He may even become a meal for us if things get really bad."

"Who'd eat a dog?" one man called.

"Many people eat dog and consider it a delicacy," Javik responded.

"I guess, if you ain't tried it, don't knock it," another shouted.

The meal continued, but the complaints about Mordah's food died off rapidly.

After dinner, the men dozed before taking their places on the battlements at midnight. Javik roused them and led his group out into the cold. The night was moonless, and the wind blowing across the walls stung exposed skin like a thousand hornets. Javik pulled his cloak closer around himself and hunched his head down between his shoulders. The woolen mask Dana made for him was welcome protection against the bitter cold. As he stamped his feet to maintain circulation, a call came from the tower on his left.

"Rider approaching with others in pursuit!"

Javik turned in the direction the lookout pointed and saw a lone rider galloping swiftly toward the fortress. He was well ahead of his pursuers, but his horse was showing signs of tiring.

"Archers to the walls!" Javik called, and a dozen men left the shelter of their small booths to begin climbing to their battle stations. When they were in place, Javik commanded, "Fire at the pursuers."

A rain of arrows arced toward the horsemen but fell behind them. "Again," Javik called.

The riders were gaining on their quarry, but this time, the arrows fell among them. Two riders fell to the ground and others slumped in their saddles. The leader called a command, and the remaining horsemen wheeled back to the cover of the forest.

"Cease fire," Javik called as the lone rider rode up to the walls.

"Throw over a rope ladder," Javik commanded, and two men lifted the coiled up unit over the battlement and let it fall toward the ground. The rider dismounted and began to climb.

"Keep an eye on the forest. There may be more of them," Javik called. He ran to meet the climber and arrived just as a familiar face appeared in the torchlight.

"Sigurd! What are you doing here?" Javik called.

Sigurd dropped onto the catwalk and smiled broadly at his old fellow student in the house of Tao Shan.

"Why, spying for my country, of course. Is that you, Javik?" He held out his arms and the two old enemies embraced.

"I was hoping I'd never see you again," Javik chided. "How did you know me with this mask on my face?"

"I recognized your country accent and the smell of the longhouses." Sigurd smiled as he cast his insults. "Well, it seems we're destined to antagonize each other the rest of the winter here, but can you see to my horse? I don't think there's more than those few after me, so you can open the gate safely. Take me to Samack; I have important news for him." Sigurd shoved Javik towards the stairs.

"Bring in his horse and see it's stabled and fed," Javik directed a man who nodded and moved off.

The two made their way to the command center, and Javik probed Sigurd for information.

"Why were you spying on the Sentii?"

"I speak Sentian fluently, but I detest wearing their ridiculous clothes. I can't wait to change into something more suitable to my station in life."

Javik smiled, Sigurd was still as vain as ever.

"What's new with you, Javik?" Sigurd asked.

"I'm a married man now, Sigurd."

"Congratulations," Sigurd nudged Javik playfully. "That wild girl of yours, eh?"

"No, she's gone off to find her people. It seems she's some kind of princess of a lost kingdom. Tao Shan told me her kingdom was destroyed years ago. I married a village girl instead."

"Too bad, Allana was the most beautiful woman I've ever seen. Oh well, life's that way." Sigurd shrugged.

"What news from the Sentii?" Javik asked.

"Bad, I'm afraid. They plan to attack this fortress within two days. Are all of the reinforcements here?"

"No, only the contingent from my village, but Samack expects the rest soon."

"Let's hope they arrive quickly. The Sentii army is very

large and well equipped with siege machines."

They reached the door of the command center, and Javik opened it to find Goldar and Samack standing near the wall map. Samack recognized Sigurd immediately.

"Sigurd! Why are you back here?" Samack said.

"Sir, the Sentii found me out. I barely escaped with my skin, thanks to Javik's archers."

"Come lad, and tell us all you know," Samack commanded.

Javik turned to leave, but Goldar called him back.

"You may stay for this, Javik."

Javik loosened his cloak and pulled off his mask.

Sigurd removed his coat and helmet and moved to the map.

"The Sentii main force is assembling here," he pointed to a small town. "They have siege engines and a large force of infantry and archers. They plan to attack this fortress in two days."

Samack and Goldar reeled back a bit at the news. Samack recovered first.

"The King was certain they'd target the low pass because of the chance of snow in the high passes," Samack said.

"That's what they wanted the King to think. They planted false plans with other spies and pulled the siege engines toward the low pass before turning them toward us. A powerful wizard advises their king, and he's declared there will be no snow here for a week. The Sentii believe they can reduce this fortress in that time," Sigurd said.

"They're planning on a small garrison here if they strike quickly," Goldar said.

"With luck, we'll be at full strength before the attack. I'll send messengers to the other contingents urging them to speed up. Thank you, Sigurd. You've done well. Get some rest," Samack said.

Sigurd knelt and saluted Samack, then rose and turned to Javik. "We need to talk over a mug of your blasted qush."

"I must return to my men, Sigurd, but I'll see you after our watch is over."

Javik returned to the wall, and a long night of cold and boredom.

CHAPTER 27

The morning dawned as cold as the day before. Javik was glad to see the fire in the barracks area as much as the hot tea at breakfast. He was chilled to the bone, and even Mordah curled up near the blaze to sleep for a while before demanding his meal. Javik found his bunk and pulled the furs up around his neck before drifting off into warm oblivion.

The bustle of activity associated with the arrival of another reinforcement contingent roused Javik from sleep. He pushed back his fur covering and surveyed the scene. This barracks was now full, and the remainder of the group was led off to another set of quarters. One of the new men noticed Mordah.

"We've been quartered in a stable. I see someone's hairy horse here." The other men laughed as the joker approached the dog. Mordah growled deep in his throat causing the man to hesitate.

"Careful, Kinose, that's a war dog," another man called.

"He is, and he'll take your hand off if you go any closer," Javik said.

Kinose turned to see a sleepy-eyed Javik. "Is this monster yours?"

"Yes, and he's probably very hungry. Would you like to be his breakfast?" Javik smiled as he spoke.

The men roared with laughter as Kinose backed away from

Mordah. "No, but I hope you feed him well. I wouldn't want him to mistake me for a meal."

The room settled into its usual murmur of conversation as Javik dressed and made himself presentable for the day. Mordah moved to his side and looked up with an expectant expression.

"I know, you're hungry. So am I. Come along."

Javik led Mordah into the courtyard outside the barracks and cut a large chunk from the semi-frozen deer carcass hanging outside the barracks. It was hard work, but he knew Mordah was capable of breaking up the flesh and bones. The huge dog settled down to eat, and Javik made his way to the dining room.

It was between breakfast and lunch, and there wasn't much to eat from the breakfast leavings. He envied Mordah his feast. Some strong bark tea made up for the lack of food; he'd catch up at lunch. As he sat drinking the tea, another familiar face entered the hall.

"Noka! Is that you?" Javik called.

The redheaded youth turned and recognized his old school roommate immediately.

"Javik, how good to see you," Noka crossed the room, and the two friends fell into an embrace.

"This is like a reunion," Javik said. "Sigurd is here too."

"Oh no, have you two fought yet?" Noka asked.

"No, we're old friends since Browdat adopted me and after our fight over Allana. I just got up, so I have no idea where he is. We'll see him at lunch, though. I never knew Sigurd to miss a meal."

Javik held Noka at arm's length. "You've bulked up some since I last saw you. I assume you went through Mauhad even though Tao Shan didn't recommend you."

"Yes, my father insisted I fight in the war with the Wallans. I was always in the reserves far to the rear. I heard you were in the thick of it, though."

"I was, and war is not the glorious thing some would have you believe it is. It was a horrible experience, Noka."

"Well, you got some booty, at least. I understand you have the sword of Aelin the Red."

"My father, Browdat, has it. I sold it to him to finance my second year with Tao Shan."

"Another year? How did you stand it?"

"It wasn't like our year. I learned about becoming a leader, and I didn't have to march with rocks in my pack. What's your job here?"

Noka looked down at the floor. "I'm in charge of the commissariat."

"Don't be ashamed of that. What would we do without food and supplies? The men are already complaining they don't get enough to eat. Did you bring more food?"

"Twenty wagon loads for the men and another thirty for the horses. The wagons are already on their way back to load more from the King's storehouses. I fear the men won't fare much better, though. The King expects a long siege, and we may be snowed in for the winter anyway."

"Sigurd was spying for us among the Sentii, and he says they plan to reduce this place with siege engines and move through quickly. He thinks the attack will come in a day, or two."

"The King thinks the Sentii are headed for the low pass. He's sent the bulk of his forces there along with most of the supplies," Noka said.

"We'll know soon, I expect," Javik said.

"Are you and the wild girl married?"

"That's a sad tale, Noka. She turned out to be a princess, and it went to her head. She ran off to find 'her people', as she called them. No, I married one of the village girls. She's with child and due to deliver in a few weeks. I hope we can return home before my son arrives."

"You're a lucky man. I haven't found a girl in my village who'll have me. They all want warriors."

"Every man here may see service on the walls before this is over, I fear."

Their conversation was interrupted by the sound of the alarm bell.

"What's that?" Noka asked.

"It's the alarm bell. I must report to my station. We'll talk later. Look for Sigurd." Javik ran back to the barracks for his weapons and a warm cloak. He stopped on the way to the wall to get Mordah.

Goldar met him as he gained the catwalk. "Javik, the Sentii are here." Goldar pointed toward the forest where a host of Sentii warriors were assembling just out of arrow range.

"Where are the siege engines?" Javik asked.

"They'll be here soon enough. I expect they'll ask for our surrender first. They think there's only a small garrison here. See to your men, Javik. I don't expect an attack, but we need to be prepared."

Javik moved among his men. Some of them were still overcoming sleep, but they were all at their stations prepared to fight. He watched as the throng of enemy soldiers grew larger. They pounded weapons on their shields and sang bloody war songs in Berglauni explaining how they would deal with warriors who opposed them. All of his men were veterans, and there was no need for him to steady them. It seemed the Sentii would never stop emerging from the forest, but in a little while, a group of riders carrying a white flag rode into the area between the Sentii and the fortress ditch.

"Hold your fire," Goldar commanded, then sent a man to bring Samack.

"Gallant defenders," one of the Sentii shouted. "We have no wish to shed blood needlessly. You see our strength, but that is only a fraction of our might. Tomorrow, we will bring up great siege engines capable of battering down your walls in a matter of days. Surrender now, and you may go home to your wives and families. We want only this fortress to defend our lands against you. We will take no hostages, and you may leave with all your arms, armor and horses. You may all leave except the murderer of Grucheau. If that dog be among you, we will try him for his crimes and punish him accordingly. You have until the sun sets tomorrow to answer."

Samack appeared just as the Sentii was ending his speech. "Bah! The Sentii dog lies," he said to Goldar.

"We all know that, sir. Do you wish to answer him?"

"No, we will wait on his deadline. We should have our full strength by then. I also want to see what kind of siege engines they have."

"They must be large ones. Look where they dig their trenches," Goldar said.

The Sentii troops began digging a good twenty meters in front of the forest. They were within archer range, but it was too long a shot to be effective. The siege machines would be placed behind this line of trenches, and the distance from the forest meant they were large machines, indeed.

"Trebuchets," Samack said in a low voice so that only Goldar could hear him.

Goldar's face took on a serious look, but he quickly composed himself.

"Who is this murderer of Grucheau?" Samack asked.

"One of my men. His name is Javik, and he killed Grucheau in combat. The Sentii have no case against him."

"Well, make sure the Sentii don't get hold of him." Samack turned to find Sigurd next to him. "Will they bombard us, Sigurd?"

"I don't think so, sir. They seem to want this place intact to use as a base for their invasion. I saw a siege tower among their machines before I had to make a hasty exit."

"May I let the men stand down now, sir?" Goldar asked.

"Yes, keep it to the normal watch until after the deadline. We'll need all the rest we can get."

Javik joined his men in the dining hall. He'd heard the conversation between Samack and Sigurd, and briefed them on what he overheard.

"Well, if they're going to use a siege tower, we won't have much use for pikes on the wall," one man offered.

"Why do you say that, Morgan?" Javik asked.

"They'll come off that siege tower so fast pikes'll just be in the way. You need something to do a lot of damage quick. Like this." Morgan un-slung a pollaxe from his back and handed it to Javik.

"I'm familiar with these, but why would it be superior to a pike? I'd think we could use a line of pikes to block the ramp from the siege tower while our archers picked off the attackers."

"It don't work quite that way. They'll have their own archers above us in the siege tower to pick off people on the battlements. You need to mix in with their own troops so's they don't dare shoot at you."

"Sounds like a good idea," Javik agreed as he hefted the pollaxe. "Could you show the rest of us some tricks with this?"

"Sure." Morgan took the axe from Javik and stepped to the

center of the room.

"First, you gotta keep it movin', like this." Morgan swung the axe in great arcs creating a fearsome swishing sound.

"Hah," another man said. "That's no good. I'd just come in on your side and skewer you easily."

"Try it," Morgan said.

The man drew his sword and advanced toward the axe man. As he drew near, Morgan changed the direction of the swing and knocked the sword from his hand before pushing the pointed butt end into his opponent's chest.

"See, the beauty of this weapon is you can use both ends to kill."

Another man spoke up. "What about a pike? A pike man could attack from behind you before you noticed him."

"You keep checkin' your back if you have to, but you can easily break a pike with this thing."

Javik joined in taking the axe from Morgan. "Don't forget the point on the other end also. The pollaxe kills three ways."

"Aye," Morgan said as he took the weapon back from Javik. "But, don't forget the fourth way." Morgan lunged at Javik with the axe held horizontal and stopped his blow just short of Javik's face.

"And, don't forget to use all of your weapons," Javik said as he raised a knee toward Morgan's crotch.

A surge of laughter erupted from the group. By this time, they'd attracted a crowd, but the lunch bell disrupted the entertainment.

"I want every man to draw a pollaxe from the armory tomorrow after breakfast. We'll have a class on it in the morning. Morgan, you and I will teach them."

The final reinforcement contingent arrived the next day. The garrison was now up to full strength, and the watches were reduced to four hours. Javik's men learned the basics of the pollaxe, and he felt well prepared for any coming fight.

The Sentii trenches were now complete, and several siege engines were rolled up behind them. Four trebuchets, three ballistas and a large siege tower made up the mix. That evening, the riders with the white flag reappeared. Samack was waiting for them.

"Berglauni, what is your answer?" the leader called.

"We will never surrender. I suggest you retreat now, it will save the lives of many of your men."

"Look to your own men's lives, Berglauni. The battle begins now." The leader tore the white cloth from the pole and threw it to the ground as the party galloped back behind the trenches.

Javik watched in awe as the huge tower began inching toward the wall. It moved very slowly, but its advance was steady. He estimated it would be nearly dark before it reached the ditch and wondered how they would manage to bridge it.

Archers launched fire arrows at the structure, but it was covered with skins and those were being constantly doused with water from inside the tower. Archers on top of the tower kept up a steady barrage on the catwalk forcing the defenders to keep their heads down and their bodies behind the stone battlements. The tower finally reached the ditch, and a wooden wall swung outward and up creating a roof in front of the giant machine. Javik watched as men began to fill the ditch with bundles of sticks and baskets of dirt from under the cover of the new roof.

Two smaller structures began to move forward of the trench line. They linked up with the siege tower, and Javik could see men moving more stick bundles and dirt baskets into the tower while the empty baskets were loaded on the re-supply structures. He could now see that oxen were the motive power of the smaller structures and guessed that even more of the animals were under the tower. As the ditch was filled, the tower advanced. Torches were lit near the top of the tower, and the light flooded the walls with an orange glow. Javik could now smell the oxen. Their musty odor intermingled with the smoke from the torches and the nervous perspiration of the men on the wall.

The tower advanced closer, and now, the groan of the wheels and the shouts of the men inside could be heard. Drums began to beat on the top of the tower, and the archers began a war song while beating their bows against the protective hides in time to the music. Javik felt his knees begin to weaken and his throat went stone dry. Even Mordah began to whimper a bit until Javik stroked his neck in encouragement.

The giant structure was headed for a section of the wall half way between two towers. Neither tower would have a good shot at the thing, and the wall could only house so many men. Goldar gave the orders.

"Javik, bring your men to the front of the tower. They'll drop a ramp on the battlements. We must keep them from gaining the catwalk. Crossbowmen, stay back and take any target you can. Concentrate on the archers atop the tower. You other men stay close on either side of Javik's group. You'll have to replace any man lost in the melee. Be ready men, they'll drop the ramp soon."

It seemed to take hours for the tower to inch close enough to the wall, but finally, the ramp dropped revealing a mass of shields advancing along the planks.

"Now men!" Javik shouted as he held his axe high in the air and stepped onto the ramp. Arrows were flying all around him making the noise of a thousand hornets. He felt the press of men around him as he swung his axe at the first shield. The blow staggered the man, but he quickly recovered and lunged at Javik with his sword. An easy parry sent the weapon clattering off the ramp and into the ditch far below while the return swing sent the shield spinning upward exposing the enemy warrior to the handle point of the weapon. Javik heard his scream as he felt the steel penetrate bone and flesh. Blood spurted as he withdrew the point and parried a thrust from his right.

Javik smiled as he saw the surprise in the man's eyes when the blade of the axe dug into his leg. He collapsed in a heap with another warrior stumbling over his body. A sharp blow with the pole sent blood flying from the man's face as he too fell over his comrade.

A pike appeared from inside the enemy ranks with its point aimed at Javik's middle. From his left, an axe splintered the shaft before it could reach him. He noticed Morgan smiling at him, but another sword attack turned Javik's attention back to the battle at hand.

This warrior made the mistake of holding his shield too low. Javik sidestepped the sword and brought the axe head down squarely on the man's helmet, splitting it in two and producing a great spray of gray matter and blood.

The Sentii began to retreat back into the tower, and Javik felt the ramp beginning to move upward under him.

"Back men! Back!" Javik called and began to retreat toward the wall. It was a two-meter drop to the battlements as he leapt to safety, but he managed to just make the catwalk. He looked up to see the tower backing away from the wall. He collapsed against the cold stone as Mordah came up to inspect his master.

Javik ruffled the big dog's fur. "No need to protect me, Mordah. I'm fine."

Mordah welcomed this news with a great deal of licking.

Javik rose and took count of his men. All were safe, but two nursed wounds. He inspected each one and sent them to a healer station.

"You were magnificent, Javik!"

He could not fail to recognize Sigurd's voice, and he turned to see his old nemesis holding a bloody sword and a small shield with a large chunk cut out of its rim.

"It looks like you've seen some action yourself," Javik said.

"A few of the Sentii dogs got past you, but they now lie in the ditch. You learned the axe well at Tao Shan's house."

"One of my men suggested it was a good weapon for fighting on the ramp. He saved my life out there."

"That's what your men are for, after all," Sigurd sneered. He was still as much of a snob as ever.

"Noka's here too," Javik said.

"I didn't see him on the wall."

"He's with the commissariat. I imagine he was counting arrows while we fought."

Sigurd laughed. "Poor Noka, he never was much with the weapons. Did he ever learn the sling?"

"Allana gave up on him, but he's much better with figures than any of us. Perhaps those skills will come in handy someday."

"Come, let's have a mug of qush to wash down the blood." Sigurd threw an arm around Javik, and led him to the dining hall.

CHAPTER 28

All through the night, the smaller structures made their way back and forth across the field between the forest and the fortress. They continued to fill up the ditch in spite of constant bombardment from the catapults in the four towers and a hail of fire arrows. Shortly before dawn, one of the units was disabled. Several Sentii were cut down as they fled the immobile shelter, and it finally caught fire as the water used to keep it damp evaporated. The men on the wall cheered loudly as it blazed away to charred timbers.

The sun rose over the treetops, and the great tower advanced once more, but this time, several smaller structures came with it. Each one headed for a spot where the ditch was filled in, and the sound of the alarm bell brought Javik and his men back to the wall.

"What orders, Goldar?" Javik asked.

"Now they know our garrison is much larger than they expected. They'll use ladders today to attack at several points along the wall. Use your pikes to push them away from the wall. I'll have men standing by to take care of any Sentii who gain the catwalk. Just keep those ladders off the wall."

Javik spread his men out to face two of the advancing shelters while others lined up to oppose the rest. A group of swordsmen confronted the siege tower. As the small shelters neared the wall, ladders appeared through hatches in their roofs. The catapults managed to disable one of the units, but the men simply ran to another one. The archers and crossbowmen managed to down several, but not enough to make a difference.

Javik watched as a ladder slowly rose to his part of the wall. It clanked against the wall confirming its metallic makeup. There would be no burning of these ladders. He shouted to his men.

"Push it away as soon as the Sentii start climbing."

Pikes rushed forward hooking the curved part of the points around the top rung. Javik leaned over the wall and waited patiently as the enemy warriors began to climb.

"Now!" Javik shouted, and his men strained against the weight of the ladder and its cargo of armored men. The top of the ladder moved slowly, at first, then more rapidly as the balance tipped against the Sentii. The screams of the falling men rent the air, and the thud of armored bodies in the ditch echoed off the wall. In a moment, the ladder was swinging back into place.

"Once more, men," Javik called as the ladder fell into place. Again, the pikes hooked the top rung, and once more the men pushed, but this time, the ladder did not budge. More pikes joined the effort, but it was no use. Javik saw the futility of the effort and commanded a change in tactics.

"Use your pikes to drive the climbers off the ladder as they reach the top. Morgan! You and I will use our axes to take care of any who make it to the catwalk."

"Aye, Javik," Morgan replied.

"I've got your back, Javik." It was Mikka and his contingent of swordsmen.

The first Sentii topped the wall and threw an axe at one of the pike men before he was driven back by another pike. The axe missed its intended target, but hit one of the swordsmen in the leg. He fell back in severe pain.

Another warrior vaulted over the wall and landed on the catwalk before a pike could skewer him, but he bought time for two more climbers to gain the wall. Mikka dispatched one while Morgan split the skull of the second. More Sentii appeared, and it became apparent there were several ladders now instead of just one. Javik saw the change and gave another order.

"Pike men! Repel those other ladders."

Javik, Morgan and the swordsmen had their hands full with the Sentii on the catwalk, but the pikes managed to find the other ladders and push them away. The fight continued for what seemed an eternity to Javik. He was relieved to hear the sound of a horn and see the ladder falling away. The mobile houses retreated toward the trench lines.

Bodies littered the catwalk. Some were still alive and moaning for mercy. Mikka moved among them dispatching those who still moved.

"Throw them over," Goldar commanded, and the men busied themselves looting the dead and tossing the near naked bodies over the wall into the ditch. Two of the dead were Javik's men, but they had sold their lives dearly. Over twenty Sentii fell from the walls that morning.

Before lunch, the Sentii renewed the attack using the same tactics, but a surprise awaited them. During the lull in fighting, cauldrons were filled with oil and fires lit under them. They hung on booms that could be swung out over the wall. The cauldrons could be tipped over with chains to dump the scalding contents on the attackers. When they ran out of oil, boiling water would serve almost as well. The main difference being the water would not burn, or stick to the men or the structures.

This time, the ladders would not push away, and Javik waited for a full ladder before calling for the oil. He could hear the flesh crackling as the Sentii were literally fried like cuts of venison. Their hideous screams cut through his soul like swords. A terrible way to die, he thought. Other men threw torches after the oil, and soon, the structures were ablaze in spite of the large amounts of water poured from inside the houses. Once more they retreated.

Javik heard the noise of the trebuchets before he saw the first projectile - the swish of the rock holder as it accelerated through the air and the loud creak as the wooden structure complained about the load it was forced to bear. The large rock fascinated him as he watched it arc toward the fortress. He mentally calculated its trajectory and decided there was no need to duck this one. It fell just short of the wall. Another stone smashed into the wall with a deep bass thud that was more an earthquake than a sound. It rattled his teeth, but did no damage to the wall.

The bombardment continued the rest of the day, and one section of the wall began to show some damage as a result. The war machines began to concentrate their fire on that section. Goldar called a meeting of his sergeants to brief them on the situation.

"The trebuchets are beginning to weaken one section of the wall. I'm afraid we'll have a breach by noon tomorrow. They'll attack the breach and the wall at the same time hoping to spread us as thin as possible. We've prepared hedgehogs to fill the breech, but we may have to retreat to the second wall. If you hear three horn blasts in succession, retreat to the second wall as quickly as you can. Are there any questions?"

The sergeants knew what needed to be done and the dangers involved if the Sentii exploited any breach.

"Can we sally and burn the trebuchets?" Mikka asked.

"We aren't strong enough for that tactic. They'd cut us to

pieces from the trench lines."

"A small group might be able to infiltrate their lines and set fire to the machines," Javik offered.

"That would be a suicide mission with little chance of success. I'd never send any man under my command on such a foolish venture," Goldar said. "Besides, the Sentii would have the fire out before much damage could be done."

Javik thought a moment and replied, "What if we could damage the machines quickly?"

"Javik, it would take twenty men with axes half a day to cut through the timbers and cripple the trebuchets."

"Perhaps there's another way, sir. Could you spare me from the wall the rest of the day?"

"Yes, but why?"

"Tao Shan told me the secret of a magic powder with great power. I think it may be useful in helping us eliminate the trebuchets, but I'll need time to make it and test it out. I'll also need three of my men to help me."

Goldar stood for a moment in silence considering the request, but Mikka broke in.

"I've heard of such powder, Goldar. Javik may have something."

"Very well, pick your men. You have until sunrise tomorrow. I fear the wall won't hold much past that time."

Javik returned to his men and picked three to help him leaving Morgan in command of the rest. He led them to the manure pile outside the fortress's stables.

"Men, we are going to make a magic powder to destroy the Sentii war machines, but we need to do some dirty work first. One of the ingredients may lie below this fragrant pile of horse dung. I want you to scrape away the manure down to the ground level. I'm looking for a white powdery substance. Be careful to preserve as much of it as you can."

One of the men spoke up. "I've seen that stuff before, Javik. I know what you're looking for."

"Good, you can guide the other men. I'm off to find the rest of the ingredients. I'll return as soon as I have them."

The men went to work with their shovels, and Javik headed for the storage buildings to find Noka. The redhead was busy inventorying grain stocks when Javik approached.

"Noka, I need your help," Javik called.

"You have it. What do you need?"

"I need several kilos of sulphur and all the charcoal you can find."

Noka looked at his old roommate with a jaundiced eye. "Sulphur and charcoal? What do you need that stuff for?"

"It's something Tao Shan taught me. I think I can use it to make a powder that will help our cause."

Noka's face took on a more serious appearance at the mention of Tao Shan's name. If the old mentor was part of this, it had to be a good idea. "Let's see, sulphur is over here." He led Javik to several barrels in one corner of a storage room.

"One of these will do me," Javik said. "What about charcoal?"

"We have plenty for the blacksmith, but I hate to give any of it up."

"This may mean the difference between victory and defeat, Noka."

"Well, it's over here." Noka took Javik to another storage bin the size of a small longhouse filled with charcoal.

"Have some of your people grind enough of this up to fill two small barrels. It must be finely ground. Can you do that?"

"Yes, but..."

"I need it and a barrel of sulphur in the dining hall as soon as you can get it there. I'm counting on you, Noka." Javik left a perplexed Noka standing before the charcoal and returned to the manure pile.

"We've found some, Javik," one of the men called. Javik moved to the site and was pleased to see an even layer of saltpeter exposed by the shovels.

"Good job! Scrape it up carefully into a barrel and bring it to the dining hall. I'll mix the powder there."

Javik commandeered some pans from the kitchen and a small ladle for measuring the ingredients. He was moving them into the dining hall when Sigurd walked in.

"Are you the cook today, Javik?" Sigurd asked.

"No, I think I can make some magic that may help us defeat the Sentii war machines."

"I'd like to watch that, or is it to be done in secret?"

"I promised Tao Shan I'd not disclose the secret, but I think he'd trust you too. I'll need help mixing the powder anyway, and I don't want my men to see how it's done."

"If Tao Shan is part of this, I'm in to the end."

At that moment, Noka's men appeared carrying several barrels. The placed them as Javik directed and left. Javik's men came in next with the saltpeter, and he asked them to wait outside until he called.

"Phew, your magic smells greatly of horse manure," Sigurd said.

"It's a key ingredient. We don't have time to refine it. I just hope it will work as it is."

Javik and Sigurd measured out the ingredients into a pan and mixed them thoroughly.

"Now we will test it," Javik said. He poured a small line of the black powder on the floor of the dining hall and took a glowing twig from the fireplace.

"Stand back, Sigurd. I don't know how this will react."

Sigurd shrugged and moved back one step. "What's to fear from a little powder spilled on the floor?"

Javik shook his head and lit the powder. Sigurd recoiled from the blinding flash and staggered back to regain his composure.

"Great Zhou! What is this stuff?" Sigurd asked.

"Tao Shan calls it gunpowder. He uses it in his hand cannon, and he told me it can be used to destroy walls. I think we can use it to disable those trebuchets."

"It certainly burns well, but how will that help?"

"He packs it into the hand cannon, and I think if I pack it into the ground under the trebuchets, it may create enough shock to splinter their timbers."

"Hmmm, could be. Let's try it out."

Sigurd helped Javik pour the gunpowder into one of the empty charcoal barrels, and they carried it out to Javik's men.

"We'll leave the fortress by the gate on the Berglauni side, men. Bring your shovels. I'll need a hole big enough for this barrel. Bolon, you bring the heaviest timber you can carry. We'll soon see if this powder will do our job."

Outside the walls, the men dug the hole to Javik's specifications, and then placed the barrel of powder in it. Javik made sure they tamped the earth back in around the keg as tightly as possible. Digging in the frozen ground was not easy, but Javik felt those conditions were ideal for his plan. The section of heavy timber was laid on top of the keg and several large rocks were placed on it to hold it down. Javik ran a line of powder from the keg to what he thought was a safe distance and directed everyone to take cover. The men looked at him quizzically, but he barked the command again with as much authority as he could muster. Sigurd helped.

"I've seen this stuff in action, men. I suggest you do as Javik asks." Sigurd found a large tree for shelter immediately.

Javik used his flint and steel to strike a spark into the line of powder then ran for a nearby rock. Just before he reached it, he was knocked to his stomach by a wave of heat and a blast of air like nothing he'd ever experienced before. It was over in an instant, and Javik rolled on his back trying to catch his breath at the same time. A gaping hole and a splintered timber marked the location of the barrel, but the stones were gone. Wisps of gray smoke curled up from the crater as the men slowly emerged from their hiding places. Their faces told the whole story. Each man's mouth was wide open and their eyes were wide as plates. Only Sigurd seemed calm.

"I think you have something here, Javik," he said as he brushed some dirt from his cloak.

"Did you see those rocks fly?" one of the men said.

"That small one must have flown twenty meters," another gasped.

A throng of men and women poured from the fortress gate to investigate the noise. Samack was in the lead with Goldar close behind. Samack stopped at the edge of the crater and stared down into the pit.

"What manner of magic is this?" Samack gasped.

"Something I learned from Tao Shan, Sir," Javik responded. "If you agree, I'll take some of this powder and a few men out of the fortress tonight and destroy the trebuchets."

"Come inside to my chambers, and we'll discuss this. You too, Goldar."

The bombardment continued as the men discussed Javik's plan. So far, the wall was holding, but another factor was about to become important. Inside the command center, Samack could not see that a heavy snow had begun to fall.

CHAPTER 29

Samack listened carefully to Javik's plan for destroying the trebuchets, then turned to Goldar.

"What do you think of this scheme?"

"I think it's foolish. Digging holes under the machines would take too long and make too much noise. . It's pure suicide."

"Do we have a choice?" Javik added. "Those machines will soon break down our wall if they aren't stopped."

"I agree with Goldar," Samack said. "Your magic powder is wonderful, but you'd never be allowed the time to do it. I'm sorry, Javik, but I must say no to your plan. If we aren't able to defend the outer wall, I may reconsider. It will take the Sentii several days to attack the inner wall if we abandon the outer wall. I may reconsider in that event. You're a brave man, but this is more foolishness than bravery."

Javik was disappointed, but not discouraged. He knew the plan was fraught with danger, but he had supreme confidence in his ability to carry it out.

"I understand, sir. If you change your mind, I have made enough powder to do the job."

"I think we'd all better get back to the wall," Goldar said.

The group walked outside, and Samack almost leaped for joy at the sight of the snow.

"We're saved," Samack almost shouted.

"It's only snow," Goldar sounded puzzled.

"In the valley, it's only snow. Here in the mountains it's like another army fighting with us. Look, see how much has fallen in the short time we were inside." Samack scraped down to the dirt with his boot revealing almost three centimeters of the white powder.

"How much more do you expect?" Javik asked.

"By morning we will have nearly a meter. The Sentii can't fight this and our defenses too."

They moved to the wall where men were taking any shelter they could find. The bombardment had stopped, and the Sentii lines were quiet. The siege engines stood quiet as they accumulated a coating of white.

Javik spoke up. "Sir, have the Sentii abandoned their trenches?"

Samack shielded his eyes from the driving snow. "It's hard to say. They may just be under cover."

"They'll need fires in this weather if they stay in the trenches," Goldar added. "I don't see any smoke."

Sigurd chimed in. "Sir, let me scout their lines. I can use the escape tunnel to get behind their lines. Javik can guard the tunnel exit door and let me back in."

Samack thought for a moment before agreeing. "Very well, but take plenty of men with you, Javik. If the Sentii find the entrance to the escape tunnel, we'll have a real fight on our hands."

"Yes, sir," Javik agreed.

"I'll put on my Sentii disguise and meet you in the dining hall," Sigurd said as the two left the catwalk.

Javik selected four men to go with him and met Sigurd in the dining hall.

"What you men are about to learn is a closely guarded secret of this fortress. You must all swear never to divulge the entrance or exit of the escape tunnel under penalty of death. Do you so swear by our god Zhou?"

"We do," the men responded in unison.

"Good, follow me."

Sigurd led the men into the dungeon of the fortress. Each man took two torches, lighting one and saving the other for the return trip. They proceeded through a damp corridor to a cell door.

"The tunnel entrance is in this cell. It's the worst of the lot, and the fortress commander would probably be thrown in here if the place were taken." Sigurd explained.

At the back of the cell, Sigurd pulled on an iron ring, and a part of the wall swung into the cell. The men had to stoop over to enter, but the tunnel expanded on the other side of the wall so that they could easily stand up and move two abreast. Sigurd led the way.

The tunnel was cut into rock for a long way before the construction changed to shored dirt walls and ceiling. Tree roots had crept into the space in a few places, and had to be cut away with their swords. After what seemed hours, they reached a heavy wooden door with two cross-bar bolts.

"Only I go on from here," Sigurd said. "When I return, I'll knock like this," he rapped twice quickly, waited a count, then rapped three times slowly.

"I have it," Javik said. "Good luck, Sigurd."

The two embraced before Sigurd lifted the two bolts and opened the door. It was pitch black on the other side.

"The exit is closed," Javik said.

"No, this is only the first door. Don't bring your torches any further. They may be seen from the outside. Close this door after me. I know my way in the dark from here."

Sigurd slipped into the darkness, and Javik closed the door wondering if he'd ever see his old schoolmate again.

They waited, and the torches died one by one. Javik ordered that only one of the fresh torches be lit until Sigurd's return. They'd need the remaining ones to light their way back through the tunnel and the fortress dungeons.

The first of the reserve torches burned out before Javik heard the knocks. He pulled open the door to see a cold, snow covered Sigurd.

"Good news, Javik. They've pulled back to their tents. The machines are unguarded, and there are only a few sentries in the trenches. We could easily subdue the guards and plant your powder kegs before they discovered us."

"What about your tracks back to the tunnel entrance?" Javik asked.

"It's snowing too hard. They'll be gone in a few moments. Besides, I covered them well as I got close. Come, we must tell Samack."

Samack gave his approval, and the powder kegs were prepared. Javik and Sigurd led a party of thirty men out through the escape tunnel after midnight. The snow was still falling, and it was now up to their knees making the going quite slow, but insuring they moved in silence. The sentries were killed quickly, and the men approached the siege machines.

The trebuchets loomed like giant, snow-covered monsters in the darkness. Only the light of the stars revealed their true nature. At the first one, Sigurd directed the men.

"Dig under that beam. You others go to the rest and do likewise."

The team split into smaller groups and began to prepare the holes for Javik's kegs. The ground was frozen under the snow, but the men worked quickly out of fear of being caught so far from the fortress. As the holes were completed, Javik directed the placement of the powder kegs and ran a trail of powder to form a fuse. When the job was done, he set a man at each keg with a lighted rope glowing red in the night.

"When I give the command, light the powder and run for your lives," Javik whispered to the other three men who volunteered for the job. He directed the remaining men to get back inside the tunnel and waited until they were out of sight before dispersing the ignition crew.

He watched as the men took up their positions then shouted, "Now!"

Javik lit his powder and ran as fast as he could toward the tunnel. He was surprised to see one of the men pass him up, but he kept to the pathway beaten down in the snow from their approach. As he felt the heat from the blast, he dove into the snow in time to escape the concussion. The bright flash from the explosions lit up the enemy camp a few meters away, and he could see men leaving their tents. He looked back briefly at the trebuchets to see only a pile of beams where the fearsome machines had once been. Javik jumped to his feet and ran for the tunnel as the other two men caught up with him.

Sigurd was waiting outside the tunnel entrance with the rest of the men.

"You did it, Javik. What a sight! You should have seen it."

"Enough for now, Sigurd. I fear the Sentii are close behind me. Let's get going."

The shouts of the Sentii were becoming louder now as they milled about in chaos. One of the trebuchets was burning, and it cast an eerie light over the snow as Sigurd closed the outer door to the escape tunnel.

"Well, they'll know where we came from now," Sigurd said. "Our trail will be easy to find in the deep snow."

The group passed the second door, and Javik bolted it fast.

"Will this door hold them, Sigurd?" Javik asked.

"Not for long, we'll have to collapse the tunnel."

Sigurd opened a large chest a few meters down the tunnel and produced ropes and grappling hooks.

"Take these and grapple the side support beams there," he pointed to the locations.

The men did as commanded and Sigurd moved the party further down the tunnel.

"Now pull down the beams," he shouted.

The beams were easily dislodged, and the roof fell in immediately. They moved down the passageway pulling down the ceiling as they went until they reached the rock part of the tunnel.

"I think that will be enough to discourage them," Sigurd said as he embraced Javik.

"We did it, Javik. We did it!" Sigurd said.

The men responded.

"Three cheers for Javik! Hooray, hooray, hooray!"

"We did it together. You are all heroes," Javik said.

Goldar and Samack were waiting as the team exited the cell in the fortress dungeon.

"Good work, men!" Samack said. "I've never seen anything like that in my life. Your magic powder is a miracle, Javik. You must give the secret to the King."

"I've sworn to reveal the secret to no man, sir. Only Tao Shan may release me from that oath."

"Then I'll have the King speak with Tao Shan. Come, men, a hot fire and a barrel of qush await you upstairs."

The celebration went on until the dawn with most of the garrison joining in. The men on the battlements reported the Sentii were still running around in great confusion trying to unravel the mystery of the explosions.   There would be no attacks that day.

The snow continued to fall, and the Sentii force broke camp and departed.   The men gathered in the dining hall to hear Samack's speech.

"Men of Berglaundia.   We have achieved a great victory. Your courage has driven the Sentii back into their lands in defeat.   Now that the snows are here, they will not be able to renew their campaign until spring.   I would like to be able to tell you that you are free to return to your own hearths, but I fear the snow has made travel impossible now."

The men responded with a collective groan.   Samack signaled for quiet.

"I know that's disappointing, but it is a fact of life in these mountains.   The watches will be cut in half now, but we have much work to do repairing the outer wall for those not on watch.   It will be a long winter yet.   Those of you who can sing or tell tales will be our entertainment.   We also have an excellent library for those able to read.   This dining hall is available for weapons practice, and for wrestling and boxing matches.   I recommend that all of you stay as busy as possible.   The long nights here are trying for men's minds.   We have plenty of food now, and I will increase the rations."

A cheer greeted this announcement.

"If you have any complaints or questions, give them to your sergeants.   Are there any questions?"

The leader of one of the other reinforcement groups stood.

"Sir, how long until we can travel?"

"At least two months.   The trails will be waist deep in snow for at least a month, then, the thaw will begin, but the danger of avalanche will be great for another month.   If we're lucky, that is.   I've known the snows to last much longer than that, but I'd say, three months at the outside."

The men began to grumble, but the leaders silenced them.

"As I said, you will need to keep yourselves busy. You are effectively imprisoned here until spring. Once again, well done."

Samack left the room with the other leaders, and Javik slumped back in his chair as Noka came up to him.

"Will you miss your wife, Javik?" Noka asked.

"Not for the reason you think, but I will miss the birth of my son."

"I'm sorry for that, but we'll have a great time here with you and me and Sigurd. It'll be like old times again."

"Yes," Javik sighed, "like old times."

CHAPTER 30

The short winter days at the snowed-in fortress seemed to last forever. Only so much time could be spent in training, games and gambling, and after a few weeks, each song was a familiar ballad and every war story a twice-told tale. Javik, however, had another project to occupy his time. He experimented with Tao Shan's gunpowder.

Noka took an active interest in the new material and pestered Javik until he was let in on the secret. Sigurd found several women in the fortress to occupy his time and quickly lost interest in the explosive.

Javik's first project was to find some way of igniting his charge more easily and with a higher degree of safety. Leaving a trail of powder was also risky because the wind could blow a segment away leaving a gap, or simply scuffing a gap in the line could disrupt the process. Noka watched the powder burn as Javik tried different amounts of powder for his purpose, and came up with a crucial question.

"Javik, must the powder be exposed to the air to burn?"

Javik thought for a moment and remembered the hand cannon.

"No, Tao Shan put the powder inside a metal tube, and it burned very well without the air."

I think I have an idea, then. I'll be right back." Noka left Javik to his experiments and returned in a short while with a pot of glue and some bandages.

"What are the bandages for?" Javik asked.

"Watch," Noka commanded. He laid a long piece of the bandage on a table and painted a line of glue down one edge of the cloth. Next, he poured some powder over the line of glue and rolled the bandage into a long rope, gluing the edge of the strip in place to seal the package.

"Well, what now?" Javik asked.

"We let this dry overnight, and I suspect in the morning we will have something to replace your line of powder."

Javik scratched his head. "Noka, I respect your brain, but I don't see how this is going to work."

"You said the powder doesn't need air. The powder inside the bandage will burn just as well as your line of open powder, but the wind will not blow it away, and only by cutting the bandage could anyone stop the progress of the fire. In addition, the fire will not be visible. There will be no flash of light to alert the enemy to the explosion."

"Hmmm. It could work," Javik mused.

The next morning, Noka's fuse worked just as he said it would. The pair busied themselves making more of the rolled up bandages and timing the burn from one end to the other.

"Noka, we could make our rope any length to achieve any delay we wanted. You're a genius." Javik stood to embrace his friend and knocked over his mug of tea. The hot liquid soaked two of the bandage ropes before they could move their work away from the spill.

"We've ruined these two, I'm afraid," Javik said as he held up the soggy ropes.

"Rain would do the same thing. We must waterproof our ropes," Noka said. "I think I know how we can do that also."

Once more, Noka left to return a while later with a pot of hot grease. He dipped one of their ropes in the grease and hung it up to cool and harden.

Javik tried lighting the wet ropes, but the fires stopped at the tea each time. As soon as the rope dipped in grease cooled, Javik flexed it in his hands. The soft tallow didn't crack, and the rope was still flexible. Noka poured some water over a part of the rope, and it ran off harmlessly. Lighting the fuse showed it burned as well as the original.

"This is quite an improvement for only one afternoon's work," Javik said.

Noka was pensive. "We'd need a very long piece to achieve any delay longer than a few seconds."

"The cloth comes in bolts several dozen meters in length. That would be no problem," Javik said.

"Yes, but several dozen meters of rope would be quite visible to anyone suspecting a problem. I'll have to find a way to make a shorter rope last longer. I'll think about it."

"Well, we have a good device for firing our charges now. Perhaps we should build a hand cannon?" Javik said.

"We'll need the blacksmith's help with that," Noka said. "Let's go see him."

The blacksmith's shop was a popular place on cold winter days. The forge radiated enough heat to allow blacksmithing with bare arms, and the men congregated around it to talk of female conquests and great battles.

Javik approached the huge smith with a sketch in one hand and a mug of qush in the other.

"Ho, Javik. Have you brought me some of your magic powder to fire my forge?" the smith roared.

"No, Ruggen, I've brought you a project to relieve the boredom of these long nights."

"I have my wife for that purpose, but I'll take the qush."

The men laughed at the joke, and the smith snatched the mug from Javik's hand. He downed it in one great gulp.

"Now, what have you brought me?" Ruggen said as he wiped the foam from his lip.

"A curious challenge to your skills. Can you make me this tube?"

Ruggen took the drawing and studied it carefully.

"You need a foundry for this kind of thing. It'd be a tough job to forge."

Javik knew the fortress had no foundry, and the smith could only melt small quantities of steel. His hand cannon would have to wait.

"Well, I respect your experience in these things. Where could I find a foundry?"

"Only in the capital. The King commissions statues from time to time, and they cast them there in bronze. I don't know if they could cast steel."

Noka studied the wrought iron work hanging from one of the rafters and pulled one down. It was a twisted piece of iron about a meter long.

"What if you did something like this smithy?" He handed the piece to Ruggen.

"I don't get your meaning," Ruggen said as he handed the piece back to Noka.

"I mean, suppose you worked the iron into a long, flat strip then pulled it around a circular bar in a spiral like this, except you overlapped the seams a little. You could weld the seams together and have a tube like Javik wants."

Ruggen thought about the idea. "It might work, but what would you do with the tube, Javik?"

"If we closed off one end, I could put my magic powder in it and use it to launch stones or metal balls out the other end. It's a formidable weapon."

Ruggen pulled at his beard while digesting the idea. "It would have to be made of my best steel. I saw what your powder did to those trebuchets."

"Would you give it a try?" Noka asked.

"Alright, I'll try one. You two stick around to help with my forge and tell me how you want it done."

Ruggen selected a piece he was obviously using to make a broadsword. "This piece is probably strong enough, and I can make it longer by hammering it down to size. Is this the thickness you want?" He held up the blank edgewise to Javik.

"I think a bit thinner."

"Very well. You, Noka, put some more charcoal on the forge, and Javik, work the bellows. I'll do the hammering."

The forge roared to life and soon the shop was ringing to the sound of Ruggen's hammer beating the blank into shape. When the piece met Javik's approval, the smith selected a round bar and held it out for another approval. Javik nodded agreement, and the smith inserted the rod into a hole in his anvil. He put a square peg in another hole and began to heat the blank again.

The forge roared as Javik pumped the bellows. His shoulders and back were aching with the effort, but Ruggen held the metal in the glowing coals until it shone a bright white. Quickly, he pulled it from the forge and stuck it between the square peg and the round rod. As his hammer sang a merry chorus, he wound the metal around the rod until it cooled to a dull red. He pulled the metal from the rod and put it back in the forge to reheat. He repeated this process several times until he had a coiled piece of steel nearly four hands long.

"Is that long enough, Javik?" Ruggen asked.

"It looks right to me, but you have some metal left over on each end."

"No problem." Ruggen heated the iron once more and used another tool to punch off the ends. He smiled at Javik as he reheated the tube and placed it back on the rod. A few deft strokes of his hammer and the use of some special tongs soon welded the seams of the tube and finished the ends in a smooth surface. Ruggen placed the tube back in the hearth and let it become a bright red before removing it and dropping it into a bucket of oil.

The oil bubbled and an acrid black smoke rose from the barrel as he swished the tube around in it. He pulled the tube out and dunked it into a barrel of water before handing it to Javik.

"How's that?"

"Well done, Ruggen," Javik said as he turned the object in his hands. "Now we must close one end and put a small hole at that end for igniting my powder."

"Didn't I see a mechanism on your drawing?"

"Yes, you did." Javik showed the smith the drawing again.

"I see," the smith mused. "I can make the closure part of the mechanism, but that will take some time. I can have it for you by next week."

"I'll be looking forward to it," Javik said.

The steel tube was passed from man to man in the blacksmith shop, and each one turned it over in his hands. Was this tiny thing truly the weapon of the future?

A few days later Javik checked in the blacksmith shop and found Ruggen beaming over his creation.

"Look at this, Javik. I think I've improved upon your design a bit." Ruggen handed Javik a strange looking combination of wood and metal. It did not resemble Javik's drawing except for the long metal tube. A mechanism attached to the back end of the tube ended in a large, wooden piece instead of a pole. The wood section ended in a curved arch.

"This is a strange thing," Javik said as he traced his hand over the curved wood. "What is it for?"

"I guessed that the pole was used as a handle for the weapon, but a pole is too awkward. I had our carpenter make this for me. See, you can rest it against your leg," Ruggen demonstrated by placing the curved section against one of his massive thighs, "or your stomach," another demonstration, "or your shoulder." Ruggen placed the wood against his shoulder and sighted down the tube as if he were aiming an arrow.

"Good idea, Ruggen. I see you've also changed my mechanism a bit."

"Yes, I put the priming pan behind the tube instead of at its side. The match lever is the same as you requested except it's bent a bit to use the new pan." He gave the weapon back to Javik, and the young warrior worked the mechanism several times.

"Excellent work, Ruggen. Would you like to see it in action?"

"I wouldn't miss it after seeing those trebuchets destroyed."

"I have some powder left, but I'll have to find some stones and some moss to use for wadding."

"The stones are the projectiles, correct?" Ruggen asked.

"Yes, but metal could be used also."

"Wait a moment." Ruggen rummaged through some old chests and pulled out a leather bag. He brought the bag to his anvil and dumped out some metal balls. They were about five millimeters in diameter and made of steel.

"I made these for Samack some time ago. He was testing a new device for pivoting a ballista more easily. He used these in the pivot mechanism. It worked very well until the balls became rusty. I had these left over and decided they might come in handy sometime. Could you use these as ammunition?"

"I'll try them. You wouldn't have any wadding around, would you?"

"No, but you might try Willan, the carpenter. He has some stuff he uses for caulking that might work."

"Meet me outside the back gate in an hour, and we'll see if this thing works."

Willen gave Javik some caulking material that looked to be suitable, and he gathered powder and some match rope before finding Noka and Sigurd. The group assembled outside the wall, but attracted a gallery of spectators on the battlements . After the destruction of the trebuchets, they were not about to venture any closer.

Javik loaded the weapon with a small amount of powder and several of the steel balls. He lit the rope match and placed it in the firing mechanism after priming the pan.

"Stand back. I'll aim at that large tree stump, there." Javik pointed at an old stump about twenty meters away and made sure Noka, Sigurd and Ruggen were safely behind him. He took a deep breath and said a small prayer as he pointed the tube at the stump and levered the match into contact with the priming pan.

The boom elicited a scream of horror from the spectators, and the recoil knocked Javik back several steps. As the smoke cleared, Javik noticed a large chunk was missing from one side of the stump.

"Zhou save us," Ruggen muttered.

"I think you've killed the stump," Sigurd laughed.

Noka moved closer to inspect the weapon. He put his hand near the tube and pulled it back quickly.

"As I suspected, the tube is very hot," Noka said. "Stick it in the snow to cool, Javik."

Javik did as Noka asked and noticed the snow melt quickly around the black iron. He pulled it out, and Noka examined the tube carefully.

"No apparent damage from that one. You might try more powder and a few more balls."

Javik reloaded the tube and aimed with more confidence this time. The sound was not as frightening this time, but the damage to the stump was even more impressive. A section on the left side the size of a man's head was splintered heavily.

"What do you suppose its range is?" Sigurd asked.

"Let's try that large beech tree yonder," Javik said as he pointed out his next target. He reloaded with even more powder and the same number of balls.

This time, there was no obvious damage to the tree, but the four experimenters slogged through the hip deep snow to inspect the target more closely. Several of the balls had penetrated the smooth bark of the tree, and Sigurd used his dagger to dig down to them.

"They're into the wood, Javik. These would have killed a man without armor at this range, but I think a good breastplate would have stopped the balls. Don't you agree, Ruggen?"

"Aye, a crossbow would have penetrated deeper, and some breastplates will stop a crossbow bolt."

"I'll try more powder," Javik said.

"I wouldn't do that," Noka said as he pointed to the weapon's tube.

The spiral groove around the tube had separated a bit near the back end and burn marks showed where some of the explosion had leaked out.

"Let me see," Ruggen said as he took the weapon from Javik. "Ah, I know how to remedy that. I need to make the bar thicker at this end, and it wouldn't hurt to wrap another band around the other way to reinforce the tube. I'll make you another tube, Javik."

Noka had also been inspecting the steel balls. "Would you be able to make larger balls, Ruggen?"

"Certainly, how large would you want them?"

"The size of the inside of the tube, for example?"

"Aye, but a ball that size would take a lot of work to forge. Could you use cast lead?"

"I don't see why not," Javik said.

"It would be much heavier than steel," Noka said. "It wouldn't fly as far, I'd guess."

"Unless you used more powder," Sigurd inserted.

"Then you'd need a stronger tube," Ruggen said.

"It's a vicious circle," Javik said as he scratched his head.

"We've got the rest of the winter to experiment," Sigurd brought home the bitter truth of the matter.

CHAPTER 31

Javik's hand cannon testing produced some great results. The tube was now strong enough to take a powder charge capable of hurling a lead ball over two hundred meters with some degree of accuracy. A better range was less than fifty meters, and Javik could easily hit a man-shaped target consistently at that range. Sigurd and Noka both paid Ruggen to make one for them also, and they were also becoming very adept with the weapon. Soon, all three were blasting away in the snow to the delight of a growing gallery on the fortress walls.

Javik felt his dog should get used to the hand cannon and took him out on an early test. At the first shot, the huge animal beat a path through the snow to the safety of the gatehouse. Javik called him back, and Mordah obeyed grudgingly. The next shot produced much whimpering and whining, but the dog stayed by his master's side even though he cowered in the snow covering his nose with his paws. It took several outings before Mordah became accustomed to the strange weapon, but he was soon resting comfortably while the warriors practiced.

Samack and Goldar had tried the new item with mixed reviews from each one. Javik had to agree that an archer could fire faster and a crossbowman could inflict as much damage on light armor, but he continued with development efforts.

Noka was a key factor in suggesting changes to improve the

new item's usefulness. He suggested soaking the rope in a solution of the saltpeter to keep it burning in damp weather. He'd also devised a cover for the priming pan that automatically lifted when the match was brought down on the powder. This, also, made the weapon more useful in the rain and snow.

Sigurd contributed his part by designing a powder flask that automatically measured just enough for one load. Even Ruggen helped by designing a set of pliers to use for casting the lead balls.

At night, around the fireplace, the three young warriors discussed the weapon's potential for various kinds of warfare and hunting.

"I wonder why Tao Shan never told us about this thing before?" Sigurd asked one night.

"You have to admit, it isn't a very practical weapon. We've talked about it for weeks now, and we've only come up with one or two good uses," Noka said.

"If we could make it fire faster, it could be a formidable weapon, but only at long range. We dare not use it where a crossbowman or an archer could get a shot at us or where a warrior could charge us between shots," Javik said.

"I like the use of many balls at one time," Sigurd said. "That way, you have a chance of killing several at once."

"Or, making it effective even in the hands of a warrior with bad eyes," Javik joked.

"It could be an excellent tool for hunting birds," Noka said. This was a new idea, and generated a new argument lasting until the fire burned down to embers and the qush began to dull their senses. Bed was the next order of the night.

The next morning, the men noticed a definite warming trend in the weather. It had not snowed for almost a week, and the sun was beginning to clear spots on the tops of the walls and where there was no shade during the day. Practice with the hand cannons continued, and Ruggen was swamped with orders for the devices, though he increased his price each week. Javik and Sigurd were kept busy making powder, and every manure pile in the fortress had been mined for saltpeter. The price of the ingredients kept most users from firing too often, and the three friends were making good money on the trade. The supply of sulphur was nearly gone, and the charcoal stocks were reaching a low point also. Noka was soon forced to cut off powder manufacture until more charcoal could be made and more sulphur mined.

The arrival of the first traveler from the Sentii side of the pass was a welcome sight. It meant the snows had receded enough for safe travel. He brought word that the Sentii had sued for peace with the Berglauni after the loss of their siege machines to terrible magic. He was shocked to see that his tale evoked laughter among the fortress's defenders, and Javik treated him to a demonstration of the hand cannon.

A few days later, a rider arrived from the Berglauni side, and Samack called the reinforcement contingents together in the courtyard.

"Valiant defenders of our homeland," he began. "The snows are now leaving, and the pass is safe for travel. Several recent visitors have confirmed this, and it is time to let you all go home. I have a message from the King commending all of you for your bravery and advising us of the Sentii suit for peace. Go back to your hearths with my gratitude and that of your King. Well done."

A great cheer erupted from the men, and preparations began for the trip back home. Javik was not looking forward to being home again. Polla would have had her child by now, and he would be a normal husband again, and a father for the first time in his life. It would be hard to adapt to family life after his adventures defending the fortress and developing the hand cannon. He wondered if he would be up to the task.

Sigurd found Javik after the meeting. "Well, we must part again, Javik, but we need to celebrate before we go. I have a barrel of fine qush stashed away for my personal use, and I'd be honored if you and Noka would join me in depleting its contents tonight."

"Thank you. I think I need something to make me forget I'm going home."

Sigurd stared at his friend in disbelief. "You are the only man in this fortress who's not delighted to be going home. Is married life that bad?"

"I'd be racing home to Allana, but I'm dreading my return to Polla. She made my life miserable while she was pregnant. Now that the baby is born, I don't know what she'll be like. It's really sad to see her this way. She was so happy and full of life before."

"That's why I never spend too much time with one woman. They begin to sink roots into your backside after a few weeks, but come tonight and we'll forget all our troubles for a while." Sigurd slapped Javik on the back and set off to find Noka.

That evening the three friends sat by the fire in Sigurd's room and spoke of the battle, hand cannons and old times until the wee hours of the morning. All of them were snoring on the floor long before the barrel of qush was depleted.

The spring sun shone brightly even if the temperature was a bit on the nippy side as the caravan assembled for the trip back to Holliga, Javik's village. Javik rode beside Goldar as the troops walked out the gate and over the drawbridge toward home. The snow was gone in most places by now, and the ground was soggy from melt water. Even the hard packed roadway was a morass of mud sucking the horses' hooves into small craters of muck. It was slow going, but no one wanted to stop before sighting the stockade of their home village.

Water dripped from the trees overhead with just enough force to wet down their cloaks, and render them useless against the biting wind. Javik was glad he'd put on his sheepskin tunic under his chain mail. It helped to retain his body heat in spite of his damp cloak.

It was near nightfall when they reached the village. There was no one waiting to welcome them, and Goldar became edgy.

"It's so quiet, Javik. What could be wrong?"

Javik leaned forward in his saddle and studied the stockade. Nothing seemed abnormal, and Mordah showed no sign of alarm, but he noticed there was no guard in the gate towers.

"There's no guard, sir."

"Strange, we'd best check things out before we take the entire contingent inside. Javik, Mikka, Berda, follow me." Goldar led the group inside the stockade and up to the common house.

"It looks normal to me, sir," Mikka said. "Except it's so quiet."

They dismounted and entered the common house. They were not prepared for the sight of the men, women and children lying on pallets all over the floor. Dana rushed to meet them. She looked tired and weary. Her hair was tied back in a cloth, and her face held a pale cast. Goldar realized she had not applied her usual makeup, but she was still as lovely as ever. Her eyes were the most telling aspect of her appearance. They were red and showed the strain of many days without adequate rest.

"Goldar, Javik you shouldn't be in here. We have a plague."

The men let out a collective gasp and stepped back in automatic reaction to the announcement. Only Goldar stood firm.

"What can we do to help, Dana?" Goldar asked.

"You can help best by staying healthy. Zhou knows we don't need any more people to care for. Can you set up camp outside the stockade?"

"Yes, but you need some rest. Let me send in some men to help," Goldar said.

Dana wiped her arm across her forehead and sighed heavily. "You and Javik may help, but please send Mikka and Berda out."

"Is my wife well?" Mikka asked.

"Yes, Mikka. She's helping me with the sick here," Dana responded.

"Then I'll stay also," Mikka replied.

"And my mother?" Berda asked.

"She's recovering. I'm sure she could use you at your hearth, Berda," Dana said.

"May I, sir?" Berda asked Goldar.

"Go to her," Goldar said, and Berda left the improvised hospital.

"Polla, and our son?" Javik asked, dreading the answer after seeing his mother's eyes change on hearing the question.

"You have a son, and he's well, but Polla's dead, Javik."

Javik stood silent for a moment. He fought the tears welling up from deep in his soul. He must be strong for now.

"How?" Javik asked.

"She had a hard time delivering your son, and it nearly killed her then. When the plague came she was too weak to resist it. We tried to keep it away from her, but she fell ill anyway and died within a week."

"Where is my son?"

"He's with Polla's parents now. I was keeping him until they needed me here, but they have a good wet nurse and their hearth has been free of the plague."

"I'd like to see my son, sir," Javik said to Goldar.

"Go, Javik," the war leader said.

"I'll find my wife," Mikka said as he unbuckled his sword and placed his cloak and helmet next to the door.

"And my wife?" Goldar asked.

Dana looked down at her feet before answering. "She's gone, Goldar. She was too weak from her other ailments to fight off the plague. I'm sorry. We did all we could."

"I know, I know. Is she buried?"

"Yes, we bury the plague dead as quickly as possible. Tahsla wanted to burn them, but he was overruled. A special barrow has been constructed for them north of our usual place of rest."

"I'm glad she was not burned. She always hated to see anyone burned, even the plague dead." Goldar seemed to stand a bit taller after hearing the terrible news. Dana thought the long years of her illness had drained the big war leader a bit, and now the burden was lifted from his shoulders.

"I must have my men set up camp. I'll be back as soon as I can. I'll ask for volunteers to help here. I know many men will want to hear about their families, can you come to the camp later?"

"Yes, I'll be able to leave in a little while. Go and take care of your men. I'm sure they've had a hard day's ride, and they'll be fearful for their families."

Goldar kissed Dana on the forehead. "Bless you, Lady."

The men were not happy about setting up camp in sight of their own hearths, but they understood. Six volunteered to help with the sick, and headed for the common house. Cooking fires were soon blazing, and the aroma of venison stew reminded them of their hunger, dispelling fears for the moment. Dana came to the camp and answered all questions for those she knew about. She promised to find out about those she didn't know. Goldar walked her back to the common house. A full moon lit their way as they walked through the chill night air.

"Dana, you know how much I loved Ruda, don't you?"

"Yes, I know."

"I don't want to sound like I wanted her to die, or anything like that, but…"

Dana stopped walking and held a finger to the war leader's lips.

"I understand, Goldar. I know it's a relief for you. You cared for her as well as you could. Don't feel badly that you were gone when she died. I know she understood."

"It's not that. She always understood when I had to obey my obligations. It's you, Dana. I want to be with you now, and I feel guilty about that feeling."

Dana smiled, and the moonlight made her face glow even more brightly. She took the big man's face in her hands.

"Goldar, I've known of your love for me ever since Tolda was killed. Every time we've been near each other, I felt your heart reaching out to me. You've always been a perfect gentleman, and I always knew you loved Ruda with all of your soul, but I'm not blind."

Goldar pulled her close to him and felt her warmth spreading through his very being.

"When this is all over, we'll have a proper courtship, and I'll ask Javik for your hand in marriage."

"When this is over," Dana whispered.

* * * * *

Javik entered Challa's longhouse and greeted his father-in-law.

"We have both suffered a grievous loss, Father," Javik said as he embraced Polla's father.

"I know it had to be quite a shock to you, Javik, coming home to such sorrow when it should have been a joyous reunion. Come see your son."

Challa took Javik to one of the sleeping rooms where his wife, Gilda, was rocking a small baby in a wooden cradle. She saw Javik and began to cry.

"You have a son to be proud of, Javik" she said as she wiped her eyes with her apron. "Polla was so weak from the plague when he decided to arrive. It was too much for the poor thing." Gilda began to sob and buried her face in her hands. Javik went to her and knelt beside her.

"He is a fine boy. We must take comfort in him and thank Zhou for his life," Javik said as he put an arm around the woman.

"I know yours was not a marriage of love, but you treated my little girl better than any woman in the village could ask of her husband, and I thank you for making her life happy."

Javik didn't know what to say next. Polla was miserable when he left, and he doubted she improved any in his absence. He decided to let the matter rest.

"I thank you for caring for him," Javik said.

"It's no burden to me, and your mother is needed to help the sick. She seems to have a healing touch. I only hope the plague stays away from our door. I'd hate to see young Javik fall prey to it."

"Did Polla name him?" Javik asked.

"No, she gave him no name before she died. She said that was your place to name him. We've just been calling him little Javik until you came home. What will you name him?"

Javik looked at the sleeping child. It looked like all other babies to him. There was nothing about him that evoked any image for a name.

"I will have to know him better before I name him. After the plague has passed, I will spend more time with him and find a suitable name."

Javik turned back to Gilda. "I'm sorry I wasn't here for Polla. Maybe I could have helped her find the will to live."

"Oh, Javik. Don't blame yourself. You did what you had to do," Gilda said.

"Yes, Javik, you had no choice," Challa added.

"Thank you both for understanding. I don't know if I could be so gracious. I'll always feel things might have been different if I had been here."

"The child is sleeping now. Will you have some wine with us?" Challa asked.

"Thank you, but I must see if I can help my mother with the sick. I fear she's working too hard."

"We understand. Go to her, son," Challa said.

Javik kissed Gilda on her cheek and embraced Challa before returning to the common house.

Dana was not there when he walked in, and he asked Mikka about her.

"She's gone home, Javik. She said to tell you to come home and get some sleep," Mikka said.

Javik carried his baggage to his hearth and found Dana asleep already. He went to his room and collapsed without undressing.

CHAPTER 32

The next morning Javik awoke to an empty house. He dressed and found some porridge warming on the woodstove along with a loaf of his mother's best bread. The meal was as good as he remembered, and two cups of bark tea drove the chill from his bones. He had to see Polla's barrow and try to tell her how sorry he was to be gone during her trials. Donning his warmest cloak, he walked the short distance to the village burial grounds and soon found the large mound housing the latest victims of the plague. The names were carved into a slab of gray stone at one end of the dirt hill. Javik ran his finger over Polla's name, and sank to his knees.

"Polla, Polla, I'm sorry I was not here to help you. We parted on bad terms, but I think the baby would have made a big difference in both of our attitudes. Over time, we may have come to love each other. I thank you for our son. He's a fine boy, and I'll make sure he has every advantage I can give him. He'll grow up to be a warrior you would be proud of."

A twig snapped behind Javik, and he turned to see Grazhda standing at the edge of the forest.

"Grazhda, you startled me," Javik said.

"Why do you speak to the dead?" the old hag said.

"I was trying to tell Polla how sorry I was for leaving her alone in her time of need."

"Bah! She was an evil woman who duped you into

marrying her. The child was not yours, Javik."

"No matter who conceived him, he's mine now." Javik set his jaw firmly. He would not let Grazhda impugn his son no matter what she'd done for him in the past.

"Ooohhh, do not be angry with me, young warrior. I only tell you the truth. It will make it easier for you to comply with my wish."

"And what do you wish?" Javik was becoming extremely wary. Grazhda was reputed to have vast powers, and though Javik knew all magic was trickery, he could not account for the incident with Grucheau or the fact that his wand lived.

"I want the child."

Javik's blood went cold. He'd heard stories of gruesome rituals at her cabin deep in the forest, and some of them supposedly involved the sacrifice of human children. He could not allow this to happen to his son.

"Challa's family would kill me if I suggested such a thing, not to mention my own mother and Lord Browdat. What you ask is impossible."

Grazhda waved a finger at Javik. "Not so fast. I know what you're thinking, and you're dead wrong. Challa and your mother may take care of the child, but you must give him the name I choose, and you must let me have him for one year of training before he becomes a man. He will live with me for that year, but he may visit you or anyone else as he wishes. Surely, you can agree to that."

Javik thought quickly before answering. The old hag couldn't possible live much longer. She was ancient now. As for a name, one was as good as another to him.

"What name would you choose?"

"You must name him Garen."

Javik rolled the name around in his mind. He knew no one

by that name, and it wasn't a Berglauni name at all. Still, it wasn't a bad name. He'd try it out on his mother, but he had to tell Grazhda something now.

"I agree to the name, as long as my mother agrees with it. I will also agree to allow him to train with you for a year, but I can't see what a warrior can learn from you."

"Ha, ha, ha, ha, ha!" the old woman cackled. "You men are so arrogant. You have no monopoly on knowledge. Tolda would not let you come to me, but I vowed any son of yours would not be denied the chance to learn the secrets of the spirits. You've made a wise choice, Javik, but be sure you keep your part of this bargain. I can curse as well as bless."

Inside his head, the voice or reason was arguing with a dark vision rising from the depths of his soul. Reason said there were no such things as magic and spirits, but the black monster would not go away. It sat in the back of his skull laughing derisively and issuing dire warnings.

"You have my word as a warrior, Grazhda," Javik said.

"Good enough. Now go, and do not bother to come here again. Polla did not love you, she only saw you as her path to a fine house and wealth. She is not worthy of your sorrow. Go find the one to truly match your spirit. Allana will soon be queen of Gorgos, and you must help her achieve her throne. Don't linger among the dead when the living have needs."

"Javik, Javik!" The call came from behind the barrow, and Javik stepped to one side to see who was calling. Berda was approaching. Javik turned back to bid farewell to Grazhda, but she was gone. He stood for a moment pondering the encounter before responding to Berda.

"Here, Berda!" he called.

"Javik, Browdat has been asking for you. He sent me to find you."

"Do you know what he wants?"

"No, he grabbed me as I passed by his longhouse and said to find you right away."

"Well, it must be serious. Thanks for finding me. I wouldn't want to keep Browdat waiting." Javik smiled a knowing smile at Berda who understood exactly what he meant.

Browdat was busy conversing with Goldar when Javik walked in, but he quickly rose and enveloped his adopted son in a bear hug.

"Javik, I'm proud of you. Goldar's been telling me all about how you defended the wall and how you destroyed the Sentii trebuchets. How did you do it? He said you used a magic powder of some kind."

"Yes, it's a secret recipe Tao Shan taught me. He calls it gunpowder."

"Show Lord Browdat your hand cannon, Javik," Goldar said.

"What's that?" Browdat said as his face took on a look of utter puzzlement.

"I'll go get it, father. It's in my baggage at my hearth."

"Hurry back, I have a large mug of qush waiting for you," Browdat bellowed as Javik left the room.

In a few moments Javik returned carrying his hand cannon and its paraphernalia.

"What a curious looking thing," Browdat said as Javik handed him the weapon. The big war leader turned it over and over in his hands, inspecting it carefully.

"Tell me all about it. But first, a toast to our victory." Browdat pushed a mug to Javik as he and Goldar raised theirs in salute.

"To our victory," Javik said, and the men took a healthy swig.

Javik sat down his mug and took the hand cannon from Browdat.

"Well, you put the magic powder in this tube and hold it in place with a wad of caulking fiber. Then, you add some stones or lead balls and hold them in place the same way. Next, you must prime the pan with some powder." Javik lifted the pan cover, an invention of Noka's, to show how it would be done. "Close the pan cover and light the match." Javik produced a piece of match rope from his bag of equipment. "Once it's glowing nicely, you put it into the lever, here." He threaded it into the holder and cocked the lever. "Now, it's ready to fire." He lifted the weapon to his shoulder and pulled the trigger. The match lever fell to the pan cover with a loud click knocking the cover up and driving the match into the priming pan.

"Then you hear the voice of Zhou," Goldar said.

"Is it loud?" Browdat asked.

"Like thunder in the summer," Goldar said.

"I have to see this in action," Browdat glowed with expectation.

"We'll have to have a safe place to do that," Javik said. "I think the large field outside the main gate will do, but we'll need a target."

Goldar called over one of Browdat's servants who was busy cleaning some pots and pans. "Give me your cloth, girl," he commanded. Browdat nodded agreement, and the girl gave Goldar the damp rag. He shook it out into a square about half a meter on a side. "This should do, eh Javik?"

"I think so. Come, I'll show you, Father."

The three men marched out the main gate, but only after attracting a large crowd of curious spectators due to the strange nature of Javik's weapon. Outside in the now fallow grain field, Goldar found two twigs and tied the cloth between them.

"There, Javik, is that satisfactory?"

"I need a backstop, sir. I fear the projectiles may travel too far and injure an innocent person."

"Nonsense," Browdat gruffed. "There's plenty of empty field behind that cloth."

"No, Father, there isn't. The balls will travel across this field easily."

"Why, why, that's farther than a good bow shot," Browdat blustered.

"It has a great range, but it's not very accurate at its longest range."

"Perhaps if we put it up on the stockade wall?" Goldar suggested.

"That might be better," Javik agreed.

Goldar moved the target to the wall of thick timbers and jammed it into the crevices to hold it as Javik loaded his weapon.

Goldar stood well behind Javik, but Browdat leaned close to the hand cannon.

"You'd best stand back, father." Javik waved the big war leader back with a motion of his free hand. "You may light the match rope, if you would." Javik handed Browdat the rope, and he lit it with his flint and steel.

Javik blew on the match to get the glow he wanted and inserted it into the lever.

Goldar placed his fingers in his ears, but Browdat only gave him a quizzical look.

The weapon fired, and Browdat jumped a foot.

"Great Zhou! It is as loud as you said, Goldar."

"I told you. Now, go look at the target."

The men advanced to the stockade wall as the villagers came out of hiding.

Javik had loaded six small balls in the piece, and they

showed five holes in the cloth and one in the wood just above it.

Browdat gave a low whistle as he measured the depth of the holes with a small twig.

"They've gone in a full finger width. I shudder to think what they would have done to a man," Browdat said.

"I never had to use it in defense of the fortress, but it could be formidable as a defensive weapon," Javik said.

The crowd of villagers murmured in awe at the damage done to the cloth, but they backed away quickly as Javik turned around with the weapon.

Javik laughed at the scene of the men and women cowering away from the hand cannon.

"It's safe now. It won't hurt you," Javik called, and the people sighed in audible relief.

"May I try it?" Browdat asked.

"Certainly, Father. I'll reload."

Browdat watched fascinated as Javik reloaded.

"That takes a while," Browdat said.

"That's why it would be best used in defense. The warrior using this weapon would have to be protected while he reloaded, and only a good, solid wall could do that," Javik said.

Javik blew the ash off the match and coaxed it back to a glowing, red ember before handing the hand cannon to Browdat. He didn't need to warn the villagers, they were all inside the stockade or well behind him.

"Look down the tube at your target. Place the cloth just above the end of it and squeeze the trigger."

Once more, the hand cannon thundered and Browdat staggered back several steps.

"It has the kick of a war horse," Browdat said, but the smile on his face could have lit up the underworld. "Let's see how I did."

The cloth was now almost in shreds with the addition of six more holes.

"Hah!" Browdat shouted. "All of mine are in the cloth, you only got five."

"You were always my master at all things," Javik said as he smiled at Goldar.

"Again, I must do it again," Browdat said.

"I only have so much magic powder, Father. I have to make more soon, and I'd like to save some of this for an emergency."

Browdat pleaded like a child for candy. "Just one more, son. I want to see if I can hit the cloth from farther away. Please?"

At that moment, Tao Shan arrived and greeted the trio.

"Well, I thought I heard a hand cannon. Welcome home, Javik and Goldar."

"We made some improvements on your model," Javik said as he handed his old mentor the hand cannon.

"I see, very clever." Tao Shan examined the weapon carefully. "This barrel is not cast. How did you make it?"

"Ruggen, a blacksmith devised a way to wrap iron around a bar and forge it," Javik replied.

"Very, very clever. It should be much stronger than a cast barrel."

"Why do you call it a barrel? It doesn't look like one," Javik asked.

"It's the closest your language can come to my people's word for the piece. I like this cover for the pan also."

"You remember Noka, he devised that one."

"The lad amounted to something after all," Tao Shan smiled as he remembered the red haired student. "May I try it?"

"I had the next shot," Browdat jumped in.

"By all means, after you, sir." Tao Shan smiled as he bowed and handed the weapon to the war leader.

Browdat handed it on to Javik who reloaded.

Browdat's second shot tore some wood from behind the cloth, and Tao Shan reacted with a low whistle.

"That's a powerful load. I don't think mine could do that at this range," Tao Shan said.

"I experimented with loads while we were snowed in at the fortress. This is a very light load, because I don't have much powder," Javik said.

"Remarkable, may I try it now?' Tao Shan asked.

Javik reloaded and Tao Shan finished destroying the cloth.

"I like it very much. I particularly like your change to the stock. The pole is very awkward to use, and this one fits right into a man's shoulder."

"That was Ruggen's contribution. He also improved the firing mechanism a bit. Sigurd designed the powder measure."

"My training did not go for naught, then." Tao Shan put an arm around Javik and turned to Browdat. "A son to be proud of, Browdat. Come, I'll buy the qush."

The four men entered the stockade to the applause of the assembled crowd.

* * * * *

Later that day, Dana returned to Javik's hearth. As she was preparing dinner, Javik told her of the encounter with Grazhda.

"I saw Grazhda the other day," Javik said. "She wants me to send my son to her for training before he becomes a man."

"That's what her riddle means." Dana's eyes lit up with the sudden realization of the meaning of Grazhda's words to Allana.

"What riddle?" Javik asked.

"She told Allana she would have to give up something, but it would cause her no pain in obtaining it or in releasing it. Don't you see? Garen caused her no pain because he's not her child, and thus, she'd experience no pain in giving him to the witch. Garen is that 'something'," Dana said.

"Her terms for his training are no worse than Tao Shan's," Javik said. "I fear that you and his grandparents might object if that time comes, but I doubt the old hag will live long enough to demand her year with him," Javik said.

"Beware of what you say, Javik. I've heard tales about the old woman that go back over 100 years," Dana said.

"I'll take care of that if the time ever comes," Javik said.

"I remember when she asked your father for you. He would have no part of it, but I wanted him to let you go. There are forces in nature more powerful than weapons, Javik, and Grazhda knows all of them. Let him go."

"And, the name?"

"Garen is a good name," Dana mused. "It's Wallandian, as I recall. Several of their kings had that name."

"Then you don't object to it?"

"No, not at all."

"You always give wise counsel. Your advice makes that decision easier, but it doesn't relieve me of my greatest concern."

"Allana?" Dana smiled as she removed dark brown bread from the brick oven.

"Yes, I must go after her, but I have no idea where to find her. Margan said she wanted to move on before winter, and winter has come and gone."

Dana sat down next to her son and placed an arm around his shoulders. "You will not be content until you begin searching for her. As I recall, Margan said she was last in Ullum. That would be a good place to begin."

Javik sighed and smiled at his mother. "I want to go, but I hate to leave you behind alone."

"I have Frieda and Garen, and I suspect Goldar is only waiting for a suitable time of mourning his wife before he asks me to marry him. Don't worry about me. Go and find her."

The End

Title: *The Adventures of Regen the Bremen*
Author: M. L. Hollinger
Price: $27.99
Publisher: TotalRecall Publications, Inc.
Hardcover, ISBN: 978-1-59095-110-1
Paper Back, ISBN: 978-1-59095-111-8
eBook, ISBN: 978-1-59095-112-5
Audiobook, ISBN:
Distribution arrangements: Baker Taylor, Ingram Book Co., American Wholesale Book Co. B&N, BAM, Hastings, Powels, Online, Libraries, etc.

Regen is a Bremen. By nature he loves only his pet skeen, sensual women, money, and adventure in that order.

REGEN is an earthy, pragmatic, drug smuggler who cares little for anything but money, beautiful women, and his own highly unusual pet. The animal is a skeen, and they are usually shot on sight for the pests they are. Most people marvel that Regen managed to tame such a nasty creature. On top of everything else, he named the skeen HITLER after a 20th Century Earth dictator with a personality as evil as any skeen's. Regen is a Bremen. Bremen are known for their tough exterior, sexual prowess, and their tendency to leap before they look. I hope you enjoy following this arrogant, self-confident, egotistical and narcissistic bastard through a series of adventures in disparate sectors of the galaxy.

Title: *Josh and the Cargan*
- Author: M. L. Hollinger
- Publisher: TotalRecall Publications, Inc.
- : Hardcover, ISBN: 978-1-59095-124-8
- : Paperback, ISBN: 978-1-59095-125-5
- : eBook, ISBN: 978-1-59095-126-2
- : Audiobook, ISBN: 978-1-59095-254-2

Science tells us the speed of light is absolute, but is it? If physical objects can't go faster than 186,000 miles per second, maybe something else can.

Josh Smith is your average teenage boy. His hormones are raging and he can't wait to have sex with a girl. He also wants to be a rock star, and has an amateur band of his own. One evening after band practice he learns his rich, eccentric great grandfather, Charles Evans Bastin, is dead.

When the will is read, Josh inherits one of Charley's ugly sculptures while his father inherits the rest of the fortune. Back home, Josh accidentally discovers his sculpture is a CARGAN, a device used for interplanetary travel as a ghostly presence called an ENTITY. He travels to the planet destination of his cargan and finds it's a very exotic place indeed.

- Title: *Snow*
- Author: M. L. Hollinger
- Publisher: TotalRecall Publications, Inc.
- : Hard Cover: 978-1-59095-303-7
- :Paperback, ISBN: 978-1-59095-304-4
- : eBook, ISBN: 978-1-59095-305-1
- : Audiobook, ISBN: 978-1-59095-258-0

When her husband is reported as dead, she escapes to the United States and takes up a new life. Unfortunately, she runs into Jeff again, and he wants to take up where they left off. Naturally, Snow resists him until he traps her into resuming their relationship.

Title: *Josh Martin – Space Commander*
- Author: M. L. Hollinger
- Publisher: TotalRecall Publications, Inc.
- •: Paperback, ISBN: 978-1-59095-282-5
- •: eBook, ISBN: 978-1-59095-283-2
- •: Audiobook, ISBN: 978-1-59095-284-9

A bored teen-aged boy escorting his little brother at Disney World finds love and adventure on Space Mountain.

While waiting in line at Space Mountain, Buzz Lightyear presents Josh with a pin and suggests he'll enjoy the ride a lot more now. Josh and George board the sled, but Josh doesn't notice the cast member pushing a button on the sled. As they start the ride, Josh is suddenly propelled into another dimension where he's the Commander of a space ship. The ship is a battle cruiser, and receives an order to rescue a princess who has been kidnapped by pirates. With the help of the ships Executive officer and his staff Josh develop the perfect plan to accomplish the rescue. What could go wrong?

Title: *Mauhad*
- Author: M. L. Hollinger
- Publisher: TotalRecall Publications, Inc.
- : Hardcover, ISBN: 978-1-59095-104-8
- : Paperback, ISBN: 978-1-59095-105-5
- : eBook, ISBN: 978-1-59095-106-
- : Audiobook, ISBN: 978-1-59095-272-6

A boy struggles to pass Mauhad, the manhood test of his people, and falls in love in the process.

Javik lives in a country surrounded by mountains and covered in old growth forest. His ambition is to become a warrior like his father, Tolda, but he must pass Mauhad before he can realize that ambition. When is father is killed saving the others in his raiding party, Javik despairs of ever reaching that goal without his father's training. Goldar, who led the raid when Tolda was killed, convinces the King to allow Javik to train with Tao Shan, the finest mentor in the kingdom. Javik finds himself among the sons of the wealthy and must adjust to the situation quickly. While in training he encounters a girl in the forest. She is Allana an escaped slave, but Javik falls in love with her. He convinces her to come out of hiding, and she teaches the sling to Tao Shan's students.

The First book in the Javik series.

Title: *Queen of Gorgos*
- Author: M. L. Hollinger
- Publisher: TotalRecall Publications, Inc.
- : Hardcover, ISBN: 978-1-59095-289-4
- : Paperback, ISBN: 978-1-59095-290-0
- : eBook, ISBN: 978-1-59095-291-7
- : Audiobook, ISBN: 978-1-59095-292-4

Allana is held by the Turrek bandit King, Vargon.

Javik leaves to find her and learns of her predicament. With the help of her man Barinosh, Javik and his friends manage to free Allana and they set off to regain her throne. After many adventures Allana is crowned queen, marries Javik and they reign together.

Allana has begun her quest to regain the throne of Gorgos by establishing a high class brothel in another land with the help of a former madam who has been disfigured by a rejected lover. Allana gains a great deal of wealth and some allies, but she must cross the territory of a ferocious bandit king, Vargon, to reach Gorgos. She bribes Vargon with her body in order to secure his promise of safe passage, but he captures her in spite of his promise and forces her to marry him.

The third book in the Javik series.